Titles by Langaa RPCIG

Second Engagement

Susan Nkwentie Nde

Langaa Research & Publishing CIG
Mankon, Bamenda

Publisher:
Langaa RPCIG
(Langaa Research & Publishing Common Initiative Group)
P.O. Box 902 Mankon
Bamenda
North West Region
Cameroon
Langaagrp@gmail.com
www.langaapublisher.com

Distributed outside N. America by African Books Collective
orders@africanbookscollective.com
www.africanbookscollective.com

Distributed in N. America by Michigan State University Press
msupress@msu.edu
www.msupress.msu.edu

ISBN: 9956-558-66-4

DISCLAIMER

*The names, characters, places and incidents in this book are either the product of the
author's imagination or are used fictitiously. Accordingly, any resemblance to actual
persons, living or dead, events, or locales is entirely one of incredible coincidence.*

Contents

Prelude

___

She looked healthy and plump, and her face exuded years of complexion cream application. Dark hair crowded to her eyebrows where a prominent ridge rose to the end of her nose and beyond. Her once full and sensuous lips pulled down at the sides in a scowl. Dark visible veins contrasted with the fair skin of her arms. There was all evidence that she had spent a good number of years in the northern part of the country. She wore a flowery flowing gown over a loincloth. Her stylishly tied headscarf of the same material exposed a row of woven hair on the side. I admired her outfit and was intrigued with the way she looked at me.

I walked leisurely into the main section of the market. By the time I reached the first row of shops she was at the main gate. She came towards where I was looking at some wrappers displayed outside one of the shops. I had my salesmen from whom I usually bought these wrappers, but I was attracted by a new design, which had just arrived from Nigeria. The woman came to stand next to me. I stopped looking at the wrappers to look at her. My heart began thumping with fear. With the pretence of reaching for a wrapper further up the shelf she pushed me aside. I stepped back. She turned and looked at me from my feet to my head and back to my feet and sighed. I moved into the shop. The shopkeeper and two other customers who were in the shop stopped what they were doing and looked at us. The shopkeeper was ready to stop any brawl that might ensure but was relieved I did not react. I was convinced there was something wrong but I did not know what. I quickly left the shop to avoid any more provocation from the woman. When I left the market two hours later, I was disturbed. I tried to imagine where I had seen the woman before but nothing registered.

Later that evening I narrated this incident to my friend Lucilla. My friendship with Lucilla had carried over from secondary school and we were now like sisters.

"Are you not exaggerating, Lizzy? How can a woman you do not know bear a grudge against you?" she asked with her head tilted to one side and looking at me as if I were just being childish. She continued, "You are a woman to be admired. Don't you know that? Even me, I admire you."

We were sitting on the first floor of a snack bar overlooking the Commercial Avenue in Bamenda. Customers preferred these tables on the balcony, where they could sip their drinks and watch, goings-on in the street below. A brightly coloured awning shaded the balcony and protected it from view.

With the delicious smell of roasting chicken and fish coming from behind the bar, customers salivated – and washed down the slobber with each gulp of beer. Every evening since I arrived in Bamenda, Lucilla and I had been eating here. I always waited with anticipation for our plates, but this evening my worries seemed to have killed my sense of smell and I gave no thought to the appetizing chicken on its way to our table.

I studied Lucilla's peculiar beauty. The expensive nourishing creams she used to keep her skin looking smooth also enhanced her natural darkness. Her beauty is one that reveals itself over time. As you get to know her, her warm personality combines with her external features, leaving an indelible impression.

Our friendship was not the type that could be defined. Lucilla was not married but was able to hold her own. Neither of us went to the university, but after the GCE Advanced Level examination we both struggled with various Public Service Competitive Examinations until we found ourselves jobs and by taking more competitive examinations found ourselves in comfortable rungs of the public service.

I had come to Bamenda to buy loincloths to resell in Douala. We were having a wonderful time and she did not want it to be spoiled by my unnecessary worries.

"I do not know her but she knows me and definitely has something against me."

"You are leaving for Douala tomorrow. Before you leave I will do everything to find out about this woman. We must know who she is. One can never be too sure about women, especially if she did what you just told me."

"Lucilla, do you think I'm lying? Do you think a big woman like me would lie to you? I am serious. If I did not leave the shop, I am sure she would have done everything to get me into a fight with her." I was almost losing my patience with Lucilla. I could not understand why she was taking my story lightly. And this was evident in my voice.

"Alright, Lizzy. It must have been really serious if you are speaking this way."

"I am really scared. I can't imagine what I have done to that woman. What puzzles me more is that I do not even know her."

"By tomorrow evening we will know who this woman is. I will find out." My friend in her own way was trying to allay my fears. My mind kept going back to the events of the morning. Then I remembered something.

"When I was leaving the shop I heard the shopkeeper talking to her. It seems as if the man knows her. I also have the impression that she also has a shop in the market."

"That is good. It makes it easier for me. Now let's forget about her and enjoy ourselves."

I heaved a sigh of relief. I was afraid that she was going to brush my story aside leaving me in state of uncertainty, doubt and fear. I was assured that no matter what happened Lucilla was going to find out who the woman was. Before I left for Douala Lucilla did not succeed in getting the woman's name. Inquiries from the shopkeeper revealed that she was just one of his customers and he did not know her name. A visit to the shops in the market in the guise of window-shopping was in vain. I left for Douala disappointed and afraid.

Two weeks later, I received a letter from Lucilla. She gave me details about the woman who had accosted me in the market. Her name was Sheila. That evening, sitting with my husband in the parlour, another piece of the puzzle fell into place. We were watching television. The children were in their room. They were supposed to be doing their school assignments but from their silence it was evident they had fallen asleep. I got up to check, because I did not want the children to interrupt when I started asking my husband what was on my mind. The two younger children were in bed but the eldest, the boy, was sleeping at the reading table with his head on his book. I got him into bed and went back to sit in the parlour. I did not know how to bring up the topic. I looked at my husband and in a conversational tone asked, "Do you know where Sheila is, Gabby?"

"Which Sheila?"

"The one to whom you were first engaged."

Silence ebbed and flowed. Gabby looked at me steadily. I looked at him too, steadily.

We had been married for twelve years and had three children. One is in secondary school, one in upper primary and the youngest in lower primary. It was not easy having these children for each time my life was at stake. For these twelve years Gabby and I had gone through difficult times together. There were times when we almost came to the point of separation but miraculously stayed together. I have all the symptoms of a middle-aged woman. The stretch marks on my stomach give it a paunchy look. I can no longer wear a straight-cut dress. My life is like sediments at the bottom of a pond, hardly disturbed by the things that disturbed me twelve years ago.

Gabby sat with his legs stretched out in front of him. By the age of forty-six, his vibrancy had matured. His hands rested on his thighs below his paunchy stomach. "The stretch marks on my stomach have given it a paunchy look". Bits of hair held precariously to his scalp. What had not changed was the glint in his eyes. I could see it even in the narrow slits through which he studied me. There were no signs of laughter at the corners of his mouth. But I knew that he was not angry with me for asking. We have had so many misunderstandings so many times that this was not a big deal. I had also learnt that we are the architects of our own misery and was ready to calm the situation if it erupted. But it did not. As he looked at me he seemed to be retracing his journey back to that period long ago. I could also remember it as if it was yesterday. A ray of remembrance lit up his face. He smiled.

"It is long since I saw her. I don't even know where she is."

"She is in Bamenda."

"How did you know that?"

"I met her there. She recognized me first."

"How did she know you?"

"I do not know."

"Why did you ask about her?" Gabby asked.

"Well, it was just curiosity."

Gabby was about to ask another question but lapsed into silence. Then he turned to me as if to speak but turned to the television again. His eyes were now focused on the screen as if he could not afford to miss what was going on. I also turned to watch. Bilia Bell was doing one of her intricate foot works as she moved to the rhythm of drums and guitars. It was an arresting sight and we both watched her. At one point she winked at her unseen audience. By reflex, I turned to look at Gabby. He was smiling. Oh this eternal pull! I thought. Age cannot destroy it.

My thoughts went back to Sheila. What had prompted her to behave towards me like that? I wondered. Was there something she was missing, of which I had deprived her? Was it Gabby she wanted? Was I responsible for their break? I never even knew about her when I met Gabby. But I got to know so much about her from Gabby.

So much water had passed below the bridge and there was no need to stand watching to see what it could have been. I brushed away those thoughts. They were time consuming and led to nowhere. I turned my thoughts to the events that had led to making Gabby and I husband and wife.

Our psychological states are usually sustained by our own imaginations and actions. Our misery cannot be caused by something out of us. If it is, we must have created the first crack. The conflicts I have had with Gabby must have been caused by our egos and not by the diamond ring he had given to Sheila, which was suspected to have magical powers enough to prevent Gabby from marrying. Many of his friends had believed that either the ring was cursed or Sheila had cursed Gabby before disappearing to the north of the country. As far as I was concerned neither the ring nor Sheila had any influence on our lives. Sheila had disappeared and the ring was lying at the bottom of the sea. Gabby and I have stuck together all these years. Before we met there had been other women and men in our lives. After twelve years Sheila's presence was not going to make any difference. It is funny how people meet and stick together.

I continued to look at the TV screen but my mind was not there. It was back to the days after my first meeting with Gabby.

My dear readers, my encounter with Sheila has brought back so many memories, which I would have liked to share with you. But since my daily activities do not permit me to have a session with you like Sharezede of The Arabian Nights, and I am sure you too are quite busy, I have written it down for you to read at your leisure.

1

I met Gabby at a Njangi-party in Douala. I was on leave and intent on enjoying myself as much as possible. I got myself invited to parties where I could meet people. Meeting people was one of my favourite pastimes, not just because I was still single but for the fun of it. That evening I took particular care over my makeup and dress. I knew what fitted me and I made good use of this knowledge to accentuate my curves. I drew back my luxurious hair in a bun and clasped it with a hairpin. I finally decided after a lot of hesitation on a pair of low-heeled shoes, which would be good for dancing. Being of average height, this was to no disadvantage. With a last look in the mirror, I stepped out of the bedroom with confidence.

Jane, the friend with whom I was spending my leave exclaimed, "Chei, Lizzy! You look smart. You will surely leave some broken hearts in Douala when you leave."

"Who am I compared to the classy Douala girls. I am just a girl from a provincial town. I cannot compare with girls who are used to looking fashionable all the time. Remember that this is the economic capital and anything new from abroad gets to you first."

"You are just being modest. You know you look smashing. And a new face is always an attraction to the men."

I smiled but made no response. Jane had invited me to spend my leave with her but I felt uncomfortable having to follow her wherever she went. This was because she was always with her boyfriend, Benny, and I sometimes got in their way but there was nothing I could do. I tried to enjoy myself in spite of the situation.

We arrived at the home party early enough and there were still seats on the lawn. Benny suggested we sit on the veranda however, where we could watch all that was going on. He sat between Jane and myself and did his best to engage me in conversation. The party was in celebration of the fiftieth birthday of one of Benny's colleagues. It was not a speech-making occasion and after the host had made the only speech and supper was about to be served from the garage, the guests started milling around and getting acquainted. The food was superb and I took enough to arm myself for the evening and the dancing that was to follow. After a glass of Mateus wine I felt my armpits damp and my forehead moist. The wine and the heat combined to outdo my antiperspirant.

1

It was an informal occasion and the host had made it clear in his welcome speech that he had invited his guests to have a nice time that evening. A few couples were called to open the floor for dancing. The garage was on one side and out of the way, so while some people were dancing in the living room, which had been cleared of all furniture, others were still eating. The dancing was well underway when during one of the breaks, a man walked to our table. He greeted Benny in a peer-like manner and I immediately knew they were chums. After the introductions, the man had not moved away when a popular tune started. Jane stood up and took Benny's hand to lead him to the dance floor and said, "Gabby, why don't you and Lizzy try this one out?"

We went to the dance floor and were digging it out. I was dancing and enjoying myself as I had done with my other partners who had asked me for a dance. I just happened to be one of the unhooked girls around. They had not engaged me in any conversation except the usual, "How are you enjoying the party?" I also made sure I did not engage any of them in a conversation. But as soon as I started dancing with Gabby he started asking me questions, which I answered as evasively as I could. I was just putting on a front because the moment he walked to our table I was fascinated by his easy mannerism and the glint in his eyes when he smiled. Although my answers were evasive, they were accompanied by a smile. At one point I caught Jane's eyes and she winked at me. By the end of the first dance Gabby knew why I was in Douala. By the end of the second he knew where I worked. By the time he left he had promised to see me again. I knew nothing about him except that he was called Gabby, was Benny's friend and worked in Douala.

When we arrived home I bid Benny a goodnight and left both of them in the car. I knew they had things to say and do with each other and I did not want to be in their way. As soon as I took off my shoes and dress, I fell on the bed and sleep claimed me.

I did not know when Jane came back to the house. I was fast asleep and dreaming about the evening. Snatches of conversation, facial expressions and especially the way I felt when Gabby held me in his arms came intermittently in my sleep.

The next day as I did the housework, I thought about Gabby all the time. At one point I had to rebuke myself for saying so much to a complete stranger and on top of that thinking about him.

Jane could not restrain herself the next day when she came back from work.

"Who were you smiling at in your sleep last night? And I have seen you smile to yourself many times since I came back."

Her question took me unawares and I had to think up an answer, which I knew was not convincing. But before I could say anything she began telling me about Gabby.

Gabby was one of those boys whom nature had favoured as far as looks are concerned. He was slim and well muscled. This must have been a result of hours in the gymnasium. His main feature was his angular face, with a line of moustache crowning his upper lip. He was always impeccably dressed and a good talker. He knew how to put people at ease He also knew when to put on the right expression to charm his listeners. He had fallen in and out of love many times but had never talked of marriage to any woman as far as Jane knew. These qualities made him a prey to many girls and women who thought they could get him to make the proposal. He was the type of man capable of making any woman feel loved. But his affections were showered on so many women. Those who thought he was serious didn't think it for long. He was a worker at the National Produce Marketing Board headquarters in Douala and earned a heavy salary. I savoured all Jane had to share about Gabby, afraid to ask any question that might betray my feelings.

We spent the rest of the evening chatting about our mutual friends in Bamenda and Douala. I prayed in my heart that the conversation would not turn to the subject of boyfriends. At the moment there was no serious person in my life after I had made up my mind to forget about Andrew. I was getting tired of the hide and seek game of boyfriends. I wanted a steady relationship even if it did not lead to marriage. I did not want to rush or be rushed into any situation. I had made no response to Jane's narration about Gabby, but this did not deter her from going on with what was on her mind.

"What do you think about Gabby?"

My heart fluttered and I tried to make as if I had not heard her question. I stole a glance at Jane to see whether she had noticed the trembling of my lips. Jane was putting nail vanish on her nails and did not look up as she spoke. She continued as if I had given a response.

"The dancing yesterday with Gabby was done more with the mouth than the legs. You did not seem to be aware of the people around you. You were just talking and talking. What were you talking about?"

"Just the normal chitchat that such situations require to maintain an amicable atmosphere," I replied.

"But you were smiling more than I have ever seen you smile," she said.

"I was just enjoying myself. That is all. By the way, is Benny coming this evening?" I asked, to change the topic of conversation.

"He said he was going to Bafoussam to see their branch manager there first thing this morning, so he'll return early this evening. We have been great friends and, not to keep you in the dark, I think something is going to come of this relationship. Benny has been urging me to make a trip with him to his village. I am not convinced enough about his plans to go with him. That is what we stayed up talking about the other night. I have never been to Bali and I am just confused as to what to do. It's been a long time since I left Bamenda and I am not current with the state of affairs between the Ngenbu and Bali people. Also, I do not know what my parents are going to say. I love Benny but I am afraid something is going to prevent us from getting married. My parents may not be in favour of our union."

"I know your parents. Jane, they are enlightened people. I am sure they will not want to destroy your happiness because of some tribal conflict. They have always had your interest at heart."

"Well, I hope so and pray everything turns out for the best."

We spent the rest of the afternoon reading novels, sleeping and chatting. Benny came back later in the evening and invited us out. I declined the invitation preferring to stay home and read a novel. From what Jane had told me that afternoon I knew they needed to be by themselves to talk about what was on their minds. When they did not insist I join them, I silently congratulated myself on my decision.

Three days later at noon, there was a knock on the door. I wondered who could be calling at this time of the day. Jane was at work and did not usually come home for break because of the distance from her office. I looked through the window to see who was outside. Then I opened the door. There was Gabby with that disarming smile on his face and his hands in his pockets.

"Hello, may I come in?"

I answered finally by extending my hand in greeting. His hand felt soft and warm, and he held my hand longer than necessary. I was in no hurry for him to let go.

"Remember, I promised to see you again," he said, looking into my eyes.

I did not know what to say and my mind was racing wildly trying to think of what to say. My broad smile came to my rescue.

"I hope you got a good night's sleep after the party," he continued.

"Yes I did. I was really exhausted," I replied, not being able to think of anything better to say. When he was seated he looked round the room. I followed his gaze. I was sure this was not his first time in this room and wondered why he had to take so much time looking around. I did not know that he too did not know how to break the ice. I had longed to see him again but never thought of what I might say to him. Now both of us were sitting in Jane's parlour with nothing to say to each other. The silence was becoming ridiculous and I put my head down and smiled. He caught

4

me at it and asked.

"What is so amusing?" I could no longer pretend and lifted up my head with the smile still on my face and replied.

"To be honest with you I looked forward to seeing you again. But now that you are here, I suddenly don't know what to say to you."

"Since you have been honest with me, I am going to be honest with you too. I have also been looking forward to seeing you. And I am surprised that now that I am here, I no longer know what to say."

"Did you have something you had prepared to tell me that you have forgotten?"

"Yes. It was all on my mind. I thought that when the opportunity lent itself I would be able to put it in words. But here I am."

"Maybe I should give you time to think about it."

"No. I do not need time to think about it anymore. All I have been thinking to tell you is that I like you. I like your company."

As he said this he looked out the window with a serious expression. I did not like this expression and tried to make light of the situation.

"How can you say you like me? You do not even know me."

"I know you enough to like you."

"What do you know about me?"

"I know your name, I know where you work, I know you're a good dancer, and you like dancing. I know you are from Bamenda. I am also from Bamenda. Are these not enough reasons to show that I know you?"

I could not respond because I remembered that I had told him much about myself as we danced. But I did not want to let him off so easily.

"Don't expect me to like you, because I do not know you."

"Why are you doing all these, Lizzy? I know you understand what I mean. As time goes on you will know more about me. If you like what you will get to know, fine, if not too bad for me. But you just said that you've been looking forward to seeing me. That is a good sign that you are going to like what you will learn about me."

"I hope so."

He did not respond to this and we lapsed again into silence. The nature of our sparring was evidence of the fact that we understood each other more than we were ready to accept. Thinking of nothing to say I offered him lunch. It seemed as if he had just left the office and come straight to see me. He did not want to eat alone, so I brought a plate and took some food for myself to keep him company as he ate. Over the meal I got to know what he had been doing since we met. I was tempted to ask him more searching questions but the easy manner in which he responded to my questions assured me that I would get to know whatever I wanted in due course. He left promising to come back in the evening.

As soon as Jane came back from work I told her what had happened. I watched her face to see her reaction. She only smiled and kept quiet. When I told her I would like her to come along with me because Gabby had invited me out that evening, her smile became broader.

"Jane, why do you look so happy?" I asked.

"I am happy for you," she replied. "Gabby is a nice man." Then she changed the topic.

"I was getting a bit worried."

"About what?" I asked.

"Lizzy, you are a young woman. And we have been friends for long so I understand you very well. Since you told me about Andrew I have been thinking and watching you."

"You were thinking of ways to make me forget?"

"Of course, why should a young and beautiful woman like you spend her energy on someone who does not even think of her?"

"Oh, Jane you are incredible. So what makes you think what you are thinking?"

"It's all over you. I can see it in your eyes. Just give him a chance."

"I have to give myself a chance too."

"Now you are talking," she said as we hit our palms together as a sign of mutual understanding.

At seven thirty that evening Gabby came to take me out. I told him that Jane was coming along with us. I did not even think of how he would react to this. I just did not see myself going without asking Jane along. There was no secret between us and I wanted her to be present on this first day to give me an objective opinion later on. But I did not miss the slight look of disappointment that passed across Gabby's face before he covered it up with one of his dazzling smiles. Before we left, Jane left a note on the table informing Benny of where we were. We had just ordered drinks in a nearby snack bar when Benny appeared. As the evening progressed I found Gabby's leg increasingly brushing against mine under the table. I offered no resistance. In fact I was enjoying it all. As we left the bar two hours later he clasped my hand and held me back. Benny and Jane went ahead of us.

"Good night, Lizzy," he whispered in my ears. "I want to see you again. But this time alone."

In response, I squeezed his palm and we hastened our steps to join the others. The rest of the two weeks I had decided to spend in Douala passed like a whirlwind.

It was like the beginning of an adventure and I waited anxiously for it to get to the next stage. It was evident from the start that we were interested in each other. The looks, the gestures, the deep feeling of excitement and

6

the inexplicable attraction or thunderbolt as it is often called were all present. Here was this handsome, suave man-about-town Gabby who could have any woman at his beck and call falling for a woman like me. What had I in comparison with the sophisticated Douala girls? I was impressed when I first met Gabby but feared his attention was just a bit of flirting. I got this feeling there was something I could not really place my finger on. Gabby's unwavering attention was too good to be true. I decided that if he wanted to continue the game, that would be fine with me. I was ready to play along. But I was not going to allow myself to be exploited. He looked like the type of man who would take a girl for a ride just to satisfy some macho male desire. My guard was up and I watched him closely. The closer I watched the more I discovered about him. I wanted to discover things that would help me shy away in good time. Instead I found things that endeared him to me. For example, I have long hair and when permed, it falls to my shoulders. I see no need to attach artificial hair to it. Although I admire it on other women's heads I did not want to do it. Attaching artificial hair to one's hair is a sign of sophistication, and I expected Gabby to criticize me for not doing it. Instead he would smooth my hair backwards telling me how good and natural it felt. I felt flattered. He paid attention to just those things about me that I did not want him to notice. He would comment on my neat well trimmed short nails. When I think about it now I wonder whether he was just responding to the male desire to keep what is theirs pure and simple while they admire sophistication in other women. Well I was happy that he took me for what I was and prayed that I was not just one other woman in his repertoire.

Each time Gabby invited me out I made sure I went with Jane. This was not so much because I was afraid of him or what he might do. I just wasn't ready to commit myself so soon to another man.

Andrew Tasah, my boyfriend for six years, had let our friendship die out. His letters dwindled until in that last year I received just a postcard, which did not say much. I could not keep hoping on him. I wanted to make a break before it became too late. I had already written a letter to this effect, but it lay in my drawer in the office. I had wanted my emotions to stabilize before I sent it.

My trip to Douala was to help me get over this situation. A change of scene would do me good. I never thought I was going to get involved with another man so soon. I had intended to marry Andrew and a fling with a man I might not meet again was out of the question. Gabby did not look like the type of man who would easily get himself tied down with one woman as a wife. As far as such men are concerned, they believe they still have a long way to go before marriage. And they do. There is no age limit at which a man can get married. But for the woman the story is different.

7

Gabby was just the right man to give a girl a good time and make her feel special. When the weekend arrived, he commented how either Jane or Benny was with us each evening we went out. So I was not surprised when Benny explained that he and Jane had already made plans for the weekend. Since I had promised Gabby, I could not go back on my word. On Saturday at four p.m. Gabby came looking for me. I did not expect him to come that early. Jane and Benny had already left and I had no reason for not accompanying him where he wanted us to go. He took me to a restaurant in a residential building, which had been converted into a public place where people could come and have food and drink in a quiet environment. The yard in front of the building had been separated from the street with a one and a half meter plank wall. There were beach umbrellas over the tables. Customers could sit in the airy yard as they enjoyed their drinks. The wall limited contact with the surrounding buildings and at the same time provided a good view of the street on the other side. At the entrance to the restaurant from the yard hung strings of beads made into a curtain that clicked together when the breeze blew or when somebody pushed them aside to pass. Gabby led me across the yard into the building itself and made a beeline for a table set for two. It seemed as if the customers present did not occupy this table because of their numbers. The smallest group was made of three people. I wondered why there were not many people. Then I remembered that it was a Saturday and the afternoon period for that matter. When I looked around I found another reason why there weren't many people. The décor was superb. There were potted plants placed at strategic locations to create an exotic atmosphere. The tiles on the floor, even on the extension outside, were good and expensive. Even the cloths on the tables were a step ahead of the usual plastic ones. To crown it all, the prices of the food and drinks indicated that not just any type of person could afford to come here.

Before we were seated there was a waiter at our table waiting to take our orders. I was thirsty and wanted a cold beer, so I asked for a Gold Harp. Gabby ordered the same thing. While we waited for our drinks, Gabby suggested we move our chairs together closer to the wall so we could watch what was going on around us without his having to turn his head round. As soon as we were seated in our new positions, I lifted my right hand to place my purse on the table. When I brought my hand back and placed it on my lap he placed his own hand on it and kept it in place. He alternately squeezed and released it. I turned to look at him. He was not looking at me. His gaze was fixed at the entrance. I tried to pull my hand away but he held it firmer and whispered, "Please just let it be." All along we had not said much to each other and I had the feeling that there was something wrong. For the short time that I had known Gabby, it was

8

evident that he was the type of man to keep up the mood of any gathering. He was full of life, fun and jokes. He always kept us laughing at his jokes. I think this was one of the things in him that appealed to me the most. He took life as it came. He appeared not to be serious about anything. But this was a defence mechanism, for when he felt deeply about something you could see it on his face. I got to know this later in our relationship but on that day I was at a loss. I did not know what to say. I was not only disturbed by his mood, I could not also initiate any conversation for I was not sure of where it would lead. When our beers were brought he first poured mine then his. He held up his glass for a toast and looked at me. I did not know to what we were toasting, but I was forced to take up my own glass. He tapped his glass against mine saying, "To many more occasions like this." Then he smiled. I also smiled. His pronouncement was weighty and I could not understand why he was behaving the way he was. We drank in silence, each occupied with watching the other people rather than each other. I wished Benny and Jane were with us. I was even looking forward to going to a nightclub.

"You will surely like something to eat. There is fish, chicken and pork. Which would you like?"

I was still too uncertain to say anything which I really meant. Moreover I had been silent for so long that my jaw muscles seemed stuck. I managed to swallow saliva to clear my throat and lubricate my tongue.

"Whatever you order, I will also eat."

"Are you sure, choose something yourself."

"Whatever you choose will be good for me."

"I hope you will keep to what you have said."

"What do you mean by that?" I asked.

"Don't worry about what I have just said."

There was silence for some time. I watched Gabby. He seemed to be making up his mind about something. Then he asked me when I would be going back to Bamenda. This was safe ground and I could answer without having to choose my words. We talked for some time. As we talked he loosened up. I tried to be cheerful and enjoy myself. When he laughed he sent his arm round my shoulders and pulled me closer to him. As we ate he selected tasty pieces and put them on my plate. At first he wanted to put them in my mouth but I did not allow this. He did not mind my refusal saying he respected my reaction. The barrier caused by his earlier moodiness was wearing off and he was trying to be himself again. He was such a joker and one never knew when he was joking to know when he was serious. That afternoon I was seeing more of who Gabby really was. When he leaned closer to my ear and whispered that he loved me, I asked him if he was not making a mistake.

"A mistake in the right direction."

"A right move in the wrong direction," I corrected him. For the first time that evening he laughed out loud, and the heartiness in his voice vibrated in the air. People turned to look at us. But he did not mind their stares. He was enjoying the banter with me. He kissed me several times on my cheek. Each time I made a comment to contradict whatever intention was behind the kiss and whatever effect he wanted to create. He could not believe what he was hearing. I could see from his face that he was not used to being treated that way. Maybe he thought I would immediately fall for his charms. I wanted to keep him at bay without antagonizing him or discouraging him. I was enjoying myself and the attention he paid to me only went to increase my excitement.

After the plates were cleared he ordered another round of drinks. When the bottles were getting empty I looked at my watch. It was about eight thirty in the evening. I suggested to Gabby that we call it a day. I knew he would not welcome this for he was used to saying, "The night is just beginning." He did not object and soon paid the bill and escorted me to Jane's house. I thought she would be at home waiting to find out what had happened. When I opened the door, to my chagrin, Jane was not there. I then realized that it was a ruse they had played to allow Gabby and I to be alone. I expected him to say goodnight but he just stood there looking at me. I leaned on the wall, folded my arms and looked back at him. I felt the twitch of a smile at the corners of my mouth. He too started smiling and then moved towards me. I sent out my two arms to ward him off but he held them.

"You are a very special person, Lizzy. I have never met a woman like you." He seemed to continue with the banter of the evening. I deliberately did not want to understand what he meant.

"I hope that I am not 'Special'," I said, changing the pronunciation to sound like a brand of beer that used to be very popular. "I hope you are not going to drink me."

"That's what I intend to do if you will allow me."

"Then you will have to reduce me to liquid first."

"That's what I have been trying to do the whole evening. Only that you are too frozen to melt. I hope that with time the ice will melt and I will drink my fill."

"By the time the ice melts, if it will I will not be here."

"Then I will have to apply more heat. Could you just melt for a moment for me to kiss you?" he said, as he moved nearer. He did not wait for me to answer. His lips were already on mine. But I still refused to let him have his way.

"Lizzy, please behave yourself."

"You should be the one to behave yourself. How can you kiss a woman without her consent?" This question took him aback.

"Okay, I am sorry that I did it without your consent. Are you going to give your consent before I go?"

"Oh Gabby you are really insistent. You look like the type of man who always gets what he wants."

"That may be true. But you will have to find that out for yourself. All I want now is just to kiss you with your permission."

"I will only allow you if you promise to behave better next time."

"Oh, next time I am going to do my best."

Before the words were out of his mouth his arms were around me and he kissed me gently. The kiss was not a very engaging one as I was dying with laughter when I realized the implication of my statement and the meaning of his answer.

"Gabby, goodnight. Please just go." I did not want him to linger anymore, afraid of letting down my barrier and what I would do if he attempted to kiss me again.

In fact Gabby's presence excited me, but I had to keep a firm grip on the reins of my emotions and the events to come. Before leaving he promised to take me out again on Wednesday. He reminded me that we were to be alone. I was enjoying Gabby's company more and more but I could not really locate my feelings for him. There was this overwhelming sense of contentment as I looked forward to Wednesday.

Jane came back at two in the morning. She was so tired that I had to virtually get her out of bed to prepare for work when day broke. My presence was a big relief to her as I helped her in doing the cooking and cleaning the house. This was not much and I still had so much time on my hands. I usually went window-shopping and tried to get to know the city better. But on Wednesday I did not go anywhere. I stayed at home. After cooking and cleaning the house I took a novel to the bedroom and started to read. I soon fell asleep and was awakened by the sound of knocking and a voice calling my name. Before I got up and went to the parlour, Gabby was already inside the house. I had forgotten to lock the door when I went into the bedroom. He had come to remind me to be ready at five o'clock that evening because he was coming to take me out. Five p.m. was too early but I did not argue. He was in a hurry and left quickly. At five p.m. on the dot he was at the door. I was sitting in the parlour and Jane was sleeping in the room. I had told her that I would be going out with Gabby so I did not wake her but left a note on the table. In the taxi he looked moody again. I did not want his mood of four days ago to mar my expectations, so I asked him about his day at work. He gave me a brief description of his daily routine at the office and lapsed into silence again. We arrived at a neighbourhood and he asked the taxi man to stop. We got out and I looked around. It was a residential area with no sign of a drinking spot in sight. Gabby held my hand and led me down a side street. The side street was without tar. He stopped at a small gate which he opened, and we walked in. He was taking me to his house.

The parlour was well furnished for a bachelor's house. He had a good set of chairs and a rug on the floor. There was an expensive cupboard covering one wall and a small dining table in the area close to the kitchenette. It was quite a cosy and convenient arrangement for a bachelor. I stood and looked around for some time while Gabby watched me. He could see from my face that I appreciated what I was seeing. I went ahead to put it in words.

"You have a nice setup here."

He thanked me for the compliment and went into the bedroom to remove his coat. I sat down still looking around. There were pictures of two exotic flowers on the wall. There was the orchid with its innocent looking white petals and the sundew with its pitcher waiting for unwary insects. There was also the image of a flower made from assorted sizes of seashells. There was no picture of Gabby himself hanging on the wall and I wondered why. What attracted my attention the most was the picture of a woman with a baby on her back pounding in a long mortar. I stood up to take a closer look. From a distance it looked like a painting but on a closer look I noticed that the whole picture was made up of butterfly wings skilfully stuck together. It was a masterpiece of creativity. I was still admiring it when Gabby came out.

"That's one of my most treasured pictures. When I bought it I could not believe it was made only with butterfly wings."

I agreed with him. No mixture of colours could come out with such hues. Only nature could be so meticulous. The glass case protecting the picture gave it depth, which made it look ethereal. When he led me back to the double sitter he held both my hands and spoke as if it was a speech he had rehearsed.

"You must be wondering why I brought you here." Pause. "I did not want to say what I have to say in a public place because I do not know how you will react." Pause. "I bring girls here when I have intent. They are usually aware and willing. But with you it is different. I will not declare my love for you by telling you that I love you. You will not take me serious because you know that I have said it to many girls. The point is that I find you a special person. There is something that pulls me to you. I do not know whether it is love. I do not think so because it is different. You are not like the other girls I have met. I want a closer relationship with you than you can imagine. Am I making any sense to you?" I nodded my head. I put a pensive and serious look on my face while my heart raced with happiness. He went on. "I am tired of running around with girls. They slip through my fingers. I do not know whether the fault is theirs or mine. But I think that you are different." "What makes you think that way?" I asked. "I have been watching you. Before that, when I approached the veranda of the house where we met during the party, I thanked God that I had not come with a girl. Maybe it was God who guided me that evening." He had not answered my question but I let it be. As he spoke his arm went around me. He continued. "Is there no response to my speech?" "Gabby, you have helped to make my stay here very interesting. In fact you have played a very important role in making me happy here. As you guessed, I can't also say I love you because it means different things to different people. But I really appreciate the type of person you are." I stopped. I could not continue. He waited for me to continue. The look on his face did not border on elation but when he lifted his eyes to look at me his eyes sparkled as if what I had said only made sense to him at that moment. "That is good for now. But I hope that you are not going to end at appreciating who I am." He got up and went into the kitchenette. He pulled out a tray from the oven and came and placed it in front of me. He brought out two bottles of Gold Harp from the refrigerator and placed them on a plastic mat on the table. Next he went to the cupboard and brought out two glasses. He brought water for me to wash my hands. I watched him carry out these activities and wondered at the impressions people's actions create in us. Seeing Gabby on the street or in the office, one would not believe that he could do such homely things as pulling a tray out of an oven. In the dual personalities each of us have, it is the other one, the real us, that we try to hide from people, the real 'us' that acts as a buffer between our ego and the demands of existence, that inner self which we hardly reveal and that self that keeps us sane. It was this side of Gabby he was letting me see. It might not have occurred to him that this was what he was doing. But I saw through his actions. "I thought we should spend the evening in a quiet way here. I got the chicken and kept it warm in the oven. I hope you are going to enjoy it." I was actually smiling now. He continued, "You never really let me know what is on your mind, Lizzy. You baffle me. What are you smiling at now?"

"I am just admiring the serious way you are going about things."

"Which things?"

"You put the tray on the table so quietly as if it would protest."

"You look at things from very unusual angles. I did not even know that that was what I was doing," he said.

"You could not have. It came from deep inside you." He made no comment but looked at me as if my nose had suddenly grown out of size.

The chicken was delicious and we ate it all. The homely atmosphere and the fact that we were eating with our fingers made it tastier. I never really enjoyed chicken when I had to eat it with a knife and fork, pulling off the flesh and leaving the crunchy ends of the drumsticks for the sake of eating etiquette. I ate without inhibitions. I thought that if Gabby appreciated me the way I was then he would go to the end. He also enjoyed pulling the flesh off with his fingers and licking the dripping oil. I have a way of laughing at nothing when I am happy. I laughed and Gabby thought I was laughing at the way he was licking his fingers. He made me laugh more when he said the juice was too tasty to be wasted.

After the meal he brought out a bottle of whisky. I got up and carried the tray and empty bottles to the kitchenette. Then we sat back to savour the whisky and the pleasure of each other's company. The combination of chicken, beer and whisky was having a marvellous effect on me. I do not know whether it was the effect of finding something where and when you did not expect it that made me to feel so contented. We talked about a number of issues. I cannot remember any. All I remember is that we talked as if we had known each other well before then, and that all we were doing was reminiscing. One thing I noticed about Gabby that persists until today is that he can, without a warning, throw in a remark which on the surface looks unrelated to the topic of conversation but which on closer examination carries an understatement. This usually brought a lull in the conversation and if his listener were not attentive and tactful the conversation would be left suspended uncomfortably. You would be left wondering what he meant. Both of us appreciated Bamenda but when he told me that in future I would live in Douala, I did not see what connection it had with what we were saying. At that moment I did not for one second think that things were going to turn out the way they did. It was only later that the meaning of his remark became clear. I made as if I did not hear his remark and the conversation continued.

When I look back on that first day in Gabby's house, I wonder why he did not attempt to take me to bed. I was so at ease and had such a warm longing for him that if he had made a move I do not think I would have resisted. When I narrated the events of that evening to Jane she just smiled.

I could see she was contented with the way things were moving between Gabby and me. I had just one more week in Douala. Going out with Gabby had become a routine. He knew I had nothing to occupy myself, so he did everything to keep me happy. The four of us went to the nightclub my last weekend in Douala. Then my leave came to an end and I had to leave for Bamenda. Gabby reassured me of his love and promised to keep in touch. To me out of sight was not out of mind.

2

B ack in Bamenda I had to adjust both physically and emotionally. I could not believe that Bamenda was so cold although I had spent much of my life there. I also had to accept the fact that although Gabby was not with me my love for him was not going to diminish. In fact as I thought more about him, I longed to go back to Douala. Thinking about him made me moody instead of elated. Maybe I felt that way because my wish could not be fulfilled. I was so much in my own world that I was not aware of the fact that my colleagues had noticed a change in me.

"Why are you so moody Lizzy?" asked the woman in the room next to mine. "Since you came back from leave you have not been yourself." This woman often sat in for me when I could not be available. She was also a private secretary and took my place when I went on leave. Her question put me on the watch out. If she took the time to ask me, it meant that my other colleagues must have been talking about it. I tried to be myself but things could not be the same. I even stopped going out with some of the men with whom I used to spend some evenings out for a drink or a visit to the nightclub. Although I was not as communicative with my colleagues as I used to be, I excelled in my work. To keep myself from thinking about Gabby all the time I buried myself in my work, producing documents for my boss in record time. At home I occupied myself with various activities just to keep my mind occupied. I even started doing some embroidery.

Doing things with my hands was something I loved right from primary school when I could hold two broomsticks in my hand and spin some wool round my finger. I could not see any piece of wool lying about without picking it up and attaching it to others I had picked up earlier. I put all sorts of colours of wool together and the resultant muffler was as multicoloured as Joseph's coat. In the upper primary when we were introduced to needlework, particularly crocheting which was locally known as tumakasa, it became easier. Miniature skirts, blouses and pants were made from wool picked up here and there. The completion of an item was a triumph, to be displayed to friends and then discarded. When knitting or crocheting I could escape from housework. I disappeared for hours hunched up in a corner, usually behind the house with a broomstick and some wool.

When I was in secondary school I started crocheting a bedspread, which I never completed. What I was working on now was a set of chair covers, which I had also started but not completed. These bouts of crocheting, like reading a novel, were a means of escaping from my thoughts. But unlike reading a novel which I could not leave, I could leave crocheting and pick it up again months or even years after. This was one of such bout.

Two weeks after I returned from leave my boss rang for me. I got up with mixed feelings. I dreaded going into his office. It had seemed as if God was putting me to the test. I had always tried to maintain a friendly but respectable attitude toward my boss. I respected him and did my best to make his work easier. Because of this I was often willing to stay late and do some urgent work for him. He appreciated this.

One afternoon three weeks before I went on leave just the two of us were left in the office. A team of directors was holding a meeting in town and he had to attend that meeting with some statistics. We were working late to get the documents ready. He left his room and came into mine and sat in the visitor's chair. I looked up waiting for the question I thought he was going to ask about how far I had gone with the typing. But he just looked at me and smiled. I was puzzled and continued typing to hide my confusion.

"Elizabeth, why are you pretending as if you do not understand what I have been trying to tell you though not in words?"

"What have you been trying to tell me, sir?" I asked.

"Oh, Lizzy, don't behave like a small girl. I want to invite you out this evening." I was too surprised to give an answer. I had not been blind to the moves he had been making. But I had thought that my indifference would tell him that I was not interested. His outright invitation that afternoon left me speechless. But I covered up by continuing to type. He placed his hand on mine on the keyboard and I had to stop typing. I did not wait for him to say anything.

"Thank you sir, for the invitation, but I am sorry that it cannot be possible."

"Why Lizzy? I knew that you were going to say something like that. I am sorry to be prying. But do you have a boyfriend? I have the impression that you do not have any serious boyfriend."

I was caught. But there was no reason why I should tell him the truth. When I was agonizing over Andrew I hadn't needed a shoulder to cry on.

"I am not in a position to answer that question now, sir. But that does not mean I have rejected your invitation. We can go out some other day but not today."

He did not look pleased with my response. I had answered without answering his question. After this incident he did not change his behaviour towards me. I could not understand why after what had happened he was still so solicitous. I had noticed this differential attitude towards me in the office but thought it was just his way of appreciating my work.

Things came to a head two weeks later during a send-off party organized for some staff who were retiring. The party was well advanced and everybody was in a dancing mood. All evening I had been avoiding my boss. He was the type of man who loved enjoying himself. He loved dancing and could not sit down while a good record was on. I found myself dancing next to him. When the record ended and another started, I was about to go and sit down when he held my hand and prevented me from going back to my seat. We started dancing. There was a stretch of three Makossa tunes, which he danced with me. As he danced he held me close whispering in my ears and caressing me. I did not know whether he was drunk or it was a premeditated action. Before this he had been dancing with other women and might have forgotten that his wife was present. She was left sitting alone on the high table for five successive records and did not like it. She could bear it no longer and left the high table. I did not know whether she had gone to the ladies water closet or she had gone home. One of my friends noticed her prolonged absence and whispered in my ears and I informed my boss. He excused himself at the end of the record to go and find out what was happening to his wife. She was standing outside by the car waiting for him. There was a nasty row at home and I was the target. I did not like this and made it clear to him. I was relieved to be going on leave the next week. Since I came back I did not think of what had happened until that morning.

When he came in that morning he answered my greeting with a grunt. So when he rang for me I was very uncomfortable. I steeled myself and knocked at the door before going in. As I walked in he stood up with a smile and extended his hand in greeting. I was surprised at his change of mood. I sat down and looked at a point above his head so that I could see his face without actually looking at him.

He was a good administrator and knew how to handle his personnel. He not only encouraged a healthy relationship among his staff, but he also made sure he maintained a similar relationship between his staff and himself. He had a way of handling situations, which never gave the person concerned time to prepare a defence. Even if you foresaw and prepared, he would disarm you before beginning. If he had to scold you for not obeying one of the office regulations, something he often did before giving a written query, he called you into his office and put you at ease by asking about your family, before launching into questioning about the indiscretion. He would speak quietly but firmly about your obligations and commitment to duty. Now he was speaking quietly but with concern.

"I have been worried about you. Since you came back from leave you have been quiet even when the other girls are conversing. Is there anything wrong?"

"No, sir."

"Please do not get me wrong. I really want to be of help. Forget about what happened. There is no string attached to my offering you help. You are one of the girls I admire for their steadfastness and discipline. If I did not call you to find out what is happening I could not have felt fine with myself."

"There is nothing wrong, sir." I answered smiling as if the smile would dispel his fears. But he continued.

"Life is too short to be spent the way you are doing. Why don't you go out and enjoy yourself as you used to do? I hear some of the things your friends say. It seems as if you are no longer interested in enjoying yourself. If I invite you out it is because I genuinely want to make you cheerful again and to make amends for what happened."

"Thanks for your concern sir. I appreciate what you are doing for me…" At that moment there was a knock at the door and a man opened and walked in.

"I did not see your secretary so I thought I should find out if you were inside," the man said as he walked towards my boss. I could see that they knew each other.

"It's okay, Jimmy, I was just giving my secretary instructions on some documents she has to prepare for me."

The man sat down without being invited.

"That is all for now. When you are through with the typing let me see the draft copy first."

"All right, sir, I will do that." My presence was no longer needed and I stood up to go out. Back at my seat I thought about what my boss had just said. I saw nothing wrong with having a drink with him if he was as sincere as he sounded. I made up my mind. There was no need to give in to a situation, which did not exist. My anger against his wife was not enough for me to get back at her in any way. Moreover rejecting his invitation would create an unhealthy atmosphere between us in the office. It would be mean for me to take advantage of the situation and make good of her suspicions. I valued a genial relationship with my colleagues as well as my boss. I had it firmly fixed in the back of my mind that I would not allow this atmosphere to be tainted. On the other hand I did not want to put him in a situation of expectancy – expecting things to be different one day. If I had wanted to exploit the situation and get money from him I could have done so. But I respected him and valued my position as his private secretary too much to behave in an unbecoming manner.

"Can I give you a lift?" It was a Saturday morning a week later and I was standing by the roadside waiting for a taxi to go to the market. My boss was sitting at the wheel smiling at me. This was one of the few times I saw him driving himself. He was going to Sacred Heart College to see his son. He had to drop me at the main market entrance before continuing on his journey. He had picked me up along Cow Street. At the Ngeng's junction the narrow bridge slowed down the movement of vehicles. The traffic jam continued right up to the Veterinary Junction. All this while, we were quiet, as he concentrated on his driving. When we got to the Veterinary Junction, instead of continuing with the other vehicles along Sonac Street, he turned left taking the Ayaba Hotel road.

"I think this is a good opportunity for me to renew my invitation. I hope you are not going to say no."

"How can I refuse an invitation so graciously offered? I do not know how to thank you for your concern. You have been so good to me. You are like a father to me." He laughed at this.

"Am I that old?"

"Oh, you misunderstood me. I was referring to your attitude not only towards me but also towards your whole staff. Everybody appreciates the way you relate with us."

"Thank you too for that, I appreciate your telling me this."

I had wanted to drive home the fact that there was no way he could get intimate with me. But he seemed to have sensed it and I had to quickly cover up with a more pleasing compliment.

Eight p.m. that evening found us at the Independence Hotel. It was one of the earliest hotels built in Bamenda. Many others like Ayaba Hotel, Mondial Hotel and Monte Christo had been built after it and overshadowed it in modern architecture and furnishing. In spite of these new fangled hotels, the Independence Hotel still maintained a dignity in atmosphere and décor, which only those with the feeling of the old timer would appreciate. While the younger folks flocked to the modern hotels with their blaring lights and ear-jarring disco music, the veterans preferred this old reliable spot. They preferred this hotel because they still had the urge to have a nice time with their families or friends in a peaceful and respectful environment with their own type of music in the background. The location of the hotel was one of the factors that made it exclusively for the older folks who had cars and could drive there when they wanted. Taxis did not usually go there except on hire. The prices of drinks were another deterrent for the younger generation. People paid for the comfort, privacy and discreet arrangement. Although there was just one entrance into the hotel

21

premises, the paths leading to the bar, restaurant, nightclub and rooms from the parking lot were cut off from each other by a high hedge of shrubs so that somebody passing to the rooms would not be seen from the other parts except by the receptionist. What attracted my attention as we entered the lobby to the restaurant and bar was a board on the wall on which was written the following warning:

WHAT YOU SEE HERE
WHAT YOU HEAR HERE
WHAT YOU DO HERE
REMAINS HERE.

The lettering was done in gold colour and shone even when the lobby was dark. When we entered the lobby Don Williams was crooning one of his tunes with its eternal appeal. We went into the bar and he ordered drinks. He was quite familiar with the environment and the stewards treated him with respect. I wondered if he had ever brought his wife here. I could sense that he loved and valued his wife but this did not prevent him from having a fling of excitement every now and then. There were many people in the bar drinking and chatting. The dimmed lights produced a cosy atmosphere. It was such a convenient arrangement. The restaurant was just next door and one could have his drinks taken there through a connecting door. This is what my boss requested. Like the bar, the restaurant was also busy. It seemed as if a seminar was in progress or had just ended. There were many people eating at the other tables. Many of them were in groups of four or six. At a far corner a couple was seated. They did not seem to be seminar participants, just as we were not. They had finished eating and were waiting for their bill. When they paid their bill, they left with the man holding the woman close by his side. They moved towards the door. At the door the man left her and went to the reception. He did not come back. The woman too soon disappeared. I did not see in which direction she had gone. My mind went back to the inscription at the lobby. It was really a convenient arrangement. This place catered for everything. There was provision for every pressing need to be fulfilled. And whatever happened here was supposed to remain here.

The meal was delicious and my boss kept up a lively conversation. He made witty remarks about what was happening around us. I was discovering another person. We were like colleagues having a meal. The cloak of the boss was off and he was just being a man. After the meal he suggested we go to the nightclub and see what it looked like. I was also curious to see how it looked. Though it was not time for the club to be full, dancing was in full swing. A party was going on and because he was a familiar face in town he met many friends. We fitted in as if we had been invited. I felt ill at ease because I met many people who knew me. I pushed this uneasiness aside because the damage had been done and there was nothing I could do about it. I concentrated on enjoying myself. The atmosphere, the dance and two bottles of small Guinness blended with two shots of Campari put me in a better mood. My boss was a real gentleman that evening. He did not dance. He just watched the people dancing. I wanted to dance but could not dare ask him. The evening was his to direct in whatever direction he wanted. He pointed out people to me and commented on the way certain people were dancing. At ten thirty when the party was rounding off for the nightclub to start, he said we should go home. He dropped me off at my house and instead of me thanking him he thanked me for the evening. I did not know what to say, except to smile and add, "Thank you."

Two weeks after my evening out with my boss, Jane telephoned to tell me she was coming up to Bamenda with Benny. I immediately guessed the purpose of their visit and was happy for her. She spent her first night in Bamenda with me and by the time we fell asleep she had briefed me about what had been happening in Douala. What affected me most was the part about Gabby. There were rumours that some workers of the Produce Marketing Board where Gabby worked were going to be laid off following the country's Structural Adjustment Programme. If he were one of them then what would become of him and of me? I thought as I listened to her story. I dared not mention this. Although Jane knew there was more between Gabby and myself when I left Douala, I had not wanted to create a situation when I was not sure of its outcome.

I accompanied Benny and Jane to Bali. When I think of it now, I thank God that she had invited me along. I do not know what she would have done. In addition to the fluttering in a woman's stomach when she meets her future in-laws for the first time, there was the added fear of the antagonism of two warring villages to spoil everything. I kept my fingers crossed when we approached the compound. It was morning and his parents were still at home. The children in the compound saw us first and started to shout words of welcome to Benny and rushing towards us. His mother came out and held him close to her chest. He towered over her and had to bend for the embrace to be effective. In their excitement we did not exist, Jane and I. Benny soon drew her attention to us by introducing us. He just said that we were his friends. I am sure he did not want to let the cat out of the bag so soon. All eyes were now turned on us. At this moment his father came out of his house. Benny left us and moved towards him. He embraced his son briefly and Benny shook hands with him while holding his hand with both of his. All this time his father did not look at his son but beyond him to where we were standing.

When an unmarried son shows up with a girl in his father's compound, the scrutiny is focused. But when he shows up with two, there is confusion. Jane and I were led to his mother's house while Benny went with his father. They were there for a while and then Benny came out. He crossed the yard to join us in his mother's house. I looked at his face trying to figure out the effect of what he had discussed with his father. If there was anything not in favour of their union, Benny succeeded in hiding it.

Before he came his mother had sat with us for sometime asking about our journey. It was just a manner of being polite for there was not much we could talk about. She soon excused herself and set about preparing food for us. She stole glances at us as she went about her chores. I am sure she was wondering which one of us was Benny's woman, for the purpose of the visit spoke for itself. If we were alone we could have communicated our assessment of the situation to each other. But now we had to keep quiet for Benny's mother was within hearing distance. We were led to the father's house where we were received anew. It was evident from the father's face that he knew what was going on and where Benny's interest lay. But it was not evident whether he was pleased or not. He kept an interested but uninvolved demeanour throughout the visit.

The food was served in the father's house, which was reasonably well furnished. As we ate an old woman came to the compound. We only knew of her presence when Benny suddenly left his food and went outside. He came back leading the old woman by the hand. She greeted us and sat down. She declined the food offered and continued to talk to Benny's father in the mother tongue. It was evident from their voices and facial expressions that they were disagreeing on something. At one point she looked at us, took up her stick, struggled to her arthritic legs and walked out. Benny made to follow her but his father restrained him. The silence that reigned after her departure was pregnant with meaning. I looked at Jane. Her attention was fixed on the food before her but she was not swallowing what was in her mouth. She kept turning it in her mouth. Benny's father was skilful in explaining what he had been saying with his sister and before we left we had forgotten about the old woman.

When we went to Mbengwi two days later, Benny did not accompany us. He waited for us in Bamenda. Jane had to tell her parents first to get their reaction before Benny came into the picture. Her parents also welcomed the idea. All was now set for negotiations to begin between the two families. Before they left for Douala, Benny had arranged for a delegation of elders in his family to pay a courtesy call on Jane's family in Mbengwi to inform them of their intentions.

This courtesy call is locally called 'knock door'. The people to go on this important mission were well chosen. Benny's father was head of the delegation but he was not the spokesperson. Before leaving for Mbengwi, they agreed Benny's maternal uncle would be the spokesperson. His mother was not allowed to go along. Benny's paternal uncle and his elder sister made up the group of four. They were going to knock at the door of the family to see whether they would be accepted. What Benny's relatives thought was going to be a brief visit turned out to be a whole series of events. Jane's people had been informed about their coming. So they were waiting for them.

It was on a country Sunday that the delegation left Bali for Mbengwi. They carried a calabash of palm wine with some kola nuts. As a modern family they also carried a bottle of schnapps, a bottle of Whisky and a bottle of Brandy. Jane's father had invited his best friend and the women had cooked some fufu corn and vegetable. Two cocks had been killed to receive the guests. The delegation arrived at midday and was led to the compound by two boys who had been asked to wait at Mbengwi Park for them.

The guests were taken to the family house and asked to sit down. There was nobody there except them. They looked round and were pleased at what they saw. The room where a man received his guest told much about the man. The building had four rooms that opened to a central parlour. The doors to the rooms were closed so their attention was focused on the furniture and pictures on the walls. Jane's father was a businessman and had a number of taxis plying the Bamenda- Mbengwi road and went to the surrounding villages on their market days. He was rich enough to buy a good set of chairs on which his guests were sitting. These chairs convinced the visitors that their son was not marrying into a poor family who would shift their responsibilities to their son. After a few minutes Jane's father came in and greeted his visitors. Then his wife came in and did the same. It was like a well rehearsed performance. Ma Lucy, Jane's mother, after greeting the visitors excused herself and went out. This was a men's affair and she could only return when asked. In addition, she was still readying food for the visitors. Still in cooking pots, it had to be put into food flasks for presentation to the guests.

Pa Fokam, Jane's father, was dressed in an embroidered jumper with matching trousers. After conversing with his guests he called out.

"Benjamin! Benjamin!" There was no answer. So he excused himself and went outside murmuring to himself.

"Where has this child gone to? I asked him not to go far away because I have to send him to do things for me." As he gathered energy to shout for the boy again the child appeared from the back of the house.

"Where were you? I told you to be around the house because I have to send you."

"I was behind the house, Papa."

"You were just behind the house and you did not hear me call for you?"

"I did not hear, Papa." From the way Benjamin was breathing it was evident he had been running. His father had warned him not to tell lies. But today was not a day to get angry. He whispered to the child. "Go to Pa Tekoh's compound and tell him to come." Having said this, he went back to his guests.

Neighbours had witnessed the arrival of the guests. Information got to Pa Fokam's brother and he was soon in the compound. Other close relatives who had also been informed began to arrive. The sitting room was filling with people, both men and women. When Pa Tekoh arrived his friend invited him to come over and sit by him. The guests were sitting on one side of the parlour and the relatives occupied the rest. All were now seated and looking expectantly round. Pa Fokam cleared his throat and addressed his relatives.

"Thank you all for responding to my call. You are all welcome. These people you see are from Bali. They sent me a message that they were coming to see me. When I heard the message I did not know what to do. I did not know what they were coming to tell me. I did not want to hear it alone. So I invited you all to come and hear with me what they have to say. Did I do wrong?"

"No! No! You did well." Someone added, "Our visitors are here. We thank God for bringing them safely here. Our ears are open to hear what they have to say."

Benny's maternal uncle, James, stood up to speak. He was the youngest among the men and was given this opportunity to test his skill at addressing people. Back in Bali when someone had suggested he be the spokesperson he had been laughed at by his brother who said that his tongue would stick to the roof of his mouth as soon as he stood up to speak. He had taken that as a challenge to prove his worth. To get back at his brother he had said that he had not been chosen as a delegate because he was going to disgrace the family by misbehaving after a bottle of beer. As he stood up Benny's father remembered this incident and waited with a beating heart to hear what he was going to say.

"My brothers and sisters, on behalf of my fathers," he began and looked round. Benny's eldest sister was his age and he did not know whether to call her mother as he had called the others fathers. Then he changed his mind and continued.

"On behalf of all of us from Bali, I wish to thank you for the warm welcome you have given us. We feel really at home and I am sure we feel like that because you have welcomed us from your hearts. What has brought us here is very important. It is not something which a young man like me

26

can talk about."

When he said this Benny's father's heart calmed a bit. He was afraid that the young man was going to blunder and spoil everything when it had not even started. The impression that in-laws create on the first day is a determining factor in the continuation of the negotiations. He continued. "I will call on my father, Pa Mboni, to say it. People like them are more versed in things like these." He looked at Pa Mboni and sat down. Pa stood up and cleared his throat.

"My brothers and sisters, what my son has said is very true. For us to leave Bali and come here means we are out for business. I will begin by introducing the people who are with me."

He introduced them without mentioning how they were related to each other. He just said they were his brothers and sisters. Then he continued. "We have come because we have seen something in this compound which we think we should come and ask your permission to take back with us to Bali. That is why we are here." He sat down. There was silence and Pa Fokam asked.

"What type of something are you talking about? I have many nice things in my compound. Those chairs you are sitting on are very nice. Is that what you want?" There was laughter all round. This was the atmosphere that was needed in such situations and it was welcomed.

Pa Mboni made to stand again. But Pa Fokam stopped him.

"You do not need to stand up again before you speak. We are sitting here as a family now. We are not in a court of law or in a school." This brought further laughter.

"What I mean to say is that we have seen a small hen in this compound. And we thought that we should come and ask for it because there are many cocks in our own compound."

"Aha, if that is what you came for, you should have told me earlier and I would have caught one of the hens before they all left the roost. Now that they have scattered in the neighbourhood, it will take us time to catch one. Moreover I have many hens and do not know which you would like."

There was laughter again. The delegation from Bali admired the man's sense of humour but that was not what they had come for.

"You are getting us wrong. That is not what I meant."

"Tell us. We do not seem to understand what you are saying. Maybe it is because I am a very dull man." The assembled people were enjoying the way Pa Fokam was delaying and deliberately misinterpreting what the man was saying.

"You are not dull. Indeed you have been demonstrating how sharp you are. Let me get more to the point. We have seen a girl in this compound.

We like her and we would want her to come and enrich our compound."
"Hmm… is that what you want?" Pa Fokam asked his visitors.
"You heard what he said," they agreed in unison.
"What do you say about their request?" he asked his relatives and looked round waiting for one of them to reply. When none volunteered he called on his brother.
"Sama, what do you have to say about their request?"
The man cleared his throat. It seemed as if this clearing of throat had become a preamble to any speech. "All I have to say is that there are many girls in this compound and they are free to make their choice."
Pa Fokam turned to his visitors.
"You have heard what he has said." He turned round to look for someone to send to call his wife. He saw one of his female relatives who had sneaked in while the talking was going on. She was an inquisitive woman who had not been invited and Pa Fokam was angry at her presence but he did not let it show on his face. Instead he called her to come over to him. He whispered in her ear.
"Go and call for Ma Lucy. And do not come back." The woman went quietly out of the room. Soon Ma Lucy came into the room and went over to her husband. He whispered something in her ear and she went out again.
"As I said I have many girls. They will come in one after the other and you will let us know your choice." The first girl came in and went over to Pa Fokam. He whispered something in her ear and she went out.
"Is she the one?"
The people from Bali shook their heads in denial. Another girl came in and did the same as the first and the response from the Bali people was the same. After the fifth girl they still had not seen the girl they wanted.
"You do not seem to like any of the girls you have seen. I am sorry that your journey has been in vain." Those among the crowd who understood what was happening smiled.
Benny's father asked, "Are these all the girls you have? Don't you have another daughter?"
Pa Fokam made as if he was trying to remember something.
"Yes I have. But she is not here. And I am not sure that you have seen her."
"Yes we have. She is the one we want."
"That one? No, I cannot accept. She is working in Douala and gives me a lot of money. I cannot accept."
"If that is the case, we will give you much more money than she gives you if only you accept our request."
"Is that so? How much money can you give me? Do you see me as a

28

poor man?" Pa Fokam pretended to be offended.

"No, no," Benny's father pleaded. "It is just that she is the one we want. Our son also works in Douala. Together they will give you whatever you want and even more."

"Are you telling me that the man who wants to marry my daughter is not here for me to see him? I thought he was the young man who spoke first. I was almost getting angry but decided to hold my peace."

"Pa, we cannot be as foolish as that," replied Benny's father. "You know, young men of today are getting more and more away from the tradition. We want them to know the tradition so we bring them along on occasions like this for them to learn."

"You have spoken well. That is what a father should do. Going back to what we were talking about, have these two people met each other? I ask this because children of today have their own mind. They are not like us. My father chose my wife for me. 'Is that not true, Ma Lucy?'" He turned round to look at his wife. She bent her head not wanting to look at her husband who had been equally chosen for her. He continued.

"I do not want to get involved in a situation that might not look good in the future."

Benny's father had had enough of Pa Fokam's paring and said, "I am sure that your daughter must have told you something as far as this issue is concerned."

Everything was out in the open now and Jane's father could no longer pretend. Benny's father saw the expression on his face and pressed on.

"We are here as messengers. We have come with the knowledge that everything has been arranged between the two of them. To show you that we mean business…," he said and stopped and turned to his eldest daughter, who had been custodian of the 'raffia' bag they had brought along, and asked her to bring it forward. He also asked for the calabash of palm wine to be brought forward. "This is the small thing we have brought so we may share as a family." He stopped and looked at his people and then at Pa Fokam. Then he continued.

"Or you want us to carry it back?"

"No, no," said Pa Fokam.

Benny's father left the gifts at the centre of the parlour and went back to his seat. There was silence in the room. Pa Fokam looked at his friend Pa Tekoh and shook his head.

"I cannot touch these things without asking my best friend Pa Tekoh to say something. He is like a member of this family and nothing can take place here without his being present." Pa Tekoh stood up and looked at the assembly. He focused his attention on the visitors and began.

"If a child puts scalding water in his mouth, it will burn his tongue. I

29

thank my brother for inviting me for this very important visit of our brothers from Bali. I call Pa Fokam my brother because our relationship goes far back. We have done and seen things together. He knows my mind and I know his mind. We are from Ngenbu though we have settled in Mbengwi. I hope you understand what that means."

He was speaking to Benny's father although his gaze covered the others. He stopped as if he intended to continue but he said nothing. Silence descended on the room. Everybody understood what he meant but nobody had the courage to say it. Something like that could be expected from Pa Tekoh. Pa Fokam could not have brought up the topic. It would have made Benny's people think he was looking for an excuse for refusing the marriage. And if this had been his intention then he would have told his daughter what was on his mind and this would have been communicated to them through their son. This journey would not have taken place. But Pa Fokam was tactful in the manner in which he had arranged for this to come up. He was in favour of the marriage but he had to clear his mind about how they felt about the hostilities between their two villages. Benny's father immediately understood what Pa Tekoh was talking about. They too had considered this obstacle but the way he had looked at it, it was not going to cause any problem.

"I understand perfectly what you are talking about. We thought about it before coming here. Times are changing. We are not doing today what our forefathers did. In the time of our forefathers no Bali man could dare enter the house of a Ngenbu man, but here we are today sitting and talking as brothers. The younger generation does not bear the hatred our forefathers and some of our country people bear to day. Some don't even understand the cause of these hostilities. More to that, the government is very aware of the situation and is doing everything to prevent a reoccurrence of what happened last year. What we have come to do here today will further cement the relationship between our villages. No sane person should wage a war against his in-laws. I believe that with time this whole problem between us will finish. After all, who has ever carried away land? We came and met it and will leave it behind when we go. All that will be allocated to us is six feet. And even that does not belong to us. So, why should we prevent our children from finding happiness together because of what exists between their villages? I am sure your daughter does not understand the reason for the enmity. Neither does my son. So let us not make it an obstacle."

Pa Fokam looked at Pa Tekoh and nodded his head.

"Our brother has spoken well. Times are changing and we should change with the times. My friend Pa Fokam, you can look at what they have brought." The contents of the bag were brought out for everybody to see. James, the young man who had spoken first, was asked to carry the calabash of palm wine and place it in front of Pa Fokam. "Ma Lucy, have you seen the things that have been brought?" Pa Fokam asked his wife.

"Yes, I have seen them."

"Do you accept them?"

Ma Lucy had been so quiet throughout that a layer of phlegm had coated her vocal cords. When she wanted to talk her voice came out in a croak. She stopped and cleared her throat. Though she spoke little, she had learnt to stand by her words. In a compound of three wives and being the eldest and unschooled, she had had to learn to assert herself. But in this situation she had to be careful. She had her misgivings about her daughter's future husband being a Bali man. But for her daughter's happiness she was ready to take the chance.

"I do not have anything to say. My husband has said it all. I have seen the things. I cannot refuse what he has accepted. I only wish that Jane herself were here to pour the palm wine."

"That is no problem," Pa Fokam assured her. "Her sister can pour on her behalf." The palm wine was poured into Pa Fokam's drinking horn. He normally did not drink from this horn but being the successor of the compound and with the solemnity of the occasion, tradition demanded he did. He took a drink and passed the horn over to Benny's father who also drank and then handed back the horn. Pa Fokam took another sip and called for his wife to come over and sip too. This showed the agreement had been sealed. Pa Fokam asked for food to be brought for his visitors. Everybody present was hungry for the negotiations had taken almost two and a half hours. Before the guests left it was getting to four o'clock. A satisfied group of Bali people entered the taxi that took them back home. The conversation was mainly about Pa Fokam. Benny's father was quite impressed with him and prayed that his daughter should have the same sense of humour.

Every detail of the visit was written to Benny who told Jane what had happened. When Jane told me what had happened when Benny's people went to Mbengwi, I wondered how my parents would react if Gabby and I were to get married, for we were not from the same village. My parents were always hammering on the fact that it was better for a girl to get married to a boy from her village.

3

It happened a month after. The bomb had fallen. Jane telephoned to tell me. Gabby was one of the victims. I listened to her narration. My senses deadened. I could not respond.

"Are you there, Lizzy?" Jane asked. She got no response from me. My throat was clogged with emotions.

I finally managed to answer, "Yes, Jane. Poor Gabby! It's going to be hard for him." That was all I could muster courage to say. Jane continued.

"You need to see him, Lizzy. He is so changed. I just wish you could do something for him."

"What can I do, Jane?"

"There are lots of things you can do for him. Since you left he has not stopped talking about you. I am sure you must have a pile of his letters by now." In fact, Gabby had written to me almost every week since I left. I had forbidden him from calling me in the office.

"Yes, Jane, I am listening."

"For the moment Douala is not a very conducive place for him, with all the talk going on. You know the Anglophone community here. Almost everybody knows everybody else and news goes round very fast. He does not like the pitying glances people give him when he passes by. I think that a change of scene would do him a lot of good. And with you around…"

"I will do everything to help, Jane. But I hope that he did not put you up to this."

"No, he did not. It is all my idea. Now that you have agreed, I will discuss it with Benny and we will suggest it to him. Thank you very much, Lizzy. I will keep you informed of any developments. Bye."

"Bye, Jane."

I dropped the receiver wondering whether to be happy or sad. I was happy that Gabby might come to Bamenda and happy thinking I could bring a ray of light into the situation. I wanted to see that smile on his face again but wondered whether there would be any smile, even for me. Then I remembered that his family was in Bamenda. Why did his coming up have to depend on me, I wondered. Why did Jane make my acceptance so important? Did it really matter? When I thought that it might, I felt elated. My elation plummeted down however when I remembered the reason he might come to Bamenda. Gabby had not written to tell me. When I thought of this I wondered whether if I were the one I would have needed to talk about it. It was terrible to lose a job. How would it feel like to lose a job, I wondered.

A week passed during which I worried about Gabby. I did not know whether to write to him or not. The thought of his coming up helped me keep my peace. But this was just temporary. I wondered what I would do if Gabby came up expecting to stay with me. How was I going to explain my refusal? Who would I say he was? That Friday Jane telephoned to tell me that he would be coming up on Monday the next week and he would be staying in their family compound at Atuakum.

Gabby arrived in Bamenda on a Monday afternoon. After work I went home and prepared for his arrival. I did not know when to expect him because I thought he would go to their compound first before coming to see me. But he did the contrary. He came first to my house. I was so happy to see him and for a few moments he was really happy. I could see this on his face. But I did not know how he got to know where I lived and wanted to find out.

"How did you find your way here?"

"I dreamt about it."

"You are not serious. I am sure you are joking. It cannot be true."

"Lizzy, I just had to know where you live so that I could come straight here."

"Why? You should have gone to your compound first."

"I wanted to see you first. Thank you for your concern about me."

"How can you be thanking me? Jane is the one you should be thanking not me. I did not do anything. You could not even inform me of the problem."

"I could not, Lizzy. How could I have told you? What language could I have used? But I was convinced that Jane was going to tell you. You are very instrumental for my being here. If not because of you I could not have come to Bamenda."

After a moment he asked, "Is this the way you are going to welcome me?" I had kept his bag behind the door. I did not want to keep it in my room. Although I looked forward to spending some time alone with him, I did not want my actions to appear as an invitation. If he wanted to stay, he should say it himself.

"I am sorry Gabby. This is not the way to welcome you. I am sorry. It is just that when I heard of the problem I was so worried myself." I had been sitting opposite him to have a good look at him. His face looked strained and his eyes almost bloodshot. He had taken the retrenchment very badly. I now moved to sit beside him. I kissed him on his cheek.

"This is the way I should have welcomed you."

"You can do it better than that." And before I realized it he had caught my face between his palms and was kissing me on my lips. I did not resist the kiss. It seemed as if this was just what he was waiting for. I returned the kiss and even sent my arms round him. We clung to each other. Gabby's healing process had begun. I stopped the kiss and looked at him. He smiled. I was glad to see that smile on his face again.

"I am glad to see you happy again Gabby."

"You have made me happy, Lizzy. I wish you were with me in Douala. I would not have gone through what I have gone through."

"It is all right, Gabby. I am here with you. You must be tired and hungry. Let me get you smoothing to eat."

As we ate Gabby looked more and more relaxed. He enjoyed the food and complimented me on it. We spent the afternoon catching up.

"Now that you are here can you tell me what actually happened?"

"I was very surprised myself when I saw my name on the list of those who had been retrenched. I do not understand what happened."

"What were the terms of your employment? Much will depend on them."

"There was this vacancy the company announced. They needed an accountant. I had just returned from Nigeria and was doing some freelance work. I put in my application and was employed as one of the accountants. On the day of the interview I was asked so many questions about a brochure on the company that outlined its terms and internal regulations."

"They usually do that and any person who does not read the brochure carefully misses out and cannot respond to questions about specific regulations and finds himself in real trouble because it looks like negligence."

"What did they say in the article on terminations?"

"It was written that before an employee is terminated, the company is obliged to inform the employee in advance and the employee is due certain benefits including pay offs. I had heard that some employees would be terminated. But I never thought that I would be one of them. I know that if a company wants to do some adjustments in its staffing situation those who are liabilities to the company go first."

"But you are definitely not a liability."

"Definitely not. I think that I am an asset to that company and not a liability. I have never received a query. Instead I was given a congratulatory letter at the end of my second year working there. I can't really understand how my name came to be on the list.

"Did you try to see the manager?"

"During the first week when the list came out it was impossible to see him. The outcry was terrible. I went to see the chief accountant. We talked about it and he said he too was surprised to find my name on the list. This is what gave me the courage to persist in my demand to see the manager. When I eventually saw him I came away with the impression that something was going on."

"Something must really be going on. How many people with your qualifications were suspended?"

"That is something I never thought of!" Gabby exclaimed. "I am the only one. The rest were all staff lower than me."

"Something must really be going on. Have you been given your termination letter?"

"No. I did not have the courage to go to the office since I saw the manager. It must be lying there."

"You have not taken it?" I asked, not believing what Gabby was telling me.

"I have friends in the office. Though it is not a good thing for a friend to bring you such a letter, if there were one, then one of them could have had the courage to bring it to me."

It was getting dark and I did not want the conversation to continue. Gabby had come to Bamenda to distract himself from the problems that were worrying him. But here was I getting him to talk about it.

"I am sorry Gabby. You came to Bamenda to try and forget about it. I am not helping you. I have instead made you to talk so much about it."

"You have done just the right thing. In my anger and frustration I did not ask myself the important questions I should have asked. But you are right. I came to Bamenda to forget. So I think I should be going."

Gabby tried to convince me to come along with him to Atuakum. But I declined telling him that it was not proper. I did not want to appear as a girl he picked up in Bamenda to keep him company during his stay.

During his stay we had a wonderful time together. I really enjoyed his company. He was the Gabby I had known in Douala. But there were times I caught him with a worried look on his face. Each time I saw this I told him not to be worried, for I had a presentiment that things were not going to be as bad as he was taking it. When I told him this he said that he was not worried about his job but about me. I wondered why he should be worried about me. He never mentioned it again during his stay. I too never asked him. I also did not ask how his parents and relatives had taken the news of his retrenchment. I was dying to know whether he had told them but I could not ask him.

Gabby was regaining his cheerfulness and was himself. We spent a lot of time together and really enjoyed each other's company. He often brought up the topic of marriage. I talked about it in a light hearted manner. He often teased me about it but I was evasive. When he asked about those things, which I thought were the foundation of marriage, I told him exactly what I thought. He once asked me whether there are things in my life, which I would want to hide from my future husband. I told him that it all depended on what the secret was. Moreover if the incident happened before we got married there was no need to do any post-mortem. But if the man or the woman had a secret that came into existence during the marriage, then it would be a big burden to carry. When I made this statement he had looked at me puzzled. But he did not want me to see his look and had quickly turned away his face.

Gabby stayed for three weeks during which things could no longer be hidden. He visited me in the office a number of times. My friends got to know about him. They knew I had a boyfriend who was crazy about me. They knew this from the way Gabby behaved towards me. On the days we had agreed for him to meet me at the office to go home together he was always there on time. He would hold my hand as we walked from the office to the roadside. We did everything to spend as much time as we could together by ourselves. And this was often in my house. I wanted to make Gabby's stay in Bamenda a memorable one.

On the eve of his departure, we went to Snack Concorde. After a beer each I suggested we go back to my house. I wanted to spend the last hours with him before he left the next day. He felt the same and we left. When we got home we sat on the sofa and quietness descended into the room. For some time nobody spoke. It seemed as if the implication of his departure had just dawned on both of us and we were wondering what to do about it. I did not know what Gabby was thinking about but at that moment I was really thinking about his impending departure, all that we had done together and what was going to happen from now on. I knew I was going to miss him. I turned and looked at him trying to read what was on his mind from his face. I was sitting so near him that our lips met and stayed in place. What a kiss. It lasted for I don't know how long. It bore all the restraint of the past. It was an outpouring of what we felt for each other. We moved into the bedroom and sat on the bed. Gabby could not let go. He held me as if he never wanted to let go. We were so involved with each other that before we realized it, it was one o'clock in the morning. There was no need for him to go back to Atuakum. It was dangerous going to their neighbourhood at that time of the night. Moreover, I wanted him to stay.

We fell asleep exhausted. I fell into a dreamless sleep and slept until I heard the Cathedral bells ringing at five a.m. I stirred and tried to get up but Gabby pulled me back. We made love again and I felt at peace. Gabby's stay in Bamenda had drawn me really close to him. I do not know why I felt so much peace after that night with Gabby. I knew that his absence was not going to affect me the way it had threatened to.

When we had rested from our exertions he held me close and looked into my eyes and said, "Elizabeth, ..." The name sounded strange. He always called me Lizzy. I was going to discover the reason for this switch from Lizzy to Elizabeth in the future. But for now there was no time to find out. "I have something important to ask you."

"I am listening," I replied.

"I would like you to find time and come to Douala at the end of next month."

"What for?" I asked. I realized my question threatened to make the atmosphere moody and I did not want that, so I changed my tone. "I will, if it is for something interesting," I explained acquiescently, with a mischievous grin.

"I will keep in touch so you know exactly when to come."

I got up and opened my bedside cupboard and took out an envelope and gave it to him. There was no address on the envelope and it was not sealed. He took it and held it in his hands for sometime before opening it. "Oh, Elizabeth!" he clasped me in his arms and really suffocated me. "How kind of you. How very considerate," he murmured into my ears.

"Gabby, this is the little I can do to help."

"It is not little, Elizabeth. A hundred thousand francs! Do you know how much this is going to help me?"

He could not hide his happiness. I too filled with happiness, but his next words made this feeling dissipate.

"Why this gesture Elizabeth?" I just looked at him and bent my head. I had a sinking feeling in my stomach. Maybe Gabby was thinking I was trying to entrap him. It is not unknown for girls to give money to their boyfriends to make them feel committed. In such circumstances some men even look forward to such assistance. But that was not my intention. I wanted to feel the joy of giving and to make him know that I care. I did not know that I was contributing for the future. But at that moment, I felt let down. He lifted my chin and looked at my face. I looked into his eyes for some time and lowered my gaze. In the look was all the disappointment that was in my heart. The message seemed to have gone home for he took me into his arms and wiped away the tears from my face. Then he wiped away the tears in my heart with a kiss.

"I am sorry, Lizzy. I should not have said that. Forgive me."

The sudden change from Elizabeth to Lizzy made me to look at him with a question in my eyes. Before I could put it into words his fingers were on my lips. "Don't say anything." Then he kissed me again passionately as if he wanted to wipe away the question from my lips and from my mind.

Gabby left at six thirty in the morning to pick up his bag at the family house in Atuakum. We met later at the bus stop. He was with a friend we had bumped into during his stay. He worked in the office next to ours and had made advances, which I had light heartedly ignored. He had tried to taunt me but I had been blunt and Gabby had been pleased with the discomfiture he found on the man's face. I was at ease when I met him again as I knew that he would not dare attempt to say a word to me. When the bus took off I excused myself and took a taxi home. It was a Saturday morning, and I had much work to do at home. I walked some distance away from him before waiting for a taxi to take me home. I did not want to give him the opportunity to renew his intentions or get me into a conversation. Back at home I felt an emptiness that threatened to turn into melancholia. I cheered myself up by ruminating on the highlights of Gabby's visit.

As I thought about the past week with Gabby, a speculative cloud descended. Where was all this leading? I wondered. What was to come of our awkward manoeuvres towards a relationship? I went back to Gabby's letters to find an answer. His letters were always full of information about his activities, recent happenings in Douala, news about Jane and Benny and sometimes his thoughts and wishes and aspirations. He always ended by saying how much he missed me. He said other things, which made me feel really wanted and cherished. One of his letters contained more of his thoughts than news. It did not carry the same tone as the other letters, and when I first read it I did not understand what he was saying. In the envelope in which I kept his letters, I searched for that letter. I read it again. Maybe in my excitement when I received the letter I had missed the force behind it. A sentence caught my attention and I read it again.

"In life a man needs a companion and I have discovered that when you meet that companion you become a changed person. I have been experiencing that change since I met you." What a fool I had been not to understand the implication of this statement. I was afraid that my innocent reactions and responses towards some of his teasing questions had painted a completely different picture. However, I assured myself that I was soon going down to Douala to find out. Making love with a man did not guarantee marriage. But what existed between Gabby and myself was more than just satisfying some animal desire. During his visit I had resisted giving in to him to see how far he was serious in this relationship. He had made it clear to me that he did not want to take advantage of me. Whenever I was ready he would be waiting but hoped that it would be sooner.

Before he went back to Douala his wish was fulfilled and I felt I was standing on solid ground.

I had to go to the village the following weekend to see my parents. I usually made monthly trips to visit them. Ndop town is quite near Bamenda, so distance was not the problem. But since I came back from leave I had not been to see them. I arrived on Friday evening with the intention of staying till Sunday afternoon.

As I walked down the main street that led to our neighbourhood, I marvelled at the changes that had taken place in a few weeks. The countryside that had been brown and covered with dust had a clean feel. Even the air felt cleaner as I breathed it in. The hills in particular looked neatly washed after the bush fires had burnt them into black and brown soot. The Sabga Hills always fascinate me and as I looked at them in the rays of the setting sun, they seemed to have a life of their own. Their tops in the horizon looked jagged but lower down on the slopes, grass was already forming a rich green carpet. The air was suffused with the smell of the rich earth made richer by the early rains, which had not yet soaked deep enough to make the earth heavy. This is the period for mushrooms. The wind carried their smell. The plantain trees in the nearby farms were stripped of their dry leaves. The fresh tufts of leaves left on top of the trees looked like waving gladly in the evening breeze. The air turned chilly as the evening progressed. My communion with the landscape made me momentarily forget what was on my mind. As I turned down the path that led to our compound, the sight of the houses brought it back with such force that I had to stop for a moment and map out my strategy. Standing there by the roadside and mapping out a strategy was no small feat. My mind and body were still adjusting to the new situation in which I found myself. At last I had someone to marry and I alone knew. I was anxious to tell my parents but did not know how to go about it. During my earlier visits to the village I always enjoyed this short distance from the main street down the path to our compound. It was the moment to put the stresses of town life aside and begin to savour the peace and tranquillity of the village. But today I was unable to enjoy this moment because of the happiness, anxiety and fear battling in me.

I did not know exactly how I was going to tell my parents the good news. To broach a subject like that to one's parents was not easy. In a patriarchal society where the man is supreme, the man has to make the move to inform the girl's parents. Even if the girl had worked it out with the man she still had to pretend ignorance until everything was settled behind the scenes before any overt action could be carried out. But times were changing and some cultural and societal dictates were falling away. I wondered what my parents would think about my news. None could be shared without prior investigation into how they would react. Although things were changing there were still some parents who sweet-talked their daughters into marrying a man they found suitable for her. These girls often accept because they want to satisfy their parents. But they soon take off for the nearest town abandoning their husbands. I was beyond such persuasions but still had to be sure of where I was treading.

On Saturday morning, something happened that gave me the opportunity to broach the topic to my mother. A car passed in front of our compound. The footpaths leading from one compound to another were barely motorable. Whenever a vehicle passed it left two distinct tracts at the edge of the path. I noticed some when I arrived the previous evening but made no inquiries because the path led to other parts of the village. Since vehicles carrying a corpse right to the deceased compound was a common occurrence it did not occur to me to ask. But the passage of the car awoke my interest. It was a silver coloured Toyota Cressida. I wondered who might be the owner. There was no family in our neighbourhood whose son had a car. As soon as my mother came back from the market I asked.

"Mama, a car passed here this morning. Has Ngwana bought a car?" Ngwana was the son of one of our neighbours across the stream. He lived in Yaounde and was the only one I could think of who might be in a position to buy a car.

"No," my mother replied. "They are a lucky family."

"Who?" I asked becoming more interested.

"It is the son of Pa Mbane who lives over in Nchugha. He wants to marry your friend's younger sister who is at the university. Since he came he has not allowed our ears to rest. Woo! Woo! Up and down. I wonder what they are doing in that compound."

This was my chance and I immediately took it.

"Pa Mbane lives in Nchugha, doesn't he? It seems as if the girls of this village are getting married only to boys from this village. Can a girl not get married to a man who is not from her own village?"

"Who? You?"

"No, mother not me. I was just asking."

My mother looked at me for while and kept silent. She seemed to be thinking hard. I could see this from the ridges on her forehead. I knew she was worried about my single status. I wanted to bring up the topic about Gabby but something held me back and I also kept quiet. She soon broke the silence.

"My child, a woman is not obliged to marry from a specific tribe or clan."

I made no response to this but was secretly happy that my problem had been solved. Moreover, I did not want to push the matter further and make her realize that I was particular. I smiled to myself as I remembered the musician's words, 'L'amour n'a pas de frontières'. Her own mother, my grandmother was from another village. She continued.

"But as far as I am concerned, intermarriage among the Mamagie villages is acceptable though getting a wife or husband from one's village is preferable." The weight was lifted off my mind but I continued questioning her to keep up the conversation. The conversation was flowing smoothly because she loved talking about the past and what used to happen as compared to what is happening today. She seemed to be astride two generations. She understood and appreciated some of the changes that were taking place but would adamantly reject those she considered detrimental to the cohesion needed in a family. For example, she was against the fact that women should move semi-naked when their husbands died, but when it came to parents deciding on what they thought was good for their children, she was adamant. Basically she was the traditional woman at heart but accepted some liberal ideas because she realized that they would exist whether or not she condoned them.

"What of marrying a man from Nso, Metta or even from the South West Province?"

"Times are changing and a woman cannot know where her luck lies," she replied.

This constant reference to the changing times was a new phenomenon. Maybe it was an indirect way of telling me that if the worst came to the worst, a son-in-law from anywhere would be welcomed. From the tone of her voice I sensed that the fact that none of her children was married was worrying her. But one does not get a husband from the air. We went on to talk about the merits and demerits of men and women from the various tribes we could think of within the national territory and even beyond.

I teased her on subjects on which I knew she had very strong views and was not ready for a compromise.

"If I get married my husband will have to share the housework with me."

She looked at me. I did not lift up my face to look at her. I did not want her to see the laughter in my eyes.

After a moment she asked, "Why don't you ask him to help you give birth?"

"Mother, it is not the same thing," I protested.

"What is the difference? Would you not be ashamed if your friend comes to visit and finds your husband in the kitchen washing plates?"

"Why should I be ashamed?"

"You should be ashamed because it is not the man's place to wash plates. That is a woman's job."

"And what is the man's job?"

"The man has to provide for his family and take care of his wife and children."

"Now that I work and earn a salary, do you want me to leave my job so that my husband should provide for me mother? Just as you say times have changed and if my husband wants to help me wash the plates in the kitchen I don't see why I should be ashamed. In fact, I would like my husband to help me with the housework. It would not be fair for us to come back from work at the same time and while I am in the kitchen he just sits and waits for the food. I think he would be happy to help me."

"Why are you talking as if you already have one?"

"Yes, mother." It was out of my mouth before I realized it. Although I gasped and held my mouth I was happy I had said it at last. She looked at me for a while.

"Are you serious?"

"Yes, mother. That is what I came home to tell you. I have a man who wants to marry me."

The expression on my mother's face changed. She got up and did a little dance before turning to me.

"He is from which village? Have you told your father?"

I decided to ignore the first question and answered the second. "No I haven't. I thought I should tell you first but the passing car and our conversation carried me away. The man is not from this village."

I did not say anything else. I wanted her to relate what we had been talking about with what I had just told her and draw her own conclusions. I had dropped a big task at her feet and it was up to her to think of how she was going to tell her husband about it. I did not want to be around. So, early the next morning I left for Bamenda with the excuse that I had some work to do in my house. The expression on my mother's face when I left her assured me that my message had gone home.

I went to work on Monday feeling very happy. I went through the files with a clear and steady mind. I was myself again. I laughed and joked with my colleagues in the office. They kept teasing me about the golden prince and I wondered who had first used the phrase. We were eating in a nearby restaurant one day during break when the woman who took over when I was absent commented about my being carried away by a golden prince. I had answered that we were not living in a fairyland but in the real world and I was going to take situations as they came. I did not know at that time that I was making a prophetic statement.

On Friday as I walked back to my table to start the afternoon part of the day's work, I found a letter on my table. The writing was familiar. The postmark was the same. I even took note of the stamp on the envelope. It had the picture of two doves. The letter was from Gabby. He was telling me about his journey back to Douala. I was very excited and read the letter trying not to miss anything. I now had more confidence in our relationship and replied to his letters as soon as I could. I had developed the habit of rereading the previous letter after reading the one just received so that there was a sort of continuation in my mind. Gabby had a way of writing his next letter as if the break was because someone distracted him in the course of writing the first. In this way he kept me informed of things happening in Douala, asking me about Bamenda, telling me about his work and places he went to in the course of his work. It was a way of not only sharing but also living his day-to-day experiences with me. He told me to do things for him. These were not things that benefited him in any way but things that made me think of him each day. He asked me to do the most bizarre things. I considered them bizarre at first but soon realized the advantages. He once asked me to find time to sit quiet for ten minutes every day and try to empty my mind of everything and relax. I tried it the first time and gave up. But when I tried again it was quite an interesting exercise and I tried it a few more times. When I did it before going to bed I realized that I fell asleep easily. I usually wrote to tell him how I felt after carrying out some of the things he asked me to do. There were some stupid ones as well. Sometimes he wrote asking me to put on a certain shade of lipstick for the week. These were either his favourite colours or the colours he had noted that I liked. This I could easily do for I loved trying on different shades of lipstick. I often wondered whether doing this for him pleased him or if it was just his way of ensuring that I was thinking of him. I also asked him to do things for me. I was not surprised when he forgot to do some. I had my own way of making him think of me. Once in a while, I asked him to guess what colour of a dress I would wear on a particular day. When he did guess, even if he was wrong, I sometimes said he was right just to make him happy.

A fortnight later I had a phone call. I took up the receiver expecting to hear an officious voice asking for my boss. The voice was asking whether this was the Regional Office of the Chamber of Commerce. I could not make out the person. Being used to answering phone calls, I knew when someone was calling to talk with my boss. If it were Jane her voice was already so familiar that from the first word I knew she was the one. When I asked who was on the line the next words made me listen with curiosity.

"Hello! Is that Lizzy? You are a witch. You must have made some magic. I was called back to work two days ago and it seems as if I have never left the place..." I let him go on and on without interruption. He told me that when he got back he was told by one of his friends that the company still needed his services. There must have been an error or someone had tried to play foul. He had waited with a beating heart praying that my optimism should be rewarded.

"Oh, Lizzy, you are my lucky angel."

He went ahead to tell me when I was to come down to Douala.

He tried to persuade me to stay with him when I would come down, but I refused. I was not yet so sure of my relationship with him to go that far.

Although Jane was very instrumental in bringing Gabby and me together, the situation was still too uncertain for me to say anything. It is funny how we kept quiet about this particular situation.

Usually, we discussed such situations and made decisions in advance about what to do. My emotions and words in relation to Gabby were under such control that they provided no entry point for Jane. The question she had asked after my first meeting with Gabby had not given her anything to hang on to. After Gabby's visit to Bamenda, I had told her that the visit was successful and that she was going to see the change for herself and that I had done as she requested. I did not tell her about the gesture I had made or about what I had discussed with Gabby. I did not believe that everything was going to be as smooth as I saw it coming. My recent experience with Andrew had left me wary and I still had to get this fear out of my system.

It seemed as if both of us were on guard. I do not know whether she knew of what was happening from Gabby. If she did she never made it evident. From Jane's general attitude I knew she was anxious for me to settle as she had done. She never said this openly but from their attitude and reactions to each other, they were telling me that marriage is good. To have a partner who cares is good. To have someone to talk to at those moments when you feel down is good. To have someone with whom you share your joys and sorrows is good. Such joy is the result of mutual understanding. To have a baby born out of love is good. I saw all these things in them. But I could not be so sure of Gabby. When I looked at Jane, she was taking this whole business of marriage so seriously that I wondered whether our friendship was going to be the same. I wondered whether she was going to put into practice those things we had planned to do when we got married. Already my silence about Gabby and her reticence about asking were keeping us apart. I could see that things were not going to be the same between us again.

The thirtieth of June, in just five days, seemed an eternity away. It was the last Saturday of the month and many parties were thrown on that day. I took an early bus and arrived in Douala at two o'clock in the afternoon. Many people do their shopping on Saturday and it took some time for me to get a taxi to get me to the *Rond Point* intersection from where I could get a taxi to Akwa where Benny lived.

Everything had been settled between the two families but because Jane was pregnant, no more could be done until she gave birth. But it was less expensive to live together. When I arrived they were at home. Jane was in her third month of pregnancy and was not feeling well. The early months of pregnancy, especially for the first pregnancy, are often very trying. They were very happy to see me and I could sense that there was something else that was making them happy and not just my presence. Benny left to go to town and we were left to catch up on our gossip. More importantly I wanted to know how she was feeling. The pregnancy was so fascinating. There was not much to show that she was pregnant except her breasts, which were larger than usual. What interested me the most was what she was thinking about each day. What stuck in my mind as I sat and conversed with Jane was the image of this new creation growing in her minute by minute, and day by day. I pictured a foetus curled up in her abdomen, and I imagined God using a woman's womb as the Garden of Eden where he nurtures man, imbuing him with his goodness and holiness. This human being created in the image of God lives in a state of innocence like Adam and Eve until she is gradually exposed to the ambiguities in life and has to make choices. Before then, she is equipped with the basic innate tendencies to make the right choices. I began seeing Jane as a participant in this great task of bringing a human being into existence. In her pregnancy, Jane was taking on greater significance. Life was really taking shape in her.

In our human limitations we often fail to perceive the completeness of God's works. We ignore the joys of everydayness and the surprises of creation embedded in the union of man and woman. We had a lot to talk about and Jane did most of the talking. It was six o'clock before we were aware of the passing of time. Benny came back at six thirty looking as if he had not done any work all day. It seemed as if the thought of his child growing in his wife kept him going and in good spirits. When I asked him he told me that he was not tired because his mind was always on what was happening back home. And what he thought about was very pleasing, so he could not be tired. As he said this he looked at Jane and winked. Jane pretended not to have heard him.

"Benny, you know we have to be at Gabby's house at eight o'clock. We cannot go there when the guests are already seated."

Jane gasped and held her mouth.

"Oh I am sorry; I did not mean to say that."

I looked at Jane, then at Benny.

"What is going on here?" I asked. Benny looked at Jane trying to look annoyed with her but not succeeding. Jane's head was bent as she tried to hide the laughter bubbling in her.

"What is at Gabby's place?" I asked.

"Gabby is throwing a party. It is nothing big. Just a few friends coming round for a drink," Benny explained.

"What is he celebrating? Please tell me. Don't make me appear as a fool when we get there."

"I think he just wants to celebrate his return to work," Benny replied. I was puzzled by the mischievous smile that hovered at the corners of Jane's mouth. I realized there was something going on which they did not want to tell me. Gabby had asked me to come to Douala when he had not yet been called back so this party could not have had anything to do with his being called back to work. These doubts were going round and round in my mind but there was no way for me to voice them. As I dressed up to go with Benny and Jane I wondered what Gabby was up to.

We arrived at Gabby's house at a quarter to eight and I noticed a car parked outside. We went in and he greeted us warmly. There was nobody there yet. Jane and I sat in adjacent chairs while the men went into the bedroom. After greeting me and asking about my journey Gabby did not speak much to me. But I watched his every word and action closely. He served us drinks. Soon some guests started coming in and by nine o'clock the house was full. Everybody had something to drink and conversations were going on in groups or between two people just catching up on recent events in town. Such occasions made it possible for people to meet their friends and acquaintances whom they hardly meet because everybody is too busy chasing after money and other things they think will give them fulfilment and satisfaction. Everyone laughed and some until tears misted their eyes. I saw people's real selves emerging. They were relaxed and happy. From the expressions on their faces I saw that humans are made to be happy, yet we tie ourselves up with illusions that keep us from being ourselves. We are the victims of our illusions, which prevent us from enjoying the good things God has given us free of charge. We look for satisfaction in just those things that keep us dissatisfied. We look for money, fame, property, cars and appliances, yet we are still dissatisfied once we acquire them. Here was a microcosm of society, sharing jokes and experiences and enjoying one another's company. Joy that comes with no tiring search. As I watched, I wondered why it had not occurred to humans that this was the type of life we should live more often, instead of pretending that pleasure comes from big amounts of money hidden in banks and trying to cover up the agony plaguing big mansions with beautiful wives, handsome husbands, and frustrated children. The humming of voices came to me in waves until I heard Gabby's voice begging for their attention.

"Ladies and gentlemen…" There was silence for a while then a burst of clapping. I could see from the people's reactions that they loved Gabby and I was happy for him. He continued when they stopped.

"You must be wondering why I called you all here this evening. I just want you to share in my joy at being able to acquire something to help me move around easily." There were shouts of approval. Gabby stopped and looked round the room. He was looking for me and when our eyes met he winked. He continued, "I appreciate the help all of you gave me when I had to depend on you for transportation. You will find my new companion standing outside. I will call on Mr. Bernard Bila to pour the libations for us."

Benny stood up with a bright smile on his face. He told the people present how long he and Gabby had been friends. They were friends in secondary school and moved to high school together. After high school they were separated. Gabby wanted to go to the university and he to a professional school. The first year he wrote the entrance examination into the Higher School of Magistracy, he did not make it and had to stay out for one year. Fortunately the next year he made it and went in. They were together again in Yaounde and had to drift apart later because of the demands of academics. Gabby got admission into a Nigerian university to do a masters course in Accountancy. Although they met occasionally and visited each other, it was not the same. They were no longer teenagers. They each had a focus in life and they were determined to achieve their dreams. Their friendship regained its rightful place in their lives when their careers brought them together again in Douala. Both of them had good jobs in Douala and everything fell into place. They came together like long lost brothers. Benny spoke of how they had helped each other in times of need and shared their joy in times of success, like the current one. He felt much honoured to bless the new companion, which was obtained with Gabby's hard earned money. He went ahead to talk about the value of sincere friendship and the reward of hard work. He then insinuated that Gabby had gotten a new companion to carry him around but hoped that he would soon have another to keep him at home. At this statement, everybody laughed, cheered and clapped. He then invited everybody outside for the traditional blessing of the car. I was the last person to leave the house and stood at the door and watched them stand around the car. After invoking the blessings of the ancestors, Benny poured a whole bottle of champagne on the bonnet and the tires of the car and everybody cheered again.

A whole bottle of champagne! At that time there was money in this country. Students from high schools were employed by government and paid good salaries. Commodities in the market were cheap. I remember that a bottle of beer was one hundred and fifty CFA francs. Washing soap was a hundred and twenty five CFA francs. There were opportunities for education and business. There was economic boom and the citizens benefited from it. There was more than enough money to spend. People were extravagant in their lifestyles. Even a child's birthday party was a grand occasion with bottles of champagne and whisky gracing the tables. People had fat bank accounts from money they earned and a general state of wellbeing characterized the life of the average Cameroonian. Salaries were paid on the twentieth of every month. People looked for reasons to throw a party. Getting a car was just a way of making good use of the available money.

If Cameroonians knew that at the turn of the century there would be hardship, they would have thought twice before indulging in their bacchanalian revels and topping the list of champagne importers in Africa. Like the ant in the fable, they would have stored for the rainy day. But who could have thought that things were going to change with the benevolent father figure assuring his children that things are fine and will continue to be fine. The turn of events has taught Cameroonians a lesson. If the clock could be put back, they would learn from experience.

Gabby must have spent a good sum of money. The food was ordered from a hotel. Three champagne bottles were standing in ice buckets as well as whiskies. The whole array was impressive with bottles of beer standing at one end of the table and two battalions of soft drinks at the other, arranged by the height and size of the soldiers. The food was on trays covered with foil paper. There was salad, roasted and fried fish, roasted and fried chicken, fried ripe plantains, and more. It was just the type of food that did not need any complicated accessories that messed up the place. It was the type of party expected of a bachelor.

Gabby was so involved that he did not realize I was not in the crowd. But Jane did. As the group moved back to the house she came to my side as we went back to our seats and whispered, "Don't be so detached." When everybody was seated Gabby continued.

"Ladies and gentlemen, I want to present to you those who are most honoured this evening. First there is Mr. Modi, my immediate boss and who has been like a father to me. I want to thank him for treating me in the office like an equal though he has much more experience in the field of accountancy than I do. He is the type of person who allows the young to grow."

He turned to Mr. Modi and gave him a special thank you. He continued. "There is Mr. and Mrs. Bila. They are like brother and sister to me. There is also Miss Elizabeth who came all the way from Bamenda this afternoon for this occasion." All eyes were turned on me and I had to cover up my embarrassment by putting on a charming smile. I stood up to acknowledge the honour. As the party progressed, I found myself serving the guests. Jane assisted in serving for some time and sat down, so as not to strain much. Gabby put a Makossa tune on the stereo and some of the couples started dancing. It was a very informal occasion and soon everybody joined in the dancing. There was enough to eat and drink. At about one a.m., some of the guests started to leave. I knew that we were the last people to leave so I did not bother. At one point I went into the bathroom and took rather a long time relieving myself and adjusting my make-up. On returning to the parlour it was empty and Gabby was leaning on a table waiting for me to come out. He watched me as I looked around wondering why Benny and Jane were not there.

"Where is everybody? Where are Benny and Jane?" I asked with alarm in my voice.

"Do not worry. They won't be coming back and you are quite safe here," he assured me.

"What am I going to do now? I cannot pass the night here with just a dress on me." I protested.

"Everything is all right. Come and see."

There was my travelling bag in his bedroom. I now understood why Benny had disappeared during the party. In spite of feeling a bit angry at the trick that had been played at my expense, I admired the way men stick together when women are concerned. I was too tired to argue with him. I went back to the parlour to gather the plates and glasses to carry them into the kitchen.

"Leave those things alone. They will be taken care of in the morning."

I did not listen to him and continued collecting the plates. When I finished collecting them I went into his room, took out my toilet bag and went into the bathroom. All along I said nothing to him. The cold water was welcomed as it trickled down my back. Sweat had soaked the inner wear I had on and it felt damp to the touch. After bathing and putting on my nightdress I went back to the room. Gabby was still sitting where I had left him.

"Are you angry with me Lizzy?" he asked without preamble.

Honestly I did not know how I felt. But I understood that his question was just his way of finding out how I felt about what he had done.

"Why should I be angry with you?"

"You should be angry with me because I brought your things here without telling you. If I understand you well, it means you are not angry

50

with me. If that is so then I am happy. And you should be happy too."

"Why should I be happy?"

"You are not angry with me so you should be happy."

I had really wanted him to know that I was not happy with what he had done but there was no way now. He had turned the situation round and made it impossible for me to express any hint of disapproval.

"I am tired Gabby. I want to sleep."

"I am happy to hear that. I was afraid that you would not want to sleep on my bed."

"Why are you so happy about everything I say?"

"I am happy because you are with me. I have been looking forward to just this moment." As he said this he moved closer to where I was sitting on the bed and sent his arms round me.

"Lizzy, you do not know how much your presence means to me. I have been longing to tell you so many things. But I never had the opportunity to do so."

"I am here now so you can tell me all that you had to tell me."

Without responding he got up and went to his wardrobe. He came back with a small red case. He opened it and took out an exquisitely designed diamond ring. He looked at me. But my eyes were focused on the ring. He lifted my left hand and slipped the ring on the fourth finger of my left hand.

"Lizzy, do you want to be my wife?" he asked. I was too amazed to speak. I had hoped that our relationship would blossom to this but I least expected that it would all come out this way. I understood the significance of his gesture and held my breath. I could not believe that Gabby could give me such a ring. As I looked at the ring I had the feeling of falling from a great height. The light reflected from the ring seemed to be radiating outwards. I looked at it trying to recall how I had thought I would feel if it ever happened to me. Now it was happening and I was so filled with joy I could not have imagined.

"Yes, Gabby, if you would want me as your wife." He turned me slowly to face him and our lips met. As I kissed him I was all the time conscious of the ring on my finger. This kiss was different from the ones in Bamenda. It was a confirmation of something more intense than just our need for each other. After the kiss we were breathless. I felt as if I was going to suffocate with happiness. I had to come back to earth. I was afraid that this spell of happiness was going to finish and I would never have it again. I had to reserve some.

His tone the whole evening had been light hearted as if he would not have minded if my answer had been negative. But now I saw how devastated he would have been if it were so. I used this now to tease him. "You must be happy, Gabby. You are a lucky man to have two loves in your life the same evening." "Elizabeth, you are an incredible woman. Why did you have to bring that up at this moment?" I started laughing. "Oh, do not mind me. I love you, Gabby, and this ring is a manifestation of the fact that you also love me." "Then show me that you love me again." "I will show you all my life but for now just have this as a foretaste." I brought my lips close to his and he gripped me as if he was just waiting for me to give him the green light again. From then on I cannot remember the sequence of events until the next day. The exhaustion from the evening activities and Gabby's demands to fulfil and be fulfilled left me completely dead to the world by morning. The co-mingling of happiness, excitement and satisfaction could not be registered in my mind in any order for they kept tumbling over each other.

It was morning and in my sleep it seemed as if I was watching a spot of light coming nearer and nearer to me. As I gradually returned from the astral world, I noticed that it was a ray of light pouring into the room where the window blinds had not been properly closed. I turned away from the light and Gabby's arms held me fast. He kissed the nape of my neck, my cheeks and jaws. I held my breath and lay back wishing it would never end.

"Darling, are you awake?"

I made no response. He kissed me lightly on my lips and got out of bed. I pretended to still be asleep. As soon as his back was turned to me, I opened my eyes and looked at him. He was naked and I seemed to be seeing him naked for the first time. His hairy and muscular legs fascinated me. They were so strong and firm. I watched him walk to the wardrobe to take out his housecoat. I watched him move about the room. Each time he turned to look in my direction I closed my eyes. He was waiting for me to wake up. And when there was no sign of my doing so he came back to the bed.

"Wake up. Wake up." He shook me lightly. "If you are the Sleeping Beauty, I am ready to face all dangers to rescue you."

I could not believe it was Gabby saying this. I mused how moments of absolute happiness in the adult bring back thoughts of the perfect happiness evoked in fairy tales. If contemporary man and woman could live one third of the type of happiness evoked in these tales then marriage would not carry the amount of uncertainty it does today. A tale meant for children was making more meaning to an adult. My imaginative mind was already picturing Gabby and I 'living happily ever after'. I burst out laughing. I could not resist anymore. I sat up and my attention went immediately to the ring on my finger. It sparkled in the rays of the sun. It produced the ray of the rainbow. I looked up and he was watching me. I smiled. He stretched out his hands and helped me to get up and the titans clashed. The room was different. The world was different as it is often said in the fairy tales. Unfortunately these tales never tell of the day-to-day living experiences of those concerned. The tales only focus on the perpetual state of bliss, which was not to be for Gabby and myself. But that morning we were momentarily in that state of bliss. We cleaned the house together, then prepared and ate breakfast together. I cannot remember how many times I looked at the ring on my finger. I was reluctant to put my left hand in water. I was afraid it would lose its brilliance. Its presence on my finger was indication that Gabby had given part of himself to me. I guarded the ring jealously because I wanted to preserve this union.

The woman is often regarded as the caretaker of the man, the caretaker, not the owner. This was Gabby's own way of saying 'Now I am in your hands'. It was his way of telling me that now I had someone to think about, care about and dream about and who was ready to do all of these for me. In fact, he was mapping out his territory to keep trespassers away. It is funny how a man always wants to possess a woman. While on the surface a woman seems not to be able to possess a man. I say on the surface because for a couple to be together for five, ten or fifteen years, this calls for a lot of possession which results in give-and-take situations. It is a road with thorns and brambles, which have to be endured. A woman could worm herself into a position of control, but the heavy thumb attitude only breeds antagonism or a coercing figurehead for the family. An acknowledged sense of direction in the woman leads to mutual possession, which leads to harmony.

But society's hidden agenda has assigned certain roles to the man. The woman's roles are limited for her capacity, and she faces physical and psychological restraints. The woman can be stifled in her aspirations, but will have to be protected. It is an avenue through which the woman can create her own identity and acquire social and psychological balance. Peace and unity can come to reign through this subtle process. Was I going to free myself from society's hidden agenda as well as maintain a healthy family life with Gabby?

At one o'clock the next day, Jane and Benny arrived. I gave Benny a half-smile, half-reproach look. He understood what I meant and his eyes drifted to my left hand. Immediately it seemed as if my hand had projected itself beyond my whole being, which had become inconspicuous in the presence of the ring. Jane rushed and embraced me. At that moment Gabby came out of the bedroom and came to stand by me. We stood there as if Benny was the priest joining us in holy matrimony. The spell was broken by my laughter. The rest of them joined in the laughter. We were not laughing at anything in particular. It was just the joy of knowing that our friends cared what was bubbling in us. As we laughed, Jane looked at me and shook her head. I did not know what was passing through her mind. If it was along the same lines as what was passing in mine, then we were laughing at the incredible surprises life has in store for us. Here were two girls, who used to have such good laughs after crying over the whims of a man, now willingly allowing themselves to be enslaved by these very whims. Under the general laughter we were all having secret laughs of our own.

I had to be back at work the next morning in Bamenda, so there was no time to waste. If I left at two p.m., I would be in Bamenda at nine p.m. at the latest. After chatting about the events of the party for as long as I thought reasonable, I excused myself to get my bag ready. I felt sleepy but there was no time to sleep.

4

Although I had hinted to my mother the possibility of my getting a husband, I did not make it clear that something was in the pipeline. It was time to break the good news to my parents and get their blessing. My mother in particular would be very happy, for what was she going to do with a grown up girl still coming back to her parent's house? I was the first girl in the family and had to set a good example. I was already a cause for concern. I knew that my mother was already feeling ill at ease at my continued celibacy. Mothers always think that it is their duty to get their daughters married. Fathers never think that they too can play the role and give a lucky man a wife as they had theirs. I had noticed the look on her face when we had discussed the impending marriage of my friend's younger sister. I knew she was sensitive to the remarks that were already being made about her active participation at the wedding ceremonies of her friend's children. I knew about such talks but I could not rush into marriage just to keep their tongues from wagging. This, together with the desire to escape from a boring village life and stop being a burden on their parents, is what has made many girls get into marriage.

One of the natural roles assigned to woman is to bring forth children. It is not the number of children that matters but the type of people these children grow up to become. A child is always considered a blessing whether it is born in or out of wedlock. Some tribes even believe that it is better for a girl to have children while still in her parent's home. This was assurance of the fact that she would give birth to children when she gets married and these children would belong to the family. It causes quite a strain in relationships when a girl gets married and is forced by circumstances to come back to her parent's home with her children. The girl and her parents struggle to bring up the children and at the end when the children have made it in life that is when the father identifies with the children.

But my paternal uncle's wife had a different view. As far as she was concerned she did not bring any children from her father's compound so she was not going back with any. She had left her husband with three children and went to Kumba. She could no longer bear the type of life she lived in the village of Bai Grass. She had left the village with the understanding that her husband lived in Kumba. But things were not as she expected. She was often heard to say that she never thought she was leaving her village to go to another village. If one leaves the village one should go to a town. My mother had the responsibility to bring up the two youngest children. Her responsibility was made easier because the father of the children did his best to provide for the children. They were sent to school and were doing very well. But it was rare to find such situations. Most often the story was the reverse. It is the girl's mother who unwillingly has to carry the burden of bringing up the children.

Examples of such situations abounded in the village. The most glaring one that was often used as a reference was that of Ma Trobu. She became known by that name because of her daily lament over the predicament in which she found herself. Her two daughters had left her with five children to care for. Fortunately she was still strong enough to farm and feed the children. When her first daughter had problems with her husband she had packed her things and returned to her parent's house. Her husband was always beating her and on many occasions she ran back to her parents with a swollen eye or with wounds on her back. The last time she showed up with a bite wound from her husband on her left arm. This was going too far and she had decided never to go back to her husband. Even her mother supported her decision. A year later, the woman decided to go to town and see what she could make of herself. She was last heard of in Bafoussam. The second daughter's husband was not really cruel to her. She was living in Bamenda town with her husband who worked as a security guard at the Bamenda Provincial Hospital. He had a job opportunity in Yaounde with the Wurkenhurt Security Services where the salary was three times what he was earning in Bamenda. He had to move to Yaounde. His wife was very excited and believed she was soon going to join her husband in Yaounde. The first letter she received informed her that although his salary was better, life in Yaounde was very difficult and the money he earned was not enough to maintain a family. He sent money occasionally for his wife and children. But as the year turned into another and yet into another, there was no indication that his family was going to join him in Yaounde in spite of the visits he made to Bamenda. The wife got suspicious and made a surprise visit to Yaounde only to be told that her husband had gone to Ebolowa to work. Disappointed, she returned to Bamenda. But the three weeks she had spent in Yaounde with a tribeswoman had taught her a thing or two. She soon found her way back to Yaounde leaving two children with her mother. The grandmother of these children was often heard lamenting.

"Ifi you born pikin, na trobu. Ifi you no bornam na trobu. Wetin woman go do?" Everybody in the village knew her story and many women prayed that such ill luck should not befall them. I am sure my mother was praying too.

Ours is a family of five children: three girls and two boys. The boys are the youngest. The third girl at that time was in secondary school while the second girl was in high school. Though both were in school, by village standards they were of marriageable age. Some fathers already had their eyes on them. But with my constant talking to my father to give them a chance to be educated, they had escaped from getting into early marriages. From the way things were being done in the village, my father in his humorous moments would say that their bride price would be used to send their younger brothers to the university. This always grated on my nerves and although he said it in humour, I knew that if he had the chance he would do it. There was nothing wrong in their getting married before me, but they had to stand on their feet first.

None of the speculations about me were coming to fruition. I was going to shut up their talkative mouths. It was believed in the village that I could not give birth and that was why men were afraid to marry me. Those who thought all the ova in my stomach had gone bad were going to be astounded. Some even said that I had committed so many abortions that there was no way for me to fall pregnant. They could not believe that a big woman like me working and earning a good salary would stay without becoming pregnant. I was going to make my mother understand that I had not yet given up on the idea of getting married.

I thought of the most conducive time to tell her. I knew that if I got her on my side both of us would convince my father. I could not understand why he clung to the idea that his children must choose partners from our village, while the trend was changing all round him. He did not know that a woman can make her life bearable wherever she is just as his mother did. Gabby was not from our tribe. He was from Batibo and people from my village did not know much about Batibo people. All they knew was that they produced a lot of palm oil. From my first discussion with my mother I knew that she was not going to be an obstacle. But I could not be too sure.

I could not tell my parents what was about to happen. Gabby had telephoned to tell me that the move would be made soon. I waited to see what was going to happen.

Since Gabby had just returned to work there was no possibility that a leave of absence would be granted to him. But he had assured me that he was going to arrange everything.

A week after I returned from Douala I had a visitor in my office. I had gone to my boss's office to get some instructions on how some documents had to be treated. When I came back I found a man sitting on my visitor's chair. I greeted him and sat down. Since I had just received the directions from my boss, I had to put down the salient points before I forgot. This took some time during which I felt the man's eyes watching me intently. I looked up and our eyes met. I smiled and begged him to be a bit patient. His attitude was not like that of a man seeking information or who wanted to see the boss. These usually have an air of impatience, fidgeting with pens and pencils as if they were not yet decided on what to do, or they sit rigidly staring ahead of them not daring to ruffle even the air in the room. He was calm and had this searching look on his face. It was the type of look that sought to see inside a person, one that makes you ill at ease, making you wonder whether there is something about your person or which was out of place. He looked round my office, from the files on my table to the steel cabinet behind me, to the cupboard containing more files back to my table and finally to my face. I averted my gaze when his eyes returned to my face. If he were somebody of our divisional services I would have thought he was making a mental inventory of my office. From what I learnt later on from our conversation it became clear to me that he was trying to understand the type of person I was by looking at the way the things in my office were arranged and how I responded to people.

He had been a civil servant under colonial rule in West Cameroon before being elected as counsellor for the Bamenda Rural Council. He was the type of man who expected meticulousness in every government office. He also had the air of a man who was used to giving orders and deciding what should be. As he took his time to look around, I stole assessing glances at him. He looked like the type of worker who took his work seriously and looked with indignation at the laissez-faire attitude of this new generation of workers. This could be seen even in his dressing. A well ironed shirt, a coat and a tie was the required attire for a man in a government office even if he was just visiting. As he looked round the office I could see from his face that he appreciated what he saw. He was the type of person who would want to instil the uprightness and duty consciousness of his days into any youth ready to listen. His general attitude and the expression on his face conveyed a sense of appreciation of the innovations in the office equipment, but at the same time it seemed as if the expression 'in my days...' was just round the corner. He was well groomed as most men moving out of their fifties into the sixties who want to keep a youthful appearance.

"May I help you?" I asked when I had finished. He made no response. He kept looking at me. I looked at him too, beginning to be intrigued at the man's behaviour. Whether he wanted to brow beat me to see whether I was going to wilt, I do not know. But my curiosity was turning into annoyance for the man was preventing me from going ahead with my work. I could not concentrate on my work with those eyes on me. My patience miraculously held up and I told myself to be calm and look at him counting up to sixty at the pace of a clock, giving him time to make up his mind. He smiled before I was half way through the counting. He had been examining me closely and his smile seemed to indicate that he was pleased with what he saw. He finally spoke.

"I am Gabby's uncle."

This declaration was intended to get my genuine reaction. And he did a good job at it. Keeping me in suspense had done the groundwork.

"I am glad to meet you," I said, confused about the right thing to say at that moment. He did not give me time to compose myself and say anything reasonable but went straight on.

"You must know why I am here…"

"Please, let us go outside," I said as I held his hand giving him a warm handshake and leading him outside. I was praying for my heartbeat to slow down. I was afraid it was going to affect my voice. The grip of his hand confirmed what I had been thinking about him. His palm was soft and also marked by calluses from farm work. I knew he had not come to tell me anything but to see for himself and make his own assessment. Now I could look at him in the face without embarrassment. I now knew where I stood and felt more at ease. Outside his eyes took on an amiable glint and seemed to be saying 'do not take my gaze in there too seriously'. I took him on these bases and waited for the gradually broadening grin to take the form of words.

"I hope I have not taken you unawares. In fact, I just had to see you as soon as I received Gabriel's letter."

I waited for him to continue, watching him intently but not appearing to do so. He too was watching me, gauging the effects of his words. He just had to see the woman Gabriel had described. He continued.

"You see, he has kept us in suspense for so long…" The unfinished sentence and the expression on his face showed that he wanted to say more but decided against it. I waited in silence for him to continue.

"Gabriel is a stubborn boy…" He smiled as if at himself looking beyond me to the office door as if he did not want to meet my eye. I wondered what Gabriel had done for his uncle to tell a complete stranger that he is stubborn. He continued.

"But a smart and sensible one too."

I wondered where all this was leading. I tried to figure out what he meant by Gabby being stubborn but at the same time smart. I was confused and frightened and tried not to let it show on my face. When he had introduced himself I had imagined that he had come to warn me to keep away from Gabby. He continued.

"I am a practical man and I cannot be pretending when I say Gabriel is a sensible boy." I did not know whether Gabriel's being sensible had to do with his decision at that time to tell them about a girl he had met. I did not want to follow that trend of thought but I was inquisitive to know what stubborn thing Gabby had done so I asked him.

"What has Gabby done, a big man like him, to be described as stubborn?" He looked at me. It was evident that he had not expected that I would ask a question like that. He was momentarily taken off his trend of thought but soon recovered.

"Look, my daughter, I cannot answer your question now but you will soon know." He took both my hands and held them in his as he expressed the wish to see me later in the afternoon. I gave him a brief description of where I lived and he departed.

I met or rather he met me later that day. This time it was in my house. During his visit earlier that day, there was every indication that he wanted more time to talk with me. When he suggested coming to my house, I thought it was appropriate. If I had to become part of the family, I had to start getting used to them. They would open up a niche for me to fit into the fabric of the family. I wondered whether it was going to be a good blend or a glaring patch. There were surely in-laws whom I was going to rub the wrong way and who would in turn rub me the wrong way. It was a situation of give and take but the heart of the matter lay between Gabby and me. The relationship between Gabby and me was not going to be determined by others, although having an ally in the background would be an added support to the whole experience and day-to-day building of the edifice of marriage.

Was it not the other way round too? My sense of proportion checked in. Was Gabby not also looking for a niche in the fabric of our family? Oh yes, he too should seek to blend. He should not only seek for a piece to complete his outfit. Thinking of the intricacies of the impending union was giving me a headache and I felt the rising excitement making my stomach churn. I wanted to have a cool head.

Pa Martin struck a chord in me and I felt I already had an ally in the other camp. I had this feeling after our first meeting. It is easy for a sensitive person to notice these involuntary betrayals of a person's thoughts through gestures, facial expressions and tone of voice. He did not ask questions that would betray his trend of thought. His whole attitude was really casual and cordial. Acting as the head of the family, in fact as Gabby's father, it is normal for a prospective father-in-law to maintain a non-committal facial expression in the presence of a future daughter-in-law, especially if he has heard of a string of them with none coming to fruition. Pa Martin was taking this one seriously because it was on his home terrain and close enough for him to monitor the developments. He was taking this as a personal challenge and I could imagine how he could react if things went wrong. It showed in the set of his jaw line and the angle of his chin. Underneath his warm approach lay a firm heart. I had to be cautious and win him over completely.

I was going to entertain my first in-law. I rushed home after work, prepared a good meal, tidied myself and waited. At five o'clock he arrived. He was dressed in a brown flowery jumper with matching trousers. After I had welcomed him and he was comfortably seated he looked appreciatively around. I was sitting directly opposite him and when he had looked round the room his gaze finally settled on me, looking straight into my eyes. I held his gaze for some time and gave in. I did not want to appear too bold. I had often heard my father scolding my younger sister for looking directly into his eyes when he was admonishing her. This was considered as a sign of disrespect and insubordination. At this stage it was important for me to appear meek and soft. This is how men like their women to be. As he spoke I did not look into his eyes but arranged the expression on my face to show calm interest while I was dying to know more about Gabby's people. He sat as if he would suddenly jump to his feet. I surveyed him closely.

He was of average height and a bit bulky. His face was clean shaven. It looked smooth but the spots where the hair sprouts were visible. His chin was also clean shaven but above his upper lip was a line of moustache, which he kept neatly trimmed. This thin line looked like a caterpillar that had climbed on his face. It gave a distinct resemblance to the comedian Charlie Chaplin. His eyes had crow's feet at the corners and as he spoke he kept his eyes narrowed and seemed to be looking at me between slits. I estimated his age to be about sixty-five. His appearance showed that he had spent the better part of his life in town. If he had lived in the village he would have been considered an old man. The crow's feet and curled lips were indications that he had a sense of humour and could easily laugh. I later learnt that he was a joker. But since there was something at stake he had to be serious.

"Elizabeth," he began. "Gabriel asked me to look for you. He has informed me about everything. I want you to know that I am a straightforward person and my instincts tell me a lot. Let me not go into all that. I am happy that Gabriel has made up his mind at last and has delegated me to carry out this important mission."

He spoke with all the wisdom expected of a man of his age and experience. He not only spoke for himself, he spoke for the family as well. He spoke of the merits of marriage but did not fail to point out that there were pitfalls as well. I listened attentively not only to his words but also to what lay underneath. He made the whole venture of marriage sound so simple with his jokes. But I could read from his voice that it was a necessary evil. I was glad he was saying all these things to me, for if he had not seen something good in me he would not have bothered. He went about the mission assigned to him with keen interest. What delighted me more was the fact that he realized that I had to be directly involved in the decision making. It was not enough for them to go to my parents to start arrangements without first consulting with me. When he had spoken for some time, I interrupted by suggesting he eat something.

"I am sure that you are not in a hurry," I said as I got up to go and bring the food.

"I have come to see you and will stay for as long as you want me to." I was using one of the lessons I had learnt through conversations with my colleagues in the office. Was it not said that the way to a man's heart is through his mouth? Before arriving at the decision to offer him food I considered the implications. Hospitality is one of the most important aspects of tradition and was expected of everyone. But what would happen if he refused my offer of food? How was I going to react? It would be a bad sign indicating that things were not as I expected. But if they were like that then there was no need for his coming to my house. In my final assessment these thoughts were all superficial because I had already planned what to do. Refusals and reactions would have to take their course.

While he had been speaking and I listened, he had sat at the edge of the chair as if he was not certain of my reactions to his words. He now reclined and made himself more comfortable. His total attitude was an act of acceptance. I was glad I had taken time after cooking to have a bath and dress decently. I also put on a gentle fragrance. Oh, women, what traps you set for men! But it made me feel good and bolstered my confidence. I knew he would be scrutinizing and I gave him enough to think about as I went about setting the table. It was essential for me to make him understand that I was not just a woman in the village sense. I was mature enough to know what I was getting into. I earned my keep. I had experience of life as I saw it. I now had something to look forward to. I could speak my mind. Was that not what he had hinted at earlier in the day? Well all these would be revealed with time. For now all he had to do was watch me as I moved about. I was conscious of his eyes on me. He did not conceal it. My excitement was evident in my movement and spilled over on my face. There was a fixed smile on his face. Whether he was amused at my faintly concealed excitement or he was really enjoying himself, I could not tell. But the moment was important for me.

He watched my every movement as I placed the plates and dishes on the table. Over the meal we made little conversation. He did not forget to make a positive comment about the food. I had guessed the range of beers, which a man like him would drink. At that time Becks, St Pauli and

Heineken were popular and drinking one of them was a sign of class. I did some fast thinking. He could not on his first visit ask me for these beers. But I could not dismiss the fact that he might have better taste. So I had bought two bottles of Heineken, two bottles of Export beer and two bottles of Gold Harp. When I asked him what he would like to drink, he instead asked me what I would want him to drink. I suggested Heineken. He immediately agreed and said that I had hit the nail on the head. I could not pretend that I did not drink beer. I took one bottle of Gold Harp and we drank together.

Gabby's maternal uncle, Pa Martin as he was called, visited me on a Wednesday. It seemed as if after his visit there was a meeting of the inner core of the family. For on Saturday evening two women came to visit. I had nothing to do that evening so I sat doing some embroidery. When they knocked, I opened the door and on perceiving them, I instinctively knew that these were Gabby's relatives. I welcomed them warmly and asked them to sit down. I went over to the cupboard, lowered the volume of the radio and came back and sat down where I had been sitting. One of them, the younger one picked up the cloth I was working on and examined it; then she put it down and looked at my face. Our eyes met and she turned hers away. It seemed as if they had not yet decided on what they had to say by the time they got to my house. The younger woman looked more preoccupied with her thoughts. The elder of the two who I later learnt was Gabby's mother looked round the room and finally rested her eyes on my picture on the wall. While she looked at the picture, I looked at her. I could only see her profile as her face was turned from me. Her mouth was firmly closed and her jaw line showed that she could be very firm. As she contemplated my picture her features softened and took on an expression of suppressed laughter. It was the type of expression that a mother puts on when her little girl has done something smart in the presence of adults. This was soon replaced by a slight frown that was an insufficient cover for what she really felt. The mobility of her face was too fast to be followed closely and the emotions conveyed were not easily interpreted. But all these left a marked expression of relief. Her hair was greying at the temples but the creases of age on her face were straightening up as she relaxed and this gave her an almost youthful appearance. She was very much like Pa Martin in complexion and body build. The features that characterized Pa Martin's face seemed to have been reversed on her. The set of her mouth showed that she was hard to please – a trait I have learnt to live with.

"You di wander weti bring we for your house for di kana time," Gabby's mother began. I made no response, waiting for her to continue. But I looked closely at her trying to imagine what had brought her to my house.

I had to be prepared for whatever she had come to say. Having an ally in Pa Martin was not enough. He alone was not the family. "Abi gabreya hi mami. Di wan na hi sister." I looked at the younger woman. They did not really look identical but there was this quality about her, which declared their kinship. She looked as if she had been forced to make this visit. She was Gabby's elder sister. Here was someone who had seen Gabby as a child and grew up with him. I looked at her as if I could see something about Gabby, which did not easily reveal itself when I was with him. All I got was a brief look, a supported jaw, and then she withdrew into a world of her own. I could have given everything to know what was on her mind, but she gave no access to it. The mother continued.

"Ngu sen we letter terre we say he don get woman. We chek say na play. Na pa Martin don tere we say hi don see the woman an hi lekam. So we too say me we come see you too."

So I was becoming an object for inspection? Well let them come and see their fill. What was important to me was Gabby's love. Because of this conviction, her tone and what she was saying was not enough to make me indignant. But why go there? They had the right to see the woman who was going to be a life companion to their son and brother, the woman who was soon going to be part of the family. There was something else to it. They wanted to see the woman who had interested Gabby to the extent of getting his family involved, the woman whom Pa Martin had approved of without hesitation. Their visit was more to satisfy their curiosity, for as I learnt later Gabby's earlier engagement was something they wanted to hear from a distance as it is expressed in the local dialect. They did not want it to come close.

At this stage I could not just sit there like a dumb. I thanked them for taking the pains to come right to my house. I offered them food and drink which they declined. That did not worry me, as I had long understood that women by their nature are not as open as men in such situations. It is not uncommon for some of them to show open hostility at the first encounter. But there was no sign of hostility even from the sister. This did not prevent me from being ill at ease since there was no way that I could decipher their thoughts. By being silent they were also making it difficult for me to initiate any conversation. The mother tried to keep conversation going by asking about my work. Her effort did not improve the situation as there was not much to tell and even this would not interest them. We were from two different worlds but destined to get to know each other well. Both of them looked like women who were still closely attached to farm work although they lived in town. This was evident from the state of their hands and fingernails. They bore the markings of hard labour with short peeling nails and hard palms. I instinctively clasped my palms on my lap, trying to hide my long, well manicured nails as if they would disapprove, as if it would indicate that I could not do their kind of work. Which I couldn't. But I could work just as hard at the work I was used to.

As I accompanied them to the roadside they were speaking in their native tongue as if I were not there. I knew they were discussing me, and I tried to get the trend of their discussion by observing their countenances. On parting they reverted to pidgin English and wished me a good night. The smile that accompanied our parting gave me a bit of assurance that all was not that bad.

I was fortunate to be present when the 'knock door' was done. It was an encounter during which both parties accessed their prospective in-laws. Quite often the bride's family looks critically at the financial viability of the groom's family while the groom's family was on the alert to make sure that the bride's family was not the insatiable type. The assurance of the groom's viability was not always to ensure that the daughter would be comfortable in her husband's house, but to know the type of things that would be demanded from him. If my parents were to get back something equivalent to my worth, for what would they ask? I wondered. Is there anything equivalent to a human being? Can a human being be sold or bought? At least the time of slavery was about over. How does one sell love, affection, concern and care? How and where can one buy such virtues? Are these not the things a couple expects from each other? What was the body without the essence? Take away the essence and you are left with a shell.

There is a tendency to sentimentalize the past. Those good old days when things were the way we would love them to be today. Doing this is like expecting the human mind to stand still while time marches relentlessly on. Because the past and the present exist in the human mind and the mind is controllable anything can be changed. This happened when Gabby's people came to see my people to officially ask for a wife for their son.

News had gone round the family circles that Gabby had chosen a wife at last. Everybody was inquisitive to know who this woman might be. It was not yet confirmed since the initial 'knock door' had not been done. I knew there was talk about it among Gabby's people and I did not want to risk having my parents hear about it from some other source. It was now three weeks since my return from Douala. Pa Martin told me that they would be going to see my parents soon. I rushed to the village that weekend. I was very excited but managed to control myself. I arrived when my mother was still on the farm. Fortunately, it was not one of her distant farms. I left my bag in the house and went to meet her on the farm. She was surprised to see me and rushed towards me with a worried look on her face. It was unusual for me to come for the weekend and go right to the farm in search of her. My smile assured her that all was fine. I told her why I had come to see her on the farm. She was silent for a while. Her countenance took on a look that was between happiness and perplexity. She looked away from me at the distant trees as if expecting to hear a voice that would wipe away the thought in her mind. We walked on in silence. I dared not look at her face. I was afraid of what I might see. My thoughts kept jumping from one assumption to another trying to look for a plausible reason for her silence. Although her silence killed some of the exuberance that had accumulated over the past days, I tried to keep my thoughts on a positive trend. This soon gave way to a surge of fear. I panicked. A hot sensation warmed my stomach and a bitter taste rose to my mouth. The sudden production of adrenaline seemed to have provoked my gastric pains, and I remembered that I had not eaten that morning before going to work and after work I had not eaten anything substantial because I was preoccupied with the trip to the village.

"Have you told your father?" she asked after her silence.

"No. I wanted to tell you first so that you could discuss it with him. Is it not against the tradition for me to tell him?"

"It is. You have not made that mistake. It is a good thing." After a pause she asked, "Are you going back today?"

"Yes I am going back in the evening. I just came to let you know so that you are not taken by surprise."

My mother was curious about Gabby. It was evident in her silence. I was ready to tell her all she wanted to know, but her earlier silence and guarded questions released slowly made me choose what I wanted to her to know. Funny enough, I felt a sudden sense of revolt. Hadn't she always hinted at this? Now that it was happening she was not being enthusiastic about it. I made up my mind to conceal exactly how I felt, for nothing would stand in the way of marrying Gabby. I then understood how people feel when they elope or marry against their parents' wishes.

It was not yet time for her to go home but she took her basket and hoe and we set out for home. As we walked, I briefed her on what had led to the present situation without exposing how involved I was. She did not share in my enthusiasm. Later I understood that she was not against the idea but that mothers are very prudent in such matters. They usually don't show their total acceptance especially when they have not met their prospective son-in-law. There have been instances of marriages breaking up at the last moment bringing enmity and blames on families and even villages. The marriage of a first daughter is important, as it is believed that it sets the pace for the rest to follow. Although individuals have their destinies, the breakup of a younger sister's marriage is not taken seriously if the elder sister had suffered the same fate. Comments like 'Her sister could not stay in her husband's house. Did you expect her to stay?' and 'It is their family disease' were common among people.

"Do you like him? Do you think you can accept him as he is?" my mother asked suddenly, breaking the silence. I was tempted to ask whether she had met Gabby before. Then I realized that she was asking from a different perspective. Did I like Gabby? I loved him. I said to myself. When I realized that in our mother tongue there is no equivalence for the English word 'love', I then understood what my mother was asking. The second question was the most important. Talking about a woman liking a man was a recent development in the mentality of the people. In their time when a girl had to marry a man she had never met there was no place for 'like' or what we call today "'love'". It was more of accepting the man as he was. And the man accepted the woman on the basis of her capacity for childbearing and hard work.

She had once told us how excited she was to be taken to the coast to meet her husband in the plantations after seeing him once in the village when he was on leave. They never really got to know each other before their marriage and they have been living peacefully. She still believed that tolerance was the most important ingredient in any relationship even where what we called 'love' was absent. She did not realize that as their mentality had evolved to include the word 'like' in their vocabulary, so also had the emotions of the younger generation evolved to include the concept of 'love'. But I could not tell her this. She would feel hurt. My younger sister was fond of telling her that she was an 'old-timer' and should let us live as our time demanded. I used to see a hurt feeling cross her countenance before she settled her features into contours of resignation. I was not ready to antagonize her because I really needed her cooperation, and somehow I accepted and respected her way of viewing the world.

Gabby's parents came to see my parents on what is known as a 'country Sunday'. This is the day the villagers set aside to honour their gods. On this day nobody is supposed to go to the farm. The notables go to the palace to concert with the chief and discuss and take decisions on issues concerning the welfare of the village. It is on this day too that visits are made by friendly families or to neighbouring villages. It is on such days that marriages are contracted. What Gabby's people brought was not different from what Benny's people had taken to Bali. What they brought extra was a tin of oil. Not many people were present because I had begged my parents to keep it low key. But the family members who heard could not stay away. Finally there was a crowd that was not expected. Even neighbours who heard came when all the negotiations were over to share in the food and drinks that would be provided. My presence in the negotiating room was very brief. I was called in to acknowledge that I knew the people who had come. When I came in I greeted Pa Martin first and then the others. As

I turned to go out Pa Martin called for me and asked for a seat to be brought so that I could sit by him. There was a general protest from those present. I was not yet their wife so I could not sit by him. This had not occurred to him or he might have forgotten that he had come to ask for a wife who had not yet been given to him. Although it was the tradition I found this very amusing when I thought of all the time we had spent together in my house. But on second thoughts this setting was different and tradition had to be respected. The palm wine was presented and my father poured it in his cow horn. He was not a successor so he could not drink from a goat's horn.

I had an ally in Pa Martin. After the 'knock door', in our conversations I got to understand the family's reaction to Gabby's marriage. It was a big relief to them. The manner in which my family had treated them had also pleased them. A new woman in the family was the topic of conversation. I did not mind this for I was also anxious to get to know them. Many of the family members wanted me to know that they were now my in-laws. The women in particular would greet me in the market and if I showed any sign of not recognizing them they would not hesitate to say they were Gabriel's this or that.

Pa Martin already had this possessive attitude towards me. He was very pleased with the way things had turned out and wanted me to meet some of the family members. At first I felt reticent. I was not yet officially married to Gabby and did not know what to expect. If I were in the village, I would occasionally accompany my mother-in law to the farm. I would help her in the housewifely activities that a young girl is expected to know and do. But now, what was I going to do? I trusted Pa Martin not to allow any situation to embarrass me.

He took me to his house one Sunday afternoon. I dressed simply but elegantly. From what I had seen of the family so far, they were town bred or had lived in the township long enough to imbibe its mentality. Pa Martin was considerate enough not to invite a big crowd. Those present were his wife and some elderly members of the family. Since it was a Sunday there was some of the younger generation of the family around. After greeting the elders they retired to an adjacent room where they were entertained and stayed to spend the afternoon listening to a football match on the radio. According to tradition, the successor of Gabby's father was supposed to be the head of the family, directing what had to be done. But he was a young man still in school in E.N.A.M. So Pa Martin, though of the mother's side, was the recognized head of the family as he could ensure the unity of the family. Even with the position accorded to him, he recognized the position of Gabby's younger brother who was the successor. Later I heard gossips that Gabby would have been the successor if he had shown signs of settling down as a responsible man before his father died. We had a good meal together during which there were jokes and funny stories. Most of the people present were women and they watched my every reaction. I am a good mixer and really enjoyed my stay with them. From that day I kept meeting my prospective in-laws. I kept meeting more and more of them. They greeted me in the streets. They visited me in my house and invited me out. I did not know that I was under their scrutiny, that my every action was noted as well as where I went and with whom. On the whole they were nice to me. I had not met any of them yet who did not say something to flatter me. They were still, as it is said in the native tongue, 'throwing maize to the chicken' so they had to be nice. I knew that I was not obliged to like every one of them neither did I expect each one of them to like me. This was just natural. There was this general atmosphere of expectation and subdued excitement. I do not know whether it was because I felt like this that I thought I could see it in my in-laws. Each person that was present in Pa Martin's house had tried to please me. I looked at their little concerns with amused contentment. I felt as my mother must have felt when she had visited her in-laws as a girl. I imagined the little endearments she must have enjoyed especially when she did something good like fetching a bundle of firewood for her father-in-law or filling her mother-in-law's water pots. But what was I to do to merit these endearments? There was absolutely nothing I could do. It seemed to give them pleasure to behave as their parents did when there was a bride in the family. It was important to create this atmosphere of family unity round a situation that was of great interest to all of them, although they were out of the village and in a township where individuality was gradually eroding these values they once cherished. At one point I felt that all they were doing was sheer hypocrisy, for they hardly knew me. This put me on my guard and I decided not to take things for granted but to be on the lookout.

One afternoon, I left the office and went to the market in town to buy some provisions I badly needed. It was a hot afternoon and I stood anxiously waiting for a taxi to take me home. As I looked in the direction of approaching taxis, I saw someone walking towards me. I could not believe my eyes. There was Jean Claude. When his eyes alighted on me his eyebrows arched in surprise. When he got close he embraced me kissing me on both my cheeks. I was so happy to see him that I did not mind the people around us staring. Kissing on the streets is not an Anglophone tradition and some people actually stare when they see this happening.

Jean Claude was Gabby's friend and colleague who used to accompany us sometimes when we went out with Benny and Jane. The three of them used to treat Jane and me like queens. He was always in our company to the extent that I wondered whether he had a girlfriend. He was so nice and friendly and seemed like someone who would never harbour any evil thought. He invited me for a drink in a nearby snack. As we went along, he held my hand in his and chatted along, all the time smiling at me. He was a francophone but spoke English reasonably well. He told me what he had come to do in Bamenda. There were certain musical gadgets from Nigeria, which he wanted to supply to some traders in Douala. He had to go back to Douala that afternoon to be able to be at work the next day. I sent verbal greetings to Gabby, Benny and Jane.

I kept Jane, now Mrs. Bila, informed of what was happening. I was so involved with the events that were taking place in my life that my encounter with Jean Claude was pushed to the background. My impending marriage was in the open and was causing quite a stir in the village. At the age of twenty-seven, many people had already given up the idea of my ever getting married. In their transactions with my in-laws, my parents were very understanding and I appreciated this very much. I did not expect them to make unreasonable demands on Gabby's people. But Pa Martin being who he was had done things as a man of his calibre was expected to do.

Soon after the visit of Gabby's people to my parents my father came to town to visit me. He wanted to have a heart to heart talk. As fathers are, he too had made his investigations and wanted to know how much I knew about my in-laws, particularly the man I was to marry. During the conversation he asked me an embarrassing question.

"Are you sure he has never been married before?" I was too stunned to give an answer of any sort. Coming from my father I knew that it was not a question that had come to his lips on the spur of the moment. It was not in the category of such questions. He must have meditated on it and now wanted a response. I examined the nature of the question. It was one that demanded the re-examination of a situation. How could I be certain of a situation I knew nothing about? But since he had mentioned it I had to find out.

"Do you have any idea father, for I have none." I received only a grunt for an answer. I did not know how to ask again for his silence indicated that he did not want to talk about it again. I tried to think of how my father had come upon this information and I drew a blank. If there had been anything like this, Gabby or Jane should have told me. Although Gabby was above the considered age of marriage by village standards, I was no younger. Something must have provoked this question and if there was anything to it, as the saying goes, 'the blight that affects cocoa will also affect coffee'. Even with this dictum I did not feel convinced. I felt it was just one of those things that were being said about me in the village. But further developments were to show that he was not far from the truth. When he left I felt the full impact of his question.

70

Was I going to lose another man to whom I had given my heart? Is there any use for loving if it ended in pain? Getting Andrew and what had gone on between us out of my system had taken a long time. I had finally gotten him out of my mind and was now comfortable with my relationship with Gabby. I was enjoying the warmth and support in the supposedly unproblematic uplands of Gabby's love where I thought there were no surprises; my father was unconsciously pulling the support from under my feet making me slip down the slope of despair. This was his way of making sure that I did not get in trouble. When I think about it now I wonder how he got the information.

The marriage negotiations were moving on smoothly. I did not write to tell Gabby what was happening. It was not my place to do so. Those he had delegated surely kept him informed but I talked with him several times over the phone. My boss had made a very convenient arrangement for those in the service to receive calls out of his office. I also spoke with Jane. During one of our telephone conversations she told me of the progress of her pregnancy and the preparations she was making. She was so excited with the prospect of the coming baby that she even told me that she was the luckiest and happiest woman in the world. Benny was an angel and she did not think there was another husband like him. After this enthusiasm, there was a drop in her voice.

"Lizzy, something is worrying Gabby. He was here last night telling me a very bizarre story. I did not believe one bit of what he was telling me but I have to get the truth from you." My body became suddenly hot. I wondered what must have happened. I wanted to ask Jane what was happening. But I could not speak. I was frightened and guessed that whatever was happening had to do with my relationship with him. If it were something else he would have told me. So I waited for Jane to continue.

"It seems as if someone wrote and told him that you have another man in your life. Lizzy, whatever it is, or whoever he is, please stop it."

I was dumbfounded and the saliva in my mouth became dry. In a split second I threw a glance back at the months I had known Gabby. I tried to remember whether I had behaved indecently to the extent of arousing someone's suspicions and consequently Gabby's wrath. I thought of my boss. But as far as I was concerned there was nothing suspicious in our relationship. It was platonic. I had not taken into account the conclusions people might have jumped at when they saw us together.

"Jane, I cannot believe what you are telling me. I am not a child. I know what I am getting into with Gabby. So what is the story?"

"He is furious because this man kissed you right on the street along Commercial Avenue."

At her mention of this I burst out laughing. I laughed and laughed. I could not control myself.

"Lizzy! Lizzy! What is wrong?" Jane asked in a baffled voice.

"Listen. Jane. It is very stupid of Gabby to listen to such a ridiculous story and allow it to worry him." The laughter was finished. In its place was rising indignation.

"So it is not true?" I could feel a sense of relief in Jane's voice.

"How can it be true Jane? The person was Jean Claude. I met him along Commercial Avenue and he greeted me as francophones do. Why should Gabby think I could kiss a man on the street in an intimate way?"

"Oh, what a relief, Lizzy. Gabby did not know who the person was, so he had to be angry. You know that he loves you too much."

"If he loves me there is even more reason for him to trust me. He should have asked me instead of tormenting himself for nothing. I am not a child, Jane. I perfectly understand that Gabby loves me and I love him too. I cannot do anything to jeopardize our relationship. But he should not be such an easy victim to gossip."

"I will tell him what happened. Lizzy, please do not be angry with him."

"He is the one harbouring anger not me. I hope he has learned a lesson. During my trips to Douala, Jean Claude had shown some interest in me. I could not understand this because I was sure he knew what was going on between Gabby and me."

"Lizzy, do you think Gabby was blind to Jean Claude's interest in you?"

"I did nothing to encourage him. Moreover when Gabby got the message he did not know that it was Jean Claude. I am really disappointed with Gabby. I do not know how I am going to explain this to him without making him look stupid."

When Jane dropped the phone waves of heat washed over my body as I considered the implication of what Jane had told me. So there were people in town that wrote and told Gabby about my every movement. My anger turned to these unknown and unauthorized censures of my activities. What right had they to tell Gabby such a ridiculous story? I knew then that there was someone who was not in accordance with my relationship with Gabby. And this someone must be a family member or someone close enough to Gabby to write and tell him such a lie and he believed. I felt trapped. Was I becoming a prisoner? I then realized that I had to be careful. How careful was I going to be if such an innocent encounter was misinterpreted and magnified into such dimensions?

I looked at the ring on my finger. It sort of consoled me and reassured me that such situations must arise. The ring was a concrete manifestation of Gabby's love and nothing was going to mar how we felt for each other, not even the mean tongues of family members and friends.

5

The ring was the centre of my life. Through it I saw Gabby. In the ring, I lived with him. Everywhere I went I had the feeling that everybody was looking at my hand. Although I tried to make it obscure, the sparkle could not be hidden. My colleagues did not fail to notice it. Soon the news was all round. Each acquaintance I met there after congratulated me. I basked in the assurance that I was going to lead a settled life, like that of women and their husbands whom I had admired. I was still intrigued by my boss's reaction. He seemed not to have heard the news that was circulating in the various rooms.

One morning while going into his office he asked me to see him. He had a serious look on his face and I thought either he was angry at my engagement or there was some serious matter concerning my work. I thought the former improbable because the last time we had gone out, he had been the perfect gentleman. Once seated in front of him I was taken aback by the broad smile on his face.

"Congratulations, Elizabeth. I knew all the time that you were a serious girl. But why did you not tell me? It is good. I wish I were in his shoes."

"Thank you, sir."

"I am going out of town in three days. We have this meeting in Yaounde. To show how happy I am for you, I want us to go out and celebrate. Are you free tomorrow evening?"

I could not doubt his sincerity. The last time I had gone out with him he had not done anything suspicious. Furthermore, he was interested in another girl who was returning his attentions in full measure. At the Ideal Park Hotel we had quite a nice time together talking about the recent happenings in Bamenda, in the country and the world at large. I made sure that the conversation never turned to the topic of boyfriends, girlfriends, husbands or wives. I avoided these topics because I did not want to talk about Gabby.

As we sat over a meal of vegetable salad, rice and chicken stew, a friend of his came in with his girlfriend. I knew this girl in high school and we exchanged casual greetings. They sat two tables away from us. As they drank she stole surreptitious glances at me. I caught her eyes and frowned to make her know that I did not welcome the way she was looking at us.

I enjoyed the meal and there was no pretence when I thanked him heartily. I was in no mood for staying out late. More so, I felt so snug that

I only thought of bed. He dropped me at my place and wished me a good night. He made no attempt to kiss me or squeeze my hand. Because of this my respect for him increased. He was one of those few men in control of his emotions. He was not that mean to get some compensation for his time and money as other men would. My life had some meaning. I had something to look forward to. I had a steady job and a good salary. I had loving parents. My reputation among my colleagues was enviable. There was nobody to distract me from my goal. What else could I have wanted? My colleagues were cooperative and my boss understanding.

Humming to myself one morning I walked into the office. I moved from room to room greeting everybody before settling down to work. As I sat reading the third file a letter was dropped on my table. I looked up to see who had dropped it. The person in charge of mails was walking away and only turned to give me a smile. I opened the letter with hands trembling with excitement. The letter was from Gabby. My heart was beating expectantly. In my excitement I mistakenly tore the edge of the letter. I began reading. At each sentence my heart sank. I could not believe what I was reading. My premonition when I tore the letter was taking a concrete form. By the time I got to the end my eyes were clouded with tears. I bent down as if I wanted to pick up a piece of paper. I quickly wiped my eyes and kept my head down, afraid to look up lest someone see my tear-filled eyes. One section of the letter tore my heart to shreds. It read:

"Elizabeth, you must be a wonderful actress. How can you promise to be my wife and at the same time be having an affair with your boss? All those nights you have spent out with him…"

I was emotionally devastated. I sat there looking at the letter without seeing it. My mind was in turmoil and I was incapable of rational thought. I could not continue sitting down. I put the letter in my bag, got up and went into the ladies room where I washed my face and replaced my makeup. I composed myself and came back to the office. Any constructive work was out of the question. My sorrow turned to anger. How can Gabby write such a thing to me I wondered. What did I do to merit such words? Who must have told him about my outing with my boss? I thought of the couple that had seen us at the Ideal Park Hotel. But my anger against them was impotent, first because I was not sure they were the people who had informed Gabby and second they were not present to receive the brunt of my anger. I realized that Gabby had a weakness for gossip. He believed everything people told him.

The first time this happened I had left it to Jane to do the explaining. When he had mentioned the incident over the phone I had dismissed it telling him to forget about it, assuring him that it was not enough to blight our expectations of each other. But what had just happened was too much for me to bear. The problem was not only that Gabby believed what was told about me but also that there was someone who was out to destroy my relationship with Gabby. These thoughts kept bothering me throughout the week. I carried my thoughts like a burden. It was heavy, too heavy for me to carry alone. Should I write and explain to Gabby? I could not bring myself to do that. To whom could I unburden myself, for a problem shared is a problem half solved. I could not tell my colleagues in the office. They were too talkative to keep a secret. Moreover some of them would gloat over my predicament. I could not go to my mother for obvious reasons.

On Sunday, I decided to do something, because I couldn't go on. Martha was a plumb and vivacious girl who worked in the governor's office. Although we were friends, our visits to each other were not frequent. But once we met we had so much to talk about. In fact, she was one of those women with whom one feels at ease. A stranger would easily tell her his or her woes. She had a sympathetic ear. So, to Martha I went. I went to her place in the evening when I was sure that she would be at home. She offered me a seat and went into her room. She called for her younger sister and sent her to get us some drinks. When she asked I would drink I asked for a bottle of Fanta. I could not drink beer. I drank beer when I was happy. The ache in my whole body could not stand an additional ache from the beer. Martha came back and sat with me in the parlour. We did not say anything to each other. We sat quiet as if talking could only begin when the drinks arrived. As we drank she launched her attack. I had come to her for consolation. I knew that she must have heard about my impending marriage. I was to begin with my apologies for not telling her in person before launching into my woes. But the contrary happened. Martha was the type of woman who wanted to be in the know and be a part of whatever was happening to her friends. She did not want to be informed when the event had already passed. She wanted to be current. Anything else was considered as a slight to her friendship. And this is exactly how she felt when she saw me. I was not aware of the strength of how she felt and her first remark made me feel bad, but I could not desist from what I had come to do.

"Elisa," she began. She always called me this way as a form of endearment. "How can such a thing happen to you and you do not tell me? I heard that you were engaged. I did not make any comment when I heard this. I wanted to hear from you yourself. It is dangerous to believe whatever you hear nowadays. So is it true?"

I was trapped. I did not know what to say. I had come to tell her of my woes. How was I to begin telling her that all was not well when she was expecting to hear how things were moving on? Maybe she had not noticed the strained look on my face or she might have misinterpreted it. Ironically her approach made it easier to put my problem without preamble.

"That is why I have come to see you."

"That is very good. I thought that we were no longer friends for you to keep me in the dark about such things. So when is the marriage going to take place so that I can start looking for the dress I will wear on that day?"

I did not know how to respond to this. Either Martha was pretending or she was looking forward to the marriage more that I was. But I knew her. She could not pretend to me. So I had to tell her just what was going on.

"I do not think there is going to be a marriage, Martha." The puzzled look on her face made me to realize that she had finally understood the strained look on my face.

"When you came in I saw the expression on your face and thought that you were ill. But since you did not mention the fact that you were ill I did not want to ask. So what has happened?"

"I hope that what I am going to tell you will remain between the two of us." I began. I poured out my sorrows to her. She listened without interruption. At the end she asked.

"Where does he work?"

I told her where Gabby worked.

"Do you know his full name?"

I told her that Gabby's full name was Ngu Gabriel Andong.

"Is this man not Gabriel Aweh?"

"Aweh is one of his names," I replied.

"Hey, Elisa, is that the man you want to marry? This man who nearly killed a friend of mine? Please think twice before you go to your doom. Let me tell you what happened. I have a friend who works in Ngaoundere now. She had to ask for transfer from Victoria because of this man."

I was all ears now and Gabby was a thousand miles away. Martha continued.

"She was engaged to be married to this man. They were a perfect match for each other. At that time she was working in Victoria and I was working at the governor's office in Buea. I used to spend weekends with her in Victoria. You cannot imagine the nice times we had together."

It seemed as if Martha was telling this story for her own benefit. She seemed to be enjoying her reminiscences no matter my reaction to what she was saying. She was determined to get to the end of her story. But I wanted to know who this woman was so I asked.

76

"Who is this woman? Martha."

"Let me tell you the story first."

"Why don't you tell me the name of the woman? What is the use of a story if you do not know who it is about?"

"The story is what is important, not the person." I saw that she was not going to tell me the name so I kept quiet. She continued.

"We used to go to Douala to see him. There were times I felt jealous because of the attention and money he lavished on her. What type of dress or pair of shoes could she not buy? I wonder whether she ever used a franc of her salary." I had a feeling that Martha was playing a game with me. I could sense some jealousy in what she was telling me, for there was no reason for her to tell me the story without mentioning the name of the woman concerned. To find out the truth of the story I teased her.

"But you too enjoyed with her and even shared some of the things she got."

"Of course, I did. There was enough for me to get my share." I was becoming sceptical of the truth of the story but there was no way I could bring an end to it. So I resigned myself to listen. She continued.

"Each weekend either she went to Douala or he came to Victoria. She used to tell me how he could go on his knees in front of her if he did anything to annoy her. Most of all the engagement ring he gave her was one in town. It was a diamond ring. It was very beautiful and she made sure all of her friends saw the ring."

At the mention of the ring I was startled. I hoped Martha did not see my reaction.

I looked at my hands and was happy that I had removed the ring and kept it in my bedside drawer. I could not imagine what Martha could have said if she had seen the ring on my finger. I wanted to know more about the ring so I asked.

"What did the ring look like?"

The description Martha gave fitted the description of the ring which Gabby had given to me for our engagement. I wanted to know more yet I dreaded hearing what I was going to hear. Martha was oblivious to the disaster she was creating in me. She was my friend but I knew she had a vicious streak in her and could use it whenever she pleased.

To break the tension and agony that was building up in me I added, "I am sure she was very pleased to show the ring off to you people."

"You can say that again," Martha replied. "She displayed the ring as much as she could and each time she was asked about the ring, she would speak as a 'been to' dragging on the word 'darling'. He could not bear the fact that she should dance with another person in a nightclub."

I was becoming more convinced with the story Martha was telling me. What she was saying was tying up with what was happening to me. I did not want to hear the rest of the story but I wanted to know how it ended. So I asked.

"Did they get married?"

"Why are you so impatient Elisa? Wait and hear the story to the end." I was caught. There was no escape. I was like the proverbial cricket that chirped, betraying where it was, thus inviting its own death. I had to listen to the end. Martha continued.

"Then one day everything changed. That weekend she telephoned to find out whether he was coming to Victoria or she should come to Douala. Somebody else answered the phone and told her that he was not in the office."

I could visualize the same drama happening with me. I remembered what Jane had told me over the phone. I remembered my outings with my boss. It now dawned on me how such innocent actions can be interpreted by others. As Martha spoke I tried to put into perspective all what was happening between Gabby and me. I was no longer really interested in what Martha was saying but she continued all the same and I had to listen.

"She telephoned the next day and got the same answer." Martha was warming up with her narration. I listened because I was interested in the story and also because I wanted to pick out the inconsistencies and make them the basis of my disbelief in the story for I still did not want to believe all Martha was telling me. She went on.

"That had never happened before. She started wondering why. The next day she telephoned and got him. He said that he was coming to Victoria but the words of endearment they used to say to each other only came from her."

My silence made Martha's narration sound like a monologue. It wasn't really a monologue for I was responding to it in my mind by asking questions and weighing the reactions of the actors in this drama Martha was unfolding to me in words. This was not enough. I had to get some answers from Martha so I decided to get more involved in her narration.

So I asked, "Why did he do that?"

"Gabby had heard something and was acting on what he had heard. My friend did not know what was happening so she could not understand. For the rest of the day she was worried."

I was going through the same experience. Martha was revealing to me a side of Gabby which I had not yet known. But my love for him kept my belief in Martha's story swinging from belief to disbelief.

"What did she do?"

"What could she do but wait to see Gabby for them to sort out their differences. At eight p.m. on Friday he arrived. She met him at the door to give him a welcome kiss. Instead he pushed her aside and entered the room. She stood back looking at him uncertain about what to say. His face was contorted with fury. He asked her, 'Who is Joel? And what has he got to do with you. You told me that Joel is Carine's boyfriend so that he could come and see you pretending that he is coming to see Carine. You have played the game for too long. Can I have my ring back?' She was so shocked by his demand that she did not know what to do. She just stood there looking at him. He continued.

"'You cannot say anything because it is true. Can I have my ring back please?' In anger she pulled off the ring and flung it at him. He caught it and walked out."

"That was not correct," I commented. "She could have asked him to sit down so they could talk."

"Are you saying my friend was wrong in doing what she did?" Martha asked me. I could see from her reaction that she was in favour of what her friend had done.

"I am not blaming anyone. But I think she could have calmly asked him to sit down and talk about it."

"You do not know Gabby. He is such a proud man and he has a temper. When he is angry he does not listen to anyone." I realized that Martha was trying to defend her friend's action.

"You were her friend. What did you do to help her?"

"I was not in town when all this happened. I had gone to Kumba. I heard all of this when I came back."

"So what did she do?"

"The next day she could not get out of bed. A sudden attack of malaria left her weak and unable to get out of bed. Her eyes were swollen with weeping. Her head pounded as if it was about to explode."

"So that was the beginning of the end."

"Yes it was. She did not know what to do. She lay in bed until Carine came to visit and found her in that state. Carine persuaded her to go to the hospital without knowing what had happened. But she could not leave her bed. There was nothing Carine could do but call for Joel." As I listened to the story I could not put the pieces together. There was a missing link.

I wondered why all along Martha had not said anything about her part in all this drama and waited for the appropriate time to ask her. It would have been unlike her not to have had played a role.

"When you came back and saw her, what did you do?"

"I came to her house when Joel and Carine were about to take her to the hospital. So we all went with her. She was admitted and we had to come back home to get some bedding for her and some food."

"Who is Joel?" I asked.

"He is Carine's boyfriend."

"When Gabby heard about her illness what did he do?"

"That wicked and proud man? He did not as much as answer our calls. He did not even come to see her."

"Martha, please tell me. Was she really going out with Joel?"

"Lizzy, to tell you the truth there was something fishy going on. My friend had begun behaving in a funny manner. I am not surprised that the affair ended the way it did."

I was shocked at Martha's conclusion. I was about to ask her why she had said so when she continued. "Men cannot be trusted. They are such bastards. They are not worth fighting for."

I saw pain and frustration on her face and wondered why. Since I got to know Martha in Bamenda, she had been such a carefree person, so contented with who she was that I thought there was nothing that could pain her. I did not know about her past life. I did not want to know just now. So I diverted her trend of thought.

"What happened to your friend?"

"Can you imagine that she had to ask to be transferred to another province to get away from Gabby and all the talking and gossip that were going on?"

"Where did she go to?"

She was finally sent to Ngaoundere. Before she went away she was looking like a scarecrow. The things that men do to women! Lizzy, be careful. I know this man. He only plays games with girls. He is not a serious man.

"What do you advice me to do because that is what I came to ask you."

"I cannot tell you out rightly to leave him. But I advise you to watch out. Men are devils."

I had not expected Martha to use such invectives in talking about men and Gabby in particular. Her story had revealed so much to me. My mouth felt dry and I sent my hand to pour more Fanta into my glass and found the bottle empty. That was it. I had to go. I felt exhausted physically and mentally. I needed time to sort out Martha's story and take a stand.

Back in my house I flung myself on the bed and wept myself to sleep. I got up in the night with a throbbing headache. I could not sleep anymore. I started putting things in their right perspective. Throughout my relationship with Gabby I had never known him to get angry unnecessarily. He loved me dearly. He had even told me that real love was much more than just having an affair, and that if he loved someone and the love was reciprocated, he would tolerate certain things because no one is perfect. Everyone is open to temptations now and then and needs strength to overcome them. But temptations are always there. I decided then that I was going to hear the other side of the story. In his letter he had sounded more sorry for himself than angry. What if Joel had acted deliberately in a way to make sure that Gabby never got her? Her decision to go away, was it one of guilt or of genuine disappointment? Was the person who had written to tell Gabby that I was going out with my boss not planning the same end for me? What was their aim in all these? Even Martha, what was her intention in telling me this story without giving me any constructive suggestions? Could she not be jealous that I am getting married while she is still single? The outing with my boss had not resulted in anything. I wondered how someone could sit and frame such a monstrous story. And Gabby himself, I cannot blame him because once beaten twice shy.

But how was I going to convince Gabby that the evening with my boss had no strings attached? How was I going to get the true story of what had happened with his first fiancé? Gabby must have really loved her to buy such a ring for her. Maybe he had overreacted as he was doing now. Why had he asked for the ring the first time he had confronted her? Why had he not asked for the ring in a less hostile manner? Had Gabby ever found out the truth about Joel's interest in her? Had she ever written to Gabby to tell him what she would have told him if he had given her the chance? These questions were all going round and round in my head. What was I going to do if our relationship ended the same way? What was I going to tell my mother? Where would I hide my face? I got up and took the ring out of the drawer and looked at it. I was happy that I had taken off the ring before going to Martha's house. She would have recognized it. I did not want to imagine what she would have said. I looked at the ring again. Its sparkle was no longer enticing. It gave out an eerie sparkle and together with the silence of the night I felt frightened. I put it back into the drawer. I lay down again and fell into a restless sleep.

The next day I looked pale and wane. I took a cold bath to drive away the heaviness from my head. In the office, I could not concentrate on anything. During break time I took permission and went home. I was really sick and my colleagues sympathized with me. Back home I looked at the mirror and was shocked at my appearance. The glow in my eyes was gone. My lips were white and cracked. I had forgotten to put on lipstick before going to the office. My stomach rumbled like distant thunder and I realized that I had not eaten anything substantial since my visit to Martha's house the previous day. I had no appetite and did not feel like cooking. I slopped down on the chair. Was this what was going to happen to me?

No! Not me! He was not going to treat me the way he liked and get away with it. He was not going to treat me the way he treated.... I could not remember the name and realized at that moment that Martha during her narration had not mentioned any name. I got up and went into my room. I took out the ring and looked at it again. It still had that eerie sparkle. I looked at it for what seemed an eternity and put it back into the cupboard. I was resolved not to take this situation lying down or to run away as the other woman had done. I took some phensic tablets and slept. I got up at six o'clock the next morning feeling very hungry. I quickly prepared some fried rice and ate. Then I took refuge in a novel.

Throughout the rest of the week I put together my plan and prepared my strategy. I was going to be on the offensive. I neither wrote nor telephoned Gabby. He would sweat it out as well. I put the ring back on my finger to keep up appearances. I adjusted and readjusted my strategy until I could imagine the scene that was going to take place. Minutes seemed hours and hours seemed days. I managed to be cheerful in order to avoid unnecessary and irritating questions.

It was Friday and after taking permission from my boss to go to the village, I was on my way to Douala. I got involved in the lively conversations that usually accompany such long journeys. I did so because I did not want to dwell on the purpose of the journey, fearing that thinking about it might weaken my resolve.

I arrived in Douala and Jane was surprised to see me. I had not informed anybody of my intention to come down. I desperately wanted my presence in Douala to be unknown to Benny until I had seen Gabby, so I was relieved when Jane told me that he was out of town. I poured out my tale of woes to her leaving out nothing. She listened without interruption. During my narration I was watching her reaction, especially when I came to the part of his former engagement. She tried to be composed, but biting her lower lip when I talked about it assured me that she knew. I did not tell her my plans.

"Elizabeth," she began. "You must not listen to one side of the story and just believe without hearing the other side. You must give Gabby the chance to tell you his own side of the story."

"What about my own story? Is he going to believe me?"

"I do not know. But you must try to be calm and explain everything as you have done with me. Please do not get angry. Make him understand that people might just be jealous of both of you."

"Jane, that is not the point. If people are jealous of us it is their business. We must not make it ours."

After a pause, Jane said, "Elizabeth, why don't you allow me to help you sort this out? I know Gabby and I also know that you are telling me the truth."

"No, Jane. Let me handle this."

I was relieved that Jane believed what I had told her. She also believed in the intensity of my love for Gabby. We had played games together, Jane and I. There were many situations where we had plotted and enjoyed evenings out together eating roasted chicken and fish with a persistent admirer. It seemed just being in their company pleased them. But each time they tried to get closer we dropped them. In our escapades with men we had a number of excuses tucked away to be used when the occasion arose. They ranged from ailments, which would take some time to heal, to fake accusations of jealousy, pretending that the man was interested in the other person once we saw where his interest lay.

I was not playing games with Gabby. I could not dare. Things had gone too far. If I wanted an excuse to drop Gabby, it would not be going out with my boss. The situation was much more serious for me to just brush it aside without a thought.

"How am I going to bring up the topic of his former engagement?" I asked Jane.

"You have to leave that out for now and bring it up when things have cooled down. Gabby may look at your question as a counter accusation and men do not like that." I saw her point and came to the decision that I would ask him about his former engagement depending on the way he reacted to my explanation.

The next morning I took a taxi to Gabby's house. Jane wanted to come along but I refused. I did not want an eyewitness of what was going to happen because I myself did not know what to expect. The presence of a third party might even affect our natural response to the situation. I knocked on his door and he opened the door. There was no welcome greeting. We just looked at each other and he made way for me to enter the house. He came in and sat away from me but looking at me all the time. I held my head up and looked at him. Putting my head down would have been considered a sign of guilt. My thoughts at that time were too vague to be remembered. We looked at each other for what seemed an eternity. Finally, he got up and took the car keys from the top of the cupboard and asked me to come along with him. I got into the car apprehensive as to where we were going, and what we were going to do there. He headed for the quayside, and at a place where we had spent many a pleasant evening, he stopped. Without waiting for him I got out and sat on our favourite tree trunk.

It was a bright morning and the sun was dancing on the ripples in the sea, producing a million rainbows. Everywhere was quiet except for the sound of water lapping at the quayside. My eyes were focused on the distant boats as the men rowed endlessly in the sea. They were too leisurely in their strokes to be out for serious fishing. Some children were playing in and out of the water some distance away. I watched them as if that was what I had come to do. Gabby was sitting by me but I dared not look in his direction. I was waiting for him to begin speaking. After a while he asked.

"So what happened?"

Both of us knew we had to talk. But I did not expect the beginning to take this form. The question had been asked so I had to respond.

"Gabby," I began. "I know how you are feeling. But what I am going to tell you is the truth. We are no longer teenagers and we are quite aware of the enormity of what we have decided to do."

I went on with my story leaving out no detail. I mentioned the evening my boss and I went to Ideal Park Hotel and whom we met there. I made him aware of the fact that whoever had written to tell him about what I do in Bamenda hadn't his interest at heart. I spoke as bluntly as I could with no hint of begging him. If he believed what I was saying, and wanted me as his wife, that was up to him. When I finished I sat quietly waiting for his response.

"Are you sure that you did not go to bed with him?"

Gabby's question was much unexpected and came as a shock. This was evidence that he had not believed my story. Going to bed with someone was not a situation of doubt as to whether it happened or not. What was he trying to insinuate? I wondered. His question meant that I had not told him the truth. I could not restrain myself anymore. I could not bear the thought that Gabby could be still suspicious even after I had told him everything and made him understand the circumstances under which I had gone for dinner with my boss. I was more infuriated because I knew that he had a secret, which he had kept hidden from me, which I thought I had the right to know. Since I had got to know Gabby I had been very honest with him. I got slowly to my feet.

"Gabby, if you think that I have been deceiving you as you wrote in your letter, and that I have lied to you now, then I do not know what else to say. However, I know that I am not the first person to have worn this ring. I do not want what happened to that person to happen to me." I pulled off the ring and instead of flinging it at him, I flung it into the sea and continued. "Nobody is going to wear it after me!" I shouted at him as I walked away. Just a few steps away I felt his hand on my shoulder. I was so furious that I turned round ready to give him a slap if he slapped me.

Instead he held both my hands and with a confused look on his face said, "Elizabeth, please don't walk out of my life. Listen to what I have to say. I am sorry not to have believed you. This has been because of my previous experience, which I am sure you already know. Please, let us sit down and talk. He led me back to the tree trunk. It was my turn to ask the question.

"So what happened?"

I listened to Gabby with mixed feelings. I did not know whether I was going to believe him or if he was going to tell me the truth. But I was prepared to listen to what he was going to tell me.

Gabby had known Sheila for only five months before their engagement. She was a very beautiful girl and was wanted by most men. He was infatuated with her and did everything to get her. It was a sort of competition for her and he won. He had to do everything to keep her. Because of what he was able to provide her she lavished all her love on him. When he insinuated this in what he was saying I began to wonder how much love they had for each other if that was the basis of their love.

At that that time he was too blind to see that she was not the type of woman to be his wife. At this I smiled. How does a man know the type of woman fit to be his wife? Gabby had at first thought she was the right woman for him until things began to happen. Those things were beginning to happen to me too. I had a feeling that something was wrong with Gabby. I concluded that he was not the marrying type of man.

Her demand on his finances was too high. But because of his infatuation with her and because he could afford it, he succumbed to all her demands. This is the excuse men give for blundering. Gabby said this in a tone that carried the sound of an apology. I could not imagine who he was apologizing to. Was it to me or to the woman he had hurt? Both ways it was no longer relevant. That was in the past and had nothing to do with me. He was making his apology to the wrong person. This was his confession he was making and I was in no position to judge him.

He always engaged her in conversation about marriage as he had done with me. She had wanted a cook as soon as they got married because she did not want her long well manicured nails to be dirty or broken. She would not want any relatives to live with them. She wanted a car and everything that went to make a home comfortable, a refrigerator, a cooker, a parlour with wall-to-wall carpeting. As Gabby spoke I wondered whether he took cognizance of the fact that I had my own ideas of why he was condemning her. What if they were the same as hers? Then this was going to be my last meeting with Gabby. I dreaded it but if it happened there was nothing I could do about it. At this thought my heart gave a lurch. How was I going to live without Gabby? I looked at him to make sure that he had not seen the anguished expression on my face. But Gabby was looking out on the horizon as if his thoughts were plastered there and at each step of his narration it was difficult for him to decide which one to share with me and which one to leave out.

On top of all these she wanted a talk-of-the- town wedding. Which woman would not love that? She did not give him breathing space. On weekends when he had work to do in the office in the evening, she would want to come and sit with him. She would want him to comply with every whim of hers. Things took a different turn when one day he went to Victoria to deliver some documents in their office there. After his business at the office he had gone to her house. Finding the door open he had walked in without knocking. There was Sheila sitting with another man with his arms round her. He had behaved like a gentleman. He came in and sat down. She had jumped up and tried to embrace him. She had introduced the man to him telling him that the man was going to be married to one of her best friends called Carine. Gabby's rising anger was dispelled and the evening passed without any event. Gabby was cordial with the man and attentive again to her.

Back in Douala his suspicions were once again awoken when he heard some girls in the office talking about Sheila. They were talking about her presence in Douala some days ago. He became worried. What was she doing in Douala without his knowledge? Even if she had come to Douala because of work, she could have at least called him over the phone to let him know. Later when he had asked her about it, she had brushed it aside as useless gossip.

He wanted to find out what was actually going on. So one day he had called her disguising his voice and speaking like the man he had met in her house. She had immediately answered, "Oh Joel, are you the one? Why did you not come as you promised?" He had dropped the phone and the voice had kept ringing in his ears. He could not believe what he had heard.

He had thought about all he had done since he had met Sheila and began to realize that it was not going to work. His eyes were opened and he began to wonder if his people were going to accept a wife like her. He had talked about his marriage to his uncle Pa Martin but he had not yet taken her to Bamenda. He was relieved that he had not done so. He had decided to make a clean break from her, making sure that she had no chance to worm her way back into his affections. She was a pretty woman whom no man could resist. Breaking with her was not an easy thing because he wanted to get married for other reasons. I listened to his narrative without looking at him. My gaze was far out at sea but I saw neither the boats nor the water.

"But you loved her to the extent of buying an expensive diamond ring for your engagement," I remarked.

The sun was now getting very hot but a cool breeze from the sea reduced its effect. We went on sitting on the tree trunk, both of us looking out at sea as if the response to my remark could be found there. I quickly glanced at Gabby's profile and saw that he was trying to make a decision

he found both difficult and unpleasant. He took my hands in his.
"Elizabeth, it is now that I realized that there was something wrong with that ring."
"What!" I exclaimed. I looked at my finger. The ring was no longer there and I felt relieved.
"I bought that ring for three hundred thousand francs after a reckless bid with some of my friends. It has been six years now since I came to Douala. When I first arrived I was living with a friend who works at the port. Among the Anglophone community we were the men about town. We were popular with the girls who were attracted by the flow of cash. In fact I did not know what to do with my money. I used to go down to Kribi to amuse myself at the beach there."
"You had not met Sheila by then?"
"No."
"But you could not have gone there alone, Gabby."
"You want me to say that I was with a girl? Yes I was with a girl. I do not want to go into the details because I do not want to hurt you."
"How can that hurt me? I had not known you then. Your past is your past."
"But that past is interfering in my life now and I do not like it. I want to get over with it. But I do not want to get down to the details."
"Talking about hurting, Gabby, that is just what you are doing."
"Am I hurting you by telling you my story? Then I will stop."
"No, don't. Please continue I want to hear what happened." My interest had been pricked when he mentioned his conclusions about the ring. I know that there are some cursed items that affect those who are in possession of them. I wanted to hear the source and story of the ring. I continued.
"You want to get whatever it is out of your system. So just go ahead."
Gabby continued with his story. He often went to Kribi though he could not swim. He was scared of even learning. Each time he was jokingly provoked, he said he did not want to swim like a 'graffi man' that is to drown because people from the North West Province cannot swim because they do not have large rivers. All he did was sit and watch and admire the girls in their bikinis while sipping a cool beer. At that time things were stolen from ships and sold at give-away prices. You could buy something for three times less the value. One night he was in a nightclub with some of his friends. A man came and sat at their table. He whispered to one of the men sitting with them then he left. The man he had spoken to told them that there was a hot item for sale. He said he was going out after the man to see what it was. When he came back he told them that it was good for them to see it for themselves. Each of them went out to look at it. The

article was hot because it had to be sold off as quickly as possible. It was all a matter of secrecy. He was not interested and left it to the others to do whatever they wanted. The next day he tried to find out if any of the men with whom he was sitting had bought the article. He received only vague replies. He had given no more thought to it for the rest of his days in Kribi.

The story of the ring was becoming more intriguing. Gabby had come back to Douala, about a month later. One day he was drinking in a snack bar with some of his friends when one of them said he had something to sell. They were all anxious to know what it was. But he warned them that it was not a usual 'affair' good. This one needed a 'cheque'. This was how they called any amount above fifty thousand francs. They asked to see it and he pulled a small red case out of his inner coat pocket and opened it. He passed it round for the four of them to see. When it got to him he recognized the ring he had seen that night in Kribi. He could not take his eyes off it. It was a diamond ring. The colours that emanated from it had ensnared his heart. He had to get it. He was ready to buy it at all costs.

"Unfortunately I have thrown your precious ring away."

I waited for Gabby to react at my taunting words. But he did not. He just sat looking out at the sea. I wondered if he was angry with me for throwing the ring away. To be honest, I felt no regret about it. How could I cherish something cursed? He continued with the story of the ring. One day he was talking with some of his friends on a topic they were never tired of – girls. They were talking about the rate of stealing in Douala and the part girls were playing in it. One friend started talking about girls who went out with sailors and tourists and stole from them. Gabby listened more intently when he started telling them of how a girl stole a ring from a tourist and the man nearly went mad.

This girl had been going out with this man who seemed to have had something heavy on his mind. The girl cajoled him and made a fuss of his every need until he told her the cause of his unhappiness. He had come to Cameroon to have a change of scene and to forget about the death of his wife. His wife had died giving birth and he had lost both his wife and son. He had given away everything belonging to his wife except their wedding ring, which was the only physical link remaining between them. Each time he looked at it, memories came flooding back. The girl had stolen the ring to make the man stop thinking of his wife and his past. Instead the man had become furious and the girl had disappeared with the ring leaving it in reliable hands. From the description of the ring he knew that it was the ring he had bought. On hearing this, his heart sank and he could not believe that the ring he had bought for three hundred thousand francs was making a man mad. As he listened to the rest of the narration he was in a terrible situation but hid his emotions. Back in his house he removed the ring and looked at it. What was he going to do with it? He decided to keep it. It was not his fault that the ring had been stolen. He had bought the ring with his hard earned money. It would have been stupid of him to go looking for the man to give back his ring. It was meant to be put on a woman's finger and that was what he was going to do.

While listening to Gabby's story my mind was far away. His voice seemed to be coming from a distance. A weight was gradually being lifted from my chest. I no longer cared whether I was alive or not. Nothing seemed real. It seemed to be a dream.

"What a world!" I thought as Gabby's touch on my arm brought me back to reality. I got up slowly and walked towards the car. Gabby followed me. I got in and sat staring ahead of me. He too got in but could not bring himself to take out his car keys and start the car. We both sat without talking or looking at each other. Time no longer existed and my heart was devoid of emotions.

"Let's go home, Elizabeth," Gabby finally said, breaking the silence. The drive back was just like the drive out. Anybody looking at us could not have imagined the series of emotions, tempers and words that had issued from us. While the outward journey was full of the tension of unspoken words, unexpressed emotions, and unreleased tempers, the return journey found two deflated beings with the perspiration drying on their bodies. When we arrived at his house I sank down on the chair exhausted both physically and emotionally. Gabby came and sat beside me. In an unconscious simultaneous action our gazes met, then our lips. It was a kiss of expiation and forgiveness. The pull to a kiss is the sublimation of the most treasured emotion. The act of comprehension and tolerance is a god over remonstrance.

6

The next morning rain fell. Its rhythmical sound on the rooftop invaded my consciousness as I tried to doze back to sleep. Even at midday the rain had not stopped falling. The rain in Douala especially at this time of the year has an annoying persistence, which keeps visitors from other parts of the country uncomfortable. The wetness is humid especially when the sun shines through the rain. At certain moments the sun became so hot that the rising vapours made the street look like a steaming bath. But today there was no sign of the sun. The day looked dark and dreary. I was happy to be at home.

I could not stand the mud on the side street where Gabby lived. It was always muddy even when it did not rain. Moving in a car, one hardly noticed but moving on foot was a different story. It seemed as if the drainage by the main street was blocked and water from the houses flowed down the street. I gazed through the window at the silent drizzle. It was becoming thicker and soundless. My thoughts were so hazy that I could not identify and capture any. It began with the misunderstandings that had arisen between Gabby and me. It seemed senseless to dwell on them. They were past and gone. I was swept into another world.

I looked through the window again. What I saw outside touched a nerve in my being. I saw houses hidden and secured inside fences and just next door houses with rusted zinc for walls with leaking roofs and inhabitants exposed to the merciless weather. With the sight acting as a backdrop I saw myself as a woman with a dream. It was not a one-dimensional type of dream. It had two phases. In the first I saw a woman living in society and being part of it. In the other I saw a woman living in society but not being part of it. The walls and fences of the building caused a claustrophobic feeling in me. I saw walls I had built round myself not to exclude but to protect. I also saw walls that society had built around me not to protect but to stifle. I found the wall I had built around myself very comforting and protective. But this wall is very vulnerable to the subtle insinuations, blames, social and family expectations, frustrations and outright discriminations. I tried to break out of the grip of my thoughts. I was afraid they would overtake me. Looking at the sight before me life became a tug of war. I needed my wits, strength of will and intellectual resources to be able to cope with the forces in me pushing me to do those things I thought right for me and my society.

I could no longer focus my thoughts. The filmy drizzle seemed to be converted into a constantly changing pattern of dots like a television screen when the images suddenly go off. I strained my eyes to see the shape being formed by this pattern of dots. It never came out clear but I had the feeling it was glowing:

I remembered the ring and the story, which Gabby had told me. I did not really think about the ring after I had thrown it into the sea. It was a beautiful ring and the sense of loss that stole over me was quickly wiped away by another thought. The story of the ring was scary but I consoled myself that if there were supernatural forces surrounding it, then they were far out at sea. If the ring was the cause of Gabby not being able to marry, then I was glad to get rid of it.

The ticking of the clock made me aware of the passing of time. I tried to dwell in the present, pushing away the numerous possibilities of disaster which my mind was brewing. Marrying Gabby meant my lifestyle would change. I was getting into a situation where I was expected to be responsible, caring, understanding, careful, loving, and more. These are the finer attributes of the human personality. Society expects this. The family expects this. Well and fine. These are the outward manifestations of the individual's virtues. But the ones that go to nourish the individual as a person are overlooked. The individual as well as society should nourish hope, confidence, steadfastness, duty, consciousness, and objectivity. This makes the individual better prepared to face the storms of life.

What I had longed for was being realized. But was that all? Was that all I wanted out in life? Was I prepared to face it? What was my position vis-à-vis my expectations? Was I in the position to archive them? Was I contented with what was happening in my life presently? Was there the need to improve who I was? These thoughts were being examined one by one as I stood and continued to look through the window at the silently falling rain. Material comfort was not the solution. It never left lasting satisfaction. I had to reach out.

As if this decision had cleared my vision I started seeing people moving up and down the side street, men women and children with their feet clotted with mud. They protected their faces from the drizzle. In this position they looked as if they were charging at unseen enemies. There was no physical enemy charging at them. The enemy was their scanty clothing that exposed them to cold, which seeped without notice through the cells of their bodies to concentrate in bones and their lungs.

This street is an outlet to the neighbourhood often called 'sous quartier' where people lived in slum houses. The poorest of the poor in the community lived there. This was evident from the type of shoes and dresses they wore. Some even moved through the mud without shoes. They passed in front of my eyes as if in a film. From their malnourished bodies I could imagine the type of houses in which they lived. These types of houses are called 'calabot houses'. They are made from tree wood cut in thin slices and nailed together. These houses existed as village houses and with the encroachment of urbanity into the countryside, the houses had survived till the present day. The roofs were rusted and brown with age. The wooden walls had been eaten away by white ants and the holes they left had been stuffed with old pieces of cloth. The floors in some of these houses were still earth beaten, and the windows looked like holes in the walls. Some of the houses were built with beaten tar drums. These looked more solid but rust had worn away many parts. The rust had created holes in some places and formed sharp edges. These stuck out and were tetanus traps, just waiting for the unwary passerby to scratch against them.

The rainy season exposes the poverty of the people. It is in the rainy season that leaking roofs form new puddles on the floors in addition to those of last year. It is in the rainy season that pullovers must be bought as well as umbrellas. It is in the rainy season that many more children are taken to the hospital for treatment for malaria. It is a merciless seasonal visitor. It exposes the difficult circumstances under which they live. Leaking roofs and clotted gutters are part of their daily lives. They did not seem to be even aware of them. The floods that destroy homes and property, the standing water and muddy streams flowing in front or by their houses are yearly occurrences. Talking about malaria and blood transfusion among people is just like talking about the Buea Mountain. It is always there, massive and overwhelming. People believed nothing could be done about it. Yet the incidences of floods and gutters teaming with mosquito larvae are entertainment for television viewers. "It is not happening to me," these viewers would say. "Oh, it is in another town!" It always seemed to be out there, not affecting us. But sights of these things kill something in us as something was killed and rekindled in me that day as I watched these people.

A little girl suddenly appeared in front of me. She held a two-litre container in her hand. Everything else was obliterated from my view as I watched this child struggle through the mud, through the rain, through life to get some fuel for warmth and food for the family. She was doing it today as a child and in the future would do it as a wife. I looked at her tiny legs and arms. She was about ten years old but looked like a seven-year-old girl. Malnutrition had taken three years off her existence. There was a determined look on her face as if she knew that the family's lunch depended on the two litres of kerosene, which she had to bring back home. Her hair was too long for a child and fell in braids on her scrawny neck. The braids made her a woman. They identified her for she would have been any child moving in the rain. The expression on her face, her quick steps and her braids stuck on my imagination. An impatient mother was waiting for fuel to prepare a meal of unripe bananas boiled with groundnut paste and a bit of palm oil. Should this child grow up looking forward to nothing better than the type of life the mother was living?

I grew up in a farming community. Farming is the life wire of my parents and I could see the joy in my mother's eyes after each bountiful harvest. The joy was the reward of her effort. The seeds she puts in the soil come back a hundred fold, as a result of months of careful tending and hoping. But I was out of the farming community into a community where goals are difficult to define. But I wanted to make something of my life. I wanted to rise above the restrictions and frustrations of existence, have a life buoy to hang on to in times of depression, provide sustenance, and derive satisfaction out of life. At that moment I felt like calling out to the little girl. But what would I do with her? There were many such children. What was I going to do to improve their lot? I wondered. I felt overwhelmed with sympathy and at the same time I felt like a hypocrite because there was definitely something I could do. But was I willing to do it?

There were possibilities but walls had to be broken down before these possibilities could be realized. These walls were more man-made than hereditary. I had to be part of the society and keep my eyes and ears open to such things. In the desire to protect and preserve, society is viewed from afar.

My mind was far away when I heard a knock on the door. Gabby was back for break and I went to greet him. He held me and kissed me on the cheeks and then on my lips. I started laughing. I could not help myself. I went and sat down and continued laughing. Since the incident at the beach we had not talked about it. Each of us avoided mentioning what had gone on before and during the incident. We both made a conscious effort to make the aftermath of it a period to look back on happily. I do not know why I was so amused that afternoon. We had almost broken up because of just such a kiss. Everything had been cleared between the two of us so I could mention it now without causing any harm.

"Gabby, I hope you are not going to take offense when I say this. I do not like bringing it up again. But if I do not tell you why I am laughing you might jump to unpleasant conclusions. I have noticed that each time you come back home you greet me with a kiss. I understand it as a form of greeting that has no strings attached to it. That is what I see francophones do. That is what Jean Claude did when he met me along Commercial Avenue."

"I understand, Lizzy."

Then the devil of a thought entered my head and I teased Gabby. "I have seen you greet many women like that. Does that mean there is something going on which I do not know?"

"With those women there is nothing going on. But with you there is something going on. So it is different. Moreover, you are mine and there is nothing that can come between us again."

I was glad to hear this. A new relationship was developing between us. Our brief estrangement was like an interlude for us to re-examine ourselves, and what we meant to each other. Gabby kept talking to me as he went into the bedroom to take off his coat, and I went into the kitchen to warm his food. As he spoke his voice and what he was saying came across to me, and I also sensed something. The cadence of his voice made me realize that his life in Douala without me was not interesting. He loved talking and joking. He had many friends. He loved having people around him. The person he most loved having with him was me.

I could not match his gusto and enthusiasm. As we ate he continued talking and I listened. He told me about his day at work and, for example, about the plans they were putting together to improve the quality of services. He talked about his personal plans, which invariably included me. I enjoyed his company and just being with him kept me happy. His presence kept my moody reflections at bay. I watched him as he ate with enthusiasm. He did everything with enthusiasm, never expecting failure or disappointment. He ate well. It was his favourite dish, corn flour paste usually called 'fufucorn' and huckleberry vegetable or 'Njamanjama'. As he ate, he said all the nice things he was thinking about me. I felt flattered. Who wouldn't feel flattered? Gabby was perfect. I found no fault in him. I did not want to. My eyes were closed to whatever faults he had. Is it not said that love is blind? Love builds a wall around its victims. It keeps them in an air bubble, a small world of its own that does not allow them to look too closely. I lived in an air bubble with Gabby, praying that it should not disintegrate.

Gabby was pulsating with a new force, which came across to me. It began as a general tremor before settling in certain parts of the body. The renewed force of his affection seemed to have needed that little break before shooting off on a higher wavelength. As the days passed I wanted Gabby more and more. I wondered what was going to happen to me by the end of my stay with him. I nestled in his arms and felt the warmth of his breath on my cheeks. Each time he held me like this I felt faint with desire. Gabby was not to be rushed. He took his time. It was from Gabby that I got to know how romantic the French language is. '*Je t'aime, mon amour. Embrasse-moi, Lizzy.*' His breath came out in puffs. '*Je brule,*' he would say in a seductive way with an English accent. I buried my face in his chest.

The hair on his chest caressed my face and sent shocks through me. He said he was preparing me. I found this very exciting. I had had adventures but Gabby was bringing me into a new experience. He told me what to do and asked me how I felt. In his voice were love, concern, gratitude and satisfaction. Sex became a nurturing experience, to look forward to. It was as pleasurable and exhilarating as having a good meal or listening to good music. Instead of exhausting him it gave him more vitality. I used to worry about his going back to work in the afternoon. I soon got used to the knowledge that he was capable of bouncing off the bed and, after a shower, going off to work, fresh and crisp in his creaseless shirt and coat. That was my Gabby. He was always on his legs, enthusiastic and optimistic, looking formidable and confident but could crumble if his Achilles' heel were touched. I knew his Achilles' heel. I saw it when we had the misunderstanding.

He left for work again. I was left alone. I lay back on the bed trying to recapture the afternoon from the moment Gabby had walked in until he left. I realized that it was useless dwelling on it because there was more to come. I got up, made the bed and washed the plates piled up in the sink. I had told Gabby to meet me at Jane's place after work. I got ready to go and visit her. As I stepped out of the house I came face to face with the drizzle and the mud. I stood for a moment trying to recapture the thoughts that were cruising in my mind before Gabby came in. I had been prevented from feeling the realities of these thoughts by the window. I looked at my shoes, the mud and the drizzle. I wanted to go back to the house, but I had promised Jane I would be coming to see her. I asked myself how long I was going to escape from the mud and drizzle of life. And I stepped into the mud. A filmy layer of rain had already settled on my arms as I contemplated the mud before opening my umbrella. I was like the passersby whom I had been watching, charging at an unseen enemy. My eyes were focused on the mud but I never saw it. I saw the footprints of those who had passed before me. I saw the stones jutting out, acting as footholds. I saw the slushy water running down the slope into a pond below. The water in this pond was what was often used for household chores when there was scarcity of water in the neighbourhood. I saw the filth mixed up in the mud. I saw the discarded plastic papers, the sodden cartons and broken bottles piled up by the roadside. I imagined the bacteria and larvae thriving in the standing puddles in front of the houses. My shoes were already muddy but I made no attempt to stop and wipe off the mud clinging to the soles of my shoes. The shoes were heavy but I trudged on determined to reach the tarred road before wiping them off.

Hard thumps on the hard tar took off some of the mud. My shoes felt lighter on my feet. My heartfelt lighter too. I heaved a sigh of relief. The tension that had been building in me suddenly fell off like scales. The feeling was similar to the one I had felt when I had thrown the ring into the sea and reconciled with Gabby. The misunderstanding had been like walls created by society with us providing the mortar that held the blocks together. It had been like mud clogging our lives making it heavy. I was free from the mud temporarily and moved with ease. But in the back of my mind, the mud hovered waiting to take over again.

I looked back at my life and wondered whether I had ever been so happy and for how long this happiness was going to last. It was not yet dampened by the thoughts occupying my mind. They were a means of making me know myself better, to live a happier and more fulfilling life. How was I going to live happily in the cloister of Gabby's love yet live from day to day with these things around me? How was I going to overcome or avoid the little egocentricisms that make our lives miserable? I was going to have a serious discussion with Jane about what lay before us. It was more of what lay before me, because I doubted she harboured troubles like I did. It was going to be more of asking her opinion and advice on what was going on in my mind. I believed she was facing this new situation with more stability than I.

Since she became engaged to Benny, things were moving smoothly. Even when they were living separately their lives were so coordinated that they seemed to be together all the time. Whether it was supper at Jane's place or a quick drink at Benny's, or an evening out with Gabby, everything was so well planned and their actions so complementary that at first I felt like an intruder. I imagined my life with Gabby being just as smooth. Whether Jane was deliberately hiding their problems from me or they actually had none, I did not know. I never observed remarks, looks, gestures or comments that betrayed an unpleasant situation lurking in the background. Maybe I was so happy for her and too involved with my own pursuits to notice. But I am sure she had misunderstandings with Benny. The difference was that she handled them better I did. For who is that angel of a woman who would let herself be completely taken over by a man even if she is drowning in love? It is a paradox to say that love is blind, for it is at this time that eyes are wide open and emotions sensitive to every little fault. Why are you late? Why did you not do this? Why did you do that? Why did you not go there? These are the questions on our lips when egocentrism rears its ugly head. Nobody is free from these sentiments. The difference lies in the degree to which we are able to master our thoughts, actions and reactions. Whatever Jane felt would come through when I told her the things that were bothering me.

I arrived at Jane's house a little after three o'clock. It was located on a better street although the tar was worn away in many places leaving little pools of water in the middle of the street. The environment was cleaner and healthier. I knew where both of them lived before they got together. Their present home was an improvement on their former lodgings. It looked like putting their resources together had produced something better. And indeed it had. I think what spurred them most was the idea of starting a home in a more comfortable house in spite of the amount paid in rents. And with the baby on the way, it was a wise decision. Jane's salary was not much compared to what Benny earned. But their will to live as best as they could was the driving force. This was made possible because Jane did not have any younger sisters or brothers for whom she had to care.

Their house was made of a parlour and two bedrooms, a kitchen and a store. The store could easily be converted into a bedroom, but now it contained the odds and ends that moving from one house to another always produced. The house suited Benny. It reflected the type of person he had become. He was a man of class. He liked good things in life. Fortunately for him, money was not the problem. Even the studio in which he lived before setting up home with Jane was a haven from the scorching Douala heat. It was cooled by a fan in the wall. There was always something to drink in the small fridge. The carpet was from wall to wall and a set of four comfortable chairs occupied the available space. But now in the new house the chairs were dwarfed by the size of the parlour. It would not be long before he got furniture to match the size of his new residence. I imagined what perfect happiness could exist in such a home with a good measure of love, understanding and tolerance. Material comfort and these other qualities was a rare mixture. In Jane, Benny had found another good thing, in the parlance of bachelors. Her beauty was incomparable. With Benny who had an enviable body that never had to worry about appearances, they formed the perfect couple. In the taxi, I contemplated on these things and by now was mentally exhausted by the inconsistencies of life and the games we seem to be playing with life, or was it life playing games with us?

Jane was seated in the parlour when I came in. I stood for some time looking at her. Her stomach was so large that she really looked awkward. She could not bend down to pick up something in front of her. There were pimples on her face, something she had never had. I could never have believed that Jane could find herself in such a state. Jane who had been so meticulous about her looks and so concerned about her size. There were days she drank only lemon juice and ate only vegetables so as not to get fat. She also did this downsize to be able to wear a dress which she fancied but which was not her size. Her dressing table always had cleansing lotions and non-greasy oils.

For the first time since I had known her, she looked not too pretty. Pregnancy can transform a woman for the worse both physically and temperamentally. It had done both to Jane. I almost started to laugh and joke with her about her appearance. This might have put me in a lighter mood to discuss the things that were on my mind. But I could not because coming closer to her I discovered that there was something wrong. Her eyes lacked lustre. They looked swollen with weeping. Her face that always looked fresh no matter the time of the day was without make-up. Her lips were dry and she kept wiping her nose. There was no smile on her face even at my appearance. I rushed to her side, took her hands in mine and stared into her eyes. This was my first time seeing Jane really distressed. Her hands felt hot but she did not have a fever. When I placed my palm on her forehead it was cool to the touch. She just sat there. The only movement was the rising and falling of her stomach as she breathed, even her face showed no sign of being aware of my presence.

"What is it Jane? What happened? Why are you in such a state? Are you sick?" The questions came cascading out of my mouth. I could not believe what I was seeing. It looked as if she had given up on life. You know those moments of desperation when one feels there is nothing to live for? Life became just a matter of allowing the minutes to tick by. I had believed that nothing could come between Jane and Benny. They were such a perfect couple, always happy and considerate to each other. I had felt closer to them because I wanted my relationship with Gabby to be like theirs. But on that day I began to learn a lesson. I did not want to accept the knowledge learnt from these situations. I wanted to hide them away and go on living. But they were there imposing themselves on me.

Jane did not answer my questions. She just stared away at the window. She was so withdrawn that I felt ill at ease. Her stomach looked so big with her hands folded over it. It looked like a heavy burden, which she was carrying. I became speechless as I looked at her. She stared away. God alone knew what was on her mind. Mine was preoccupied by Jane's stomach. I had heard about delivery pangs. Nothing was more painful. It was often said that if a woman has given birth then she could withstand any pain. All these thoughts did not dispel my fright. I looked at Jane and imagined her wriggling with pain on a delivery bed. I imagined the child tearing out of her and grimaced with imagined pain. How do the husbands feel at this time? I wondered. My wonder soon turned into anger. Benny did not have the right to treat her this way. I was convinced that whatever was wrong with Jane, Benny had a hand in it. She deserved better. To make her weep was tantamount to an abomination, especially now that her life was at stake. I believed what was often said about a woman giving birth: that her life hangs on a thread because anything could happen. My anger turned into fear. It was the type of fear that could not be mentioned to anybody. I was also afraid of losing Jane's friendship. She had never behaved towards me in the way she was doing. In my preoccupation I did not hear the knock on the door. The rapping sound came again. I got up and opened the door. A woman was standing there with a bowl in her hands. I stepped aside for her to enter. She went immediately and stood beside Jane, massive and pensively looking down at her. She was a buxom woman with heavy breasts and a stomach made larger by the layers of fat that had accumulated after several deliveries. It was clear from her age that she was not pregnant although her stomach was as large as Jane's. She was a Bamelike woman and spoke the broken English that comes in handy when an uneducated francophone wants to express himself in English. She addressed Jane.

"Ma pikin, a don tere you say maki you no di cry so. A don bring you sma mbongo chobi. Try chop sma."

I realized with shock that Jane's problems had not started just that day. I felt slighted that she did not need my advice or even consolation. I sat back and watched the two of them. They were like mother and child. I was so confused that I did not know what to say. Jane's silence and the woman's attitude were making me think there was something more serious than what met the eye. I began to lose faith in human relationship.

"No bi tam dis for begin cry so. E no fan fo woman weti bele me hi di vex. You no no weti fi bi tomorrow."

I looked from Jane to the woman. I felt an like outsider but waited to see what was going to happen. Jane had not answered my questions. Was she going to remain silent? The woman lowered herself onto the chair next to Jane and opened the dish. Although Jane had not spoken there were signs she was thawing. She looked at me for a long time and sighed.

She turned to the woman and said, "Thank you, Manyi." She then got up and went into the room. I could hear water flowing. There was silence for sometime then she came out.

"Aha, na so. Woman no ge fo lef hi body because man pikin don vex hi. Jinet, you sabi maki yu yanga. Lukam how you bi siddon fo de leke woman we hi di cry die."

Jane was transformed. She had powdered her face and brightened up her appearance. There was a light shade of lipstick on her lips. She smiled and came over to me.

"Lizzy, welcome." She greeted me as if I had just arrived. She was no longer the Jane I had known. There was something missing, or was there a change I had not noticed before? I sat transfixed. I did not know what was happening. She took a spoon and started eating. While she ate the silence was only broken by words of encouragement from the woman urging her to eat more. I was seeing a different Jane. Life teaches its lessons in a very unusual manner. But the timing is wonderful. They come in very subtle ways and in situations most contrary to what we expect. They come at the time we think that all is lost if something is not done. And whatever has to be done is not an act in itself but a conveyance of expression and impressions. Sometimes it gives room for absorption and digestion. At other times it is a sudden illumination. That afternoon it was a successive unveiling of thoughts I had examined and re-examined without arriving at any conclusions. My earlier expectations had clouded my judgment and what was happening to me was like a fossilized bone, which turns up in the wrong stratum and destroys a geological theory. My previous assumptions were being destroyed. Whether Jane knew of such inconsistencies and had prepared herself for them, I could not tell. I admired her ability to bounce back.

I remembered my first misunderstanding with Gabby and how I had brooded for days. Until I met him I could not get over it. I could see determination on her face as she ate. The woman kept looking at Jane with knowing eyes. Her whole attitude showed that she was familiar with problems like the one Jane had and also that she knew Jane's problem. But here I was, her best friend, with no idea of what was happening. Manyi continued talking to Jane, consoling, advising and even rebuking her. I looked at Manyi's massive body that seemed to be a bulwark against marital problems. I learnt a lot as I listened to her. What she was saying was the product of years of experience. But how was a woman about to get married expected to know all these things? One only knew these things from years of experience.

7

Matali, now Manyi as she was popularly known in the neighbourhood, had come to Douala at the age of fifteen. She had been brought down to meet her husband to whom she had been betrothed at the age of six. Being a Bamelike, trading came to her easily. While her husband went off each day to sell dry corn and groundnuts, which he bought from Bafoussam, she stayed at home parching and selling some of the corn and groundnuts. She had a way of parching the groundnuts with wood ash, which gave them a special flavour. The corn was parched in a perforated tin container held over hot flames, which made them come out like popcorn. Her blend of parched corn and groundnuts, measured into tomato cups and sold for twenty-five CFA francs, became popular in the neighbourhood. Workers constructing an industrial site nearby nicknamed it 'concrete'. Corn and groundnuts worth one hundred francs settled in the stomach like concrete and kept hunger away for the rest of the afternoon. It was popular among the unskilled workers who could not afford the more expensive food. They had left their villages to seek their fortunes in town and had to save money for rents, food, healthcare and other demands from home. In this way, Matali the young bride had a good amount of money hidden away in her tin box, which she kept always locked. One day before leaving for Bafoussam the husband asked for all the money she had got from her sales. She brought seven thousand francs. The man was furious and asked for all. She refused and for the first time the man beat her. She was very angry and because the man was going away there was no way to retaliate. When she thought about it later on, she did not even know how she was going to retaliate. But that one incident taught her a lesson.

Her husband came back with a letter for her from her parents. In it they were telling her to be a good wife. They did not like what her husband had told them about her.

The letter from her parents made her angry. They had listened to her husband and the fault was all hers. But her anger soon turned into despair at the fact that she was not yet pregnant. The next morning her husband asked her to buy her own corn and groundnuts. Because she did not want to reveal the fact that she had hidden some money, she asked him to give her the corn and groundnuts and when she would sell them, she would give back the cost and keep the profit. That was how she started building up her capital.

Her first baby came two years after her arrival in Douala. It came so late because her husband was hardly at home. His business kept him away for most of the time. He was planning to open a building material shop and all his energies went into this venture. Fortunately her pregnancy did not prevent her from continuing to parch her corn and groundnuts. She went back to the village to have her baby. During this period it seemed as if the man had forgotten about her. But her in-laws were good to her. She gave birth to a baby boy and stayed in the village for more than a year before returning to Douala. In her absence her husband opened his shop. She continued parching and selling her corn and groundnuts.

After her second baby, she wanted to open a provisions store but hadn't enough money and the demands of the children were telling on her. Her husband lent her some money and she started a makeshift kiosk near the house. In the evening she would pack the articles back to the house.

Now she had nine children. Three were in France, two in Yaounde, and one in Gabon. The remaining boy and twin girls were with her. The boy was at the university and the girls were in high school. Her husband had annexes of his shop all over Douala and one in Yaounde. She herself had a big shop in the Douala central market. They lived in their own bungalow in the Akwa neighbourhood. Mr. and Mrs. Bernard Bila were their tenants next door. Manyi had taken a liking to Jane as soon as she was introduced to her as the wife of their new tenant. I got to know all these some days later.

As I watched Manyi speak I wondered at the circumstances that had contributed to make her what she was. She was stable, settled and confident and past all cares except for her children. From what she was saying, the way she loved her husband was different from the way I loved Gabby. I could not understand this. I wondered whether she still trembled when her husband touched her. I was amused when I imagined her ability in bed. How would it look? I wondered. I smiled inwardly at the possibility of my watching such a scene. I wondered whether I was going to react to Gabby that way when we got to that age. I could not accept just anything Gabby did if it jeopardized our relationship. For her whatever her husband did meant nothing to her.

"Upside don change," (The world has changed,) she continued. "Fo we tam, we massa di sen we for contri me we go born." (In our days our husands used to send us to the village to go and give birth there.)

I was trying to follow the trend of her speech. I looked from Manyi to Jane to see the impact of Manyi's words on her.

"Ifi hi wan make you born fo ya, no bi palava. You no sabi man pikin dem. Dem tron head too much. When woman di tere dem some ting, dem di tink se you no get sens. Dem check se all ting we den tok na correct ting. Women no get fo tok. Ma pikin, tekam na sma sma. Onli di begam daso. Na sma sma di catch monki." (If he wants you to give birth here, there is no problem. You need to understand men. They are very difficult. They do not believe that a woman has any sense. They think that they are always correct. A woman has no right to speak. My daughter, be patient. Patience wins at the end.)

My attention swerved momentarily from Jane to what Manyi was saying. I could not make sense of what she was saying. Her type of reasoning was beyond my comprehension. Her nonchalance about marital problems concealed a strong will that knows how to bend to stand up stronger, a will that seeks self-preservation rather than domination.

"Ifi a bi wan take ma massa trong, beta no fo de me. A di onli begam sma sma, a di do weti a wan do. Ifi hi wan hala trong, a stop quet. A mekam leke se a no di hear someting. Lokam Jinet, you get fo lookot you sef." (If I wanted to oppose my husband's decisions outrightly, life would have been very difficult for me. When he is angry, I keep my distance. I make as if I have not heard what he has said and I go about my business quietly. See Jane, it is important that you care for yourself.)

Gradually I understood what the problem was. The more I understood the more I became confused. I wondered how two people who loved each other so much could suddenly be against each other. I believed that love was capable of smoothening out any problem. Jane and Benny now found themselves in a situation that was to test what they felt for each other. If they had talked it out and really listened to each other with understanding I am sure this situation would not have arisen. If Benny wanted her to give birth in Douala, I did not see why she did not want to. When Jane told me her reasons later on, I agreed with her. Her points were pertinent. She was interested in safeguarding her health after delivery. A house girl brought from the village would not be of any help to her because she would have to train and educate the girl on many things. This would entail a lot of strain on her part. She wanted to be with her parents so that she would rest while the babysitter was given some basic training, especially on how to care for the baby. Jane explained this to me and I felt really upset. How could Benny be so blind to the needs of his wife? I had to talk some sense into him.

It was a dreary evening. The drizzle of the afternoon kept falling steadily. The approaching darkness made its presence more obscure. Only the wetness on the skin made its presence felt. The street lights gave an unreal quality to the atmosphere. Each moving object, first just a vague impression, became a faint outline and then suddenly a concrete presence.

The streets were full of people going home. Crowds at the taxi stops chanted their destinations as each taxi crawled by. For those who hadn't umbrellas, their shirts and blouses clung to them. The chants to each taxi held the hope of relief from aching feet that had been standing for more than half an hour and longing for the warmth of home. Some men and women chatted and smiled while others held their mouths firmly set and moved only when it was their turn to chant their destinations. The drizzle did not matter to some people while to others it was an ordeal. I was happy that Gabby was coming to take me home and I would not have had to stand in this wetness and wait for a taxi. But I was experiencing another type of drizzle, which was creating some equally unpleasant mud. Jane's happiness was clouded and her relationship with Benny was nasty. There was something keeping them away from each other and this emanated from deep inside them. It manifested itself so naturally that there was nothing wrong with it. Only a second thought would reveal the diabolic nature of this something.

My heart ached for Jane. Our conversation trailed, for our minds were occupied. I could not tell her how I felt. I was uncertain as to what was on her mind. I had always felt free to say what was on my mind to Jane. But now the situation was different. She was separated from me. The new life in her, her change in temperament, the behaviour she had displayed to me, and the rift between Benny and herself were telling on her. The whole prospect of marriage did not look as appealing as I used to think. If motherhood meant all these then it was a deceptive angel. It was love and vanity all mixed up and difficult to separate. Love that keeps us strapped to the object of our love, and vanity that makes us want to break off, to rely on ourselves and have a feeling of independence.

When I heard the gate creaking open, I suddenly realized that I did not know what I was going to say to Benny. I left for the kitchen to get a drink of water, which I did not need.

"Hey! My sweet, I see you look better this evening. Where is Lizzy?"

"Oldie, you are finished. What about going to the nightclub this evening?" This was from Gabby. I could not believe what I was hearing. I held my breath with the glass of water against my lips. The water splashed into my mouth and spilled on my hands as I controlled the choking that was threatening to overcome me. Benny held me from behind.

"Lizzy, you did well to come here this afternoon. I turned to look at him but could not say anything because my attention was focused on what was going on the in the parlour.

"I will accept your invitation one of these days if you continue to invite me," Jane warned.

"Then we will have to take everything along in case…"

"No, you will just have to hire some nurses and midwives to keep on standby while I am dancing," Jane interrupted. Benny noticed that my attention was in the parlour and led me back there. Gabby was going on with his bantering with Jane. Both Benny and Jane were behaving as if nothing had happened. Jane was laughing. Who could resist Gabby's humour? Gabby concentrated his attention on Jane while Benny kept my ears busy. But I was not paying attention to what he was saying. From the way Gabby was behaving I knew that there was an intention behind his bantering. Whether he was succeeding still had to be verified.

How could so much love be tainted by egocentricity? I wondered as I looked at all of them. What we want is always the most reasonable. Benny would love to be present when his first child is born. He would want to hear its first cries and hold it in his arms minutes after birth. He would want to be the proud father. His friends would come round and to see the baby in the hospital. He would break the news to his colleagues in the office. His heart would be full with joy and pride. His manhood would be proven. He wanted all these to happen. What else could make a man happier? He did not want to wait even for a week to see his baby after it was born. His desires were justifiable and reasonable, so too were Jane's. But who was going to give in?

Jane was putting on a good show. The swollen eyes were now glittering with tears and laughter as Gabby kept her amused with his stories and jokes. Each time she looked at Benny, I could see the hurt under the laughter. I wondered why Benny was grateful to me. I had done nothing to raise Jane's spirits. Instead I was learning from what all of them were doing. It seemed as if there was no problem between Benny and Jane. I seemed to be the only one left out. They all seemed to be taking it so lightly. It seemed as if the act was being enacted for my benefit. My position was like that of the audience who knew what was actually happening while the players on stage did not. To keep in line with the act, I invited everybody for a meal of corn fufu and vegetable. I still had some left from the afternoon meal and thought it was a good idea for Jane to leave the house that evening. Benny also accepted. We went in our separate cars. On the way I could contain my curiosity no longer.

"Gabby, what is the problem between Benny and Jane? The three of you were behaving in a strange way this evening."

"Who told you that there is a problem? You women like to create mountains out of mole hills."

"You want to tell me that there is no problem? Do you think that I am deaf and blind?"

"If you are not, then you must have seen and heard everything, so why ask?" Gabby had a way of avoiding questions, which I had gotten used to.

"Just say that you do not want to tell me. Why hide it?"

"Look Lizzy, whatever Jane has told you is the way she looks at the situation. All I know is that they will come to a compromise. But do not talk about it this evening."

I could avoid talking about it. But I could not avoid thinking about it, and how it was going to be solved. When we got to the house and the food was set on the table I watched Jane and Benny closely. They were both enjoying themselves as if they had already come to a compromise. Gabby was doing his best to make everybody happy. But Gabby did notice the look of incomprehension, which clouded my face. Benny also noticed.

"What is on your mind, Lizzy?" Benny asked. "You do not look yourself." I was taken unawares. Three pairs of eyes were focused on me. Jane's were not actually focused on me. They were focused somewhere above my head. I could see clearly that she understood why I felt that way. I had not voiced my opinion yet but she could see that I was on her side. She put on a look of apathy. I was not sure she cared about what I was going to say. Gabby's warning came ringing in my ears. My throat became dry with the tension that was building up, with uncertainty and a sense of being trapped. I swallowed with difficulty and cleared my throat. Benny was looking at me anxiously with concern written all over his face. His concern was genuine and amused me a bit. The incongruous nature of the situation was beguiling. Why should he be so concerned about me when his wife was not happy with him? Gabby looked at me with a twitch of laughter in the corners of his mouth as he pretended to be concerned. I knew that he was not affected by my attitude and was just waiting to hear what I was going to say. I fumbled for words.

"I was just thinking … I was just imagining how it would be like when the baby comes." Silence. "I am sure you will be a very happy man …" I held my breath, waiting, waiting for reactions to my halting sentences. It had come out just like that. I did not even know what I was saying. It came out in spite of myself. Benny's smile was reassuring.

"I will be more than happy. I will be the happiest man in the world. I do not know how to thank Jane for the strength she has shown so far."

While he said this he looked at his wife lovingly and his eyes wandered down to her stomach and lingered. My attention was focused on Benny but I managed to glance at Gabby and Jane simultaneously. From the expression on Jane's face it looked as if she had just realized that all was not well. She was looking at her palms folded in her lap, concentrating on them as if she were hiding something that could be seen in her eyes. She lifted her eyes briefly to look at Benny. But his attention was back on me. I was happy he did not see her face in that split second. It bore all the hurt that lay under this amiable atmosphere. When Gabby looked at her a fleeting frown passed over his face but he did not allow it to linger. He gushed out with humour looking at his friend.

"I wonder what you will do with your three days paternity leave."

Jane rushed in as if she just had to say something to vent some pent-up emotions. "Why are the men given three days off? I do not see any need for it. They do not even stay by their wives to help. They spend their time drinking with their friends."

"Just wait and see what I will do when the time comes," Benny promised. I was afraid at the turn the conversation was taking. I had done just what Gabby had warned me not to do. The atmosphere was no longer relaxed. I sat tight sweating it out.

"Eh! Jane, you will not even want us to celebrate? We will think about you in the hospital. I promise. I will bring you a whole roasted chicken." Jane smiled. Gabby has this gift of making people laugh in spite of themselves.

"Men will always be men," I interjected.

"That is the best thing you have said this evening," Gabby remarked "Men will always be men and we are not different."

The problem was now in the open in a very subtle manner. Moreover, a decision had been arrived at. Jane made no protest. She seemed to have taken Manyi's advice. Was there any need to allow a disagreement to drag out the unpleasantness in us? One person had to give in. It just had to be Jane. Benny had made his point and there was no need to go back on it. He had an ally in Gabby who made sure that the topic did not come up again. I too had inadvertently aided the reconciliation process.

There was a drizzle in Jane's life and like the people waiting by the roadside laughing and joking in spite of their aching feet and soaked shirts and blouses, she was not allowing it to get her down.

The drizzle had abated a bit when Benny and Jane left the house. We went along with them to their car to see them off. Benny first opened the passenger door for Jane to get in before going round to his own side. I could see a touch of apology in this little action. We went back to the house in silence. I was in no mood to discuss anything. My silence did not dissuade Gabby from being himself. He soon got me cuddled in his arm as I fell asleep.

"Lizzy! Lizzy! Get up." I felt hands shaking me. I felt the storm outside tearing at me. It was pulling me away. I clung desperately to Gabby's hands. I was not sure whether he was pulling or pushing me, but I felt this force tossing up and down.

It all began at the point of my departure for Bamenda. My bag was standing on the dining table. I was sitting on a chair waiting for Gabby to come and take me to the bus stop. I had done all I could to lessen the level at which Gabby was going to be involved with housework. I had washed all the unoccupied pots in the kitchen. The cooker was clean. The refrigerator was well stocked with handy food items. Meat had been boiled and packaged for it not to lose its taste. Cabbages, carrots and green beans had been parboiled and packaged. The dry ingredients had been ground. Gabby could cook for himself but I wanted to facilitate the work for him.

In the bedroom everything was where it was supposed to be. His coats and shirts were all ironed and arranged in the wardrobe. His shoes were polished and hanging on the shoe rack. I had moved from room to room making sure that everything was in order. I was pleased with what I had done and was waiting for Gabby in the parlour. As I sat looking at a magazine while I waited, Gabby suddenly burst in.

"Elizabeth, you are not going to Bamenda. You are staying right here with me!"

"But Gabby…" The words stuck in my mouth. He was carrying my bag back into the room.

"You cannot do this to me," I wailed. "I have to go back."

"Shut up! You are not going."

I stood dumbfounded. Gabby came back and took my handbag and the magazine from my hands. I opened my mouth to speak but I couldn't. There was a raging pain in my head and my body was trembling.

The scene changed to Benny's house. I was watching what was going on. I did not know where I was standing but I saw Benny pushing Jane out of the house, telling her to go to the village. Jane came out, her stomach larger than before. Her gown clung to her body highlighting all the contours. Her hair was dishevelled and she wore muddy slippers. She was trying to get back into the house but Benny was doing everything to keep her out. In my frustration I lunged at Benny but something pulled me back. My anger increased the throbbing pain in my head.

I was back with Gabby again. I made a dash for the door and got to the threshold. I had to get back to Bamenda. I was going to lose my job if I stayed. My parents would be worried about me. I could not go any further. I struggled to free myself but he held me tighter.

There was a strong storm blowing outside and it tossed me here and there. I was dizzy and sweating, trying to free myself from Gabby's hold. Even as I gained consciousness, I was still struggling with Gabby. He held me tight. My breathing was still fast as I gained control of myself. I opened my eyes to find the room flooded with light. I closed my eyes and held my palm across my face to avoid the glare of light. My heart was still thumping and I felt hot. Gabby was still holding me tenderly and asking me what was wrong. My throat was dry and felt constricted. I managed to say something. I did not know whether he even heard me for he kept asking. "What is wrong, Lizzy. What is it? Please calm down. I am sure that you have been dreaming." The presence of Gabby's arms around me when I came to myself was reassuring. I was grateful that it was a dream. It was so real and the emotions were so true. My head was still aching but I felt a sense of relief. He kept caressing my back and the trembling gradually stopped and I lay quiet for some time.

"What is it, Lizzy?" he asked again. "You were struggling and pushing so hard at me. What is it?"

How could I tell Gabby what I had dreamt about? Telling him would be revealing to him how much I had been disturbed by the events of the previous evening. I did not want him to know that I was still worried about Jane and Benny. I did not want to appear stupid. He would even think I was paranoid. Moreover, the events of the dream were just representative and could be interpreted in any way.

"I had a bad dream'"

"What was it?"

"Gabby please let's talk about it in the morning." But the morning was a long time away. I lay tossing, unable to sleep. I looked at my watch on the bedside cupboard. It was two o'clock in the morning, four hours from morning. I listened to Gabby breathing. His breath came in shallow puffs. There was no rhythmic breathing to show that he was asleep. He could contain himself no longer.

"What was it that you dreamt about, Lizzy? I cannot sleep until you tell me. You cannot sleep either, so get it out of your chest."

"Gabby, am I going back to Bamenda this weekend?" Gabby's spontaneous response bore a note of incredulity.

"Why do you ask? Do you think that I will prevent you from going? Why should I? Is that what you were dreaming about and pushing me away?"

"No Gabby, we will talk about it in the morning." We both lapsed into a silence that was soon taken over by deep somnolent breaths. Before I sank again into the world of insubstantiality, the last thing I felt was Gabby's warm breath on my cheek.

Everything else became immaterial. The events of this existence withdrew into the background giving way to the peace of mind, body, and soul, which only sleep can give. The blissful unconsciousness stretched almost to eternity, but it was only for four hours.

I was feeling cold on my feet. The warmth of Gabby's presence was absent. I stretched and pulled the covers onto my legs. I felt for Gabby. Where he had been lying was cold, but the deep depression, which had born the weight of his body, was still there. I got up with a start. The room was dark and a weak sun was trying to find its way through the clouds. The clouds were fast obliterating it. I felt a chill run through my body. I got out of bed and looked at myself in the mirror. I did not actually see the face looking at me. My eyes were drawn to a note stuck on the side of the mirror. I pulled it off and read.

I did not want to disturb you.
Sleep off the nightmare and be yourself
Before I come back.

I did not understand how I could have slept till nine o' clock. When I looked at the mirror again, I got the answer. My eyes were red and swollen as if I had been weeping. My face looked strained and pale. I felt a general body malaise and my legs ached as if I had travelled a long distance. I was still holding the note. It made me feel that someone really cared. I nestled the note closer in my palm and continued to look at the face in the mirror. It seemed to be somebody else's and my mind looked in wonder at the transformation that can go on in the human consciousness while there is an apparent stability in the outer presentations.

The note said it all. I had to sleep off the nightmare. If Jane could push the problem out of her mind, why couldn't I? The dream had been an outlet for my pent-up emotions. I had to feel better now that it was out. The change had to begin from within. I smiled. The face in the mirror smiled back. The smile and the haggard face looked incongruous. The smile looked out of place on the face. I went into the bathroom. As I brushed my teeth the face confronted me again. I looked closer, peering into the dark pools of the iris, trying to see what lay beyond. I saw a hazy darkness out of which a voice was saying.

Life is too short to be wasted in unhappiness.
Create joy out of every situation.
Be positive and optimistic.

As the shower poured streams of water down my body, I felt a soothing sensation creeping from the nape of my neck down to my toes. The water was cleaning not only the dirt from my body; it was also soothing my emotions, clearing my thought, cleansing my soul. I stepped out of the bathroom feeling fresh and even chanting a tune. I continued to sing as I rubbed oil on my body. When I opened the window sunlight flowed into the room and enhanced my mood. The sun had succeeded in dispelling the clouds. The window faced east and let in the strong rays of the sun. I stood there for sometime allowing the sun to bath my body. It was absorbed through every pore and my skin glowed and wanted more. The burning sensation had a melting effect, which cleared my clotted spirit. The tight knot in my stomach was disappearing. The ache in my head and legs was cooling off. At that moment the world lost its dreary outlook. It looked positive and optimistic. I was drenched in this state when a rumble in my stomach made me look at the clock on the wall. It was ten a.m. As I went into the kitchen I glanced at the dining table. It was set for two. Gabby had prepared and eaten breakfast before going to work. I sat down and ate ravenously. The bread and scrambled egg tasted delicious. I washed it down with two cups of coffee. I enjoyed it more because it was prepared with love and served with care. I felt so happy that I wished this moment could last forever. As soon as this thought came to my mind, I remembered Jane. I had to go and see her to know whether they had sorted out their differences. I wanted their relationship to be smooth and steady, full of consideration, tolerance and understanding so that mine with Gabby might be so too.

When I arrived at Jane's place, she was sitting on the veranda cleaning her nails. There was a stool in front of her on which she placed her leg, for she could no longer bend and touch her toes. Her stomach was a big obstacle. She was applying varnish on her toenails with such precise strokes that all her attention was focused on it. When I opened the gate she did not look up. I was almost at her side before she lifted her head. The smile was unmistaken. It was a full smile, not one that started and ended on the lips. The dimple on her left cheek creased into a hollow. And her eyes sparkled. In spite of her pimples she looked beautiful and radiant. The beauty in the mind and soul had transferred onto the face. My smile also radiated happiness. I was happy for her as well as for myself.

"How did you sleep?" I asked. She burst into laughter. I was taken aback at the sudden hilarity. Then I realized that I was using the form of greeting we had adopted when we were still single and had spent the night out dancing.

"How did *you* sleep?" I started laughing too. It seemed as if a cloud and misty night had broken into a bright new day. It was the type of feeling one had when a thunderstorm gives way to bright sunlight. Since she asked the question last I had to answer. But before I did she managed to stand and embrace me.

"I slept well," I lied. "But, Jane, I was worried about you."

"I know. I could read it all over you yesterday. You were behaving so strangely."

"I was worried. How is Benny?"

"He is fine. He has gone to work."

Why was Jane making things difficult for me? I wondered. She knew what I was dying to know, but she was not prepared to say anything. On second thoughts I asked myself what I really wanted to know. Everything was fine as I could see. But I still wanted to know whether she was going to give birth in the village or in Douala. I was direct in my question.

113

"Are you coming up to Bamenda?"

"No, I am staying right here." It was said with such determination that I thought Jane must be out of her mind. The silence was becoming uncomfortable but what could I say? There was a pensive expression on her face. I looked at her closely and beyond. What I saw was reflected in her voice and words.

"Jane, are you alright?"

"I am alright, Lizzy. Only that this pregnancy has taught me a lot of things." I looked at her again. There were physical changes that could not be avoided. But there was something more.

"I can see that."

"So much has happened within a very short time. Life is a continuous lesson. I now know where I stand. Thank God Manyi has told me so many things." This was not leading to what I wanted to hear. But since she had touched on the topic of Manyi, I had another area to explore. But there was something I wanted to get to the bottom of.

"I hope everything is fine, Jane." I picked an idea from Manyi and said, "This is no time to be depressed."

"Things have been rough between Benny and me recently. I did not tell you because I did not want to spoil your stay here. I wanted you to enjoy every moment of it."

"But how do you think I can be happy when you are not?" I asked.

"Lizzy, there are certain things that you keep within you for days turning it over and over before arriving at a conclusion." This was one of the things she had learned, to be secretive. She continued, "It helps when certain problems are shared. But there are others that should be well examined only by those concerned."

It had finally come out. My fears were confirmed. This did not sound like the Jane with whom I had shared every secret.

"I have realized that marriage is not what we used to think it was. I remembered how determined we were when we talked of how our future families would look."

As Jane talked, the things we used to believe in flashed across my mind. My husband should share in the housework especially if both of us are working. He should not impose himself on me. I have a right to my opinions and should express them without fear. I should be allowed to have a say in any major decision concerning the family. Before I marry, I should love the man so much that I should not even think of being tempted by another man. My future husband should love me in the same way. If it is this way, then there never will be any reason to quarrel.

Jane was already letting go one of the things we had looked forward to upholding when we got married. She continued speaking.

"We have tried to sort out our differences. Benny insists on my staying here. I said to myself, 'Why make everyone unhappy just because I want to have my way?' It is a give and take situation."

I hope the next time it will be Benny who gives in. I thought to myself. Why must it always be the woman who gives in? I wondered. Why couldn't it be Benny? This question had no answer for the moment. Jane continued.

"It is a decision whose source lies in the desire to preserve, the desire for stability and continuity. Giving birth here is not going to be as tedious as I had thought. Benny has arranged for my mother to come down with a babysitter before I give birth."

I discovered that I could not have felt better if things had turned out differently. I was relieved to hear this. There was some nobility in the way the problem had been solved and I felt ashamed at the way I had behaved. I admired her courage and calm. I saw love as sacrifice.

This realization was to be tested not long after I returned to Bamenda. I came back to face my past and to hold love as a shield against the forces that tried to hold me back.

8

I met Martha one afternoon after work. It was a coincidence because it was immediately after working hours and I did not expect to see her in town. When I got into a taxi to go home she was sitting in the taxi. When she started asking me about what was going on as far as my engagement was concerned I felt ill at ease, first because it was in a taxi and one never knows who the other passengers are. Secondly, I did not want to let her in on what had transpired so far.

"So you have decided to go ahead, Lizzy. I hope you are strong enough to bear what you are going to face." This was her opening statement to me. I was immediately on the offensive. I did not know how she got the information but I was not going to satisfy her hopes.

"Yes," I replied. "It's all settled."

"Chei, Lizzy! You can be secretive, so when will the happy day be?"

"There will be no particular happy day. I have been happy all this while and I intend to continue being happy."

"So you want to tell me that there will be no wedding?"

"Maybe there will be. But I am not keen on it."

"Chei, Lizzy, you are really queer! Why are you not keen on a wedding? Who would want to miss an opportunity like that, a wedding cake, bridesmaid, flower girls and all that attention? To crown it all, a honeymoon. It is a once-in-a-lifetime event. I am looking forward to it."

"You will surely not be forgotten if it happens that way."

"You are talking as if you are not serious. But I am very serious."

"Tell me, Martha, why are you so enthusiastic about it now? A moment ago you were so pessimistic."

"I was just advising a good friend not to make a mistake which she would regret later. But since the die is cast, I just have to join the bandwagon and enjoy myself." There was a pause. "You know what, Lizzy, Andy is back."

"Who is Andy?" I asked.

"Are you so head over heels with Gabby that you have forgotten Andrew? Well, he is back from Britain and asked about you."

"Has he come back? Then that is fine."

"Is that all you have to say? Do you think he has forgotten?"

"Forgotten what?"

"Lizzy, do not pretend. You know what I am talking about."

"Look, Martha, that is all over and done with. It is more than six years now."

"I am just conveying his message. He wants to see you."

"What for? Martha, you know that I am engaged. I do not want his hopes to be raised."

"When he told me I did not know that you were engaged. Eh... I knew but thought that it was not going to work. I promised Andy that I was going to look for you and let you know that he was in town. But I was not lucky to see you. It seemed as if you have been out of town lately. What do I do now?"

"You can do what you like. Seeing him will not make any difference to me. Bygones are bygones."

"Lizzy, you cannot treat Andy this way. He has been writing to you, hasn't he?"

"Writing to me does not mean I have to keep waiting for him."

"He has been looking forward to coming back to you but now you turn your back on him."

"I am not sure that what you are saying is true. However, it is too late now. Thank you for the information and if you are my friend, you will know what to do."

We parted on this note. What she had said was partly true but I did not want to admit it even to myself.

Andrew and I were friends in high school. Both of us were in the science department. Our two years together were years of promises and hopes. I cannot say we loved each other. What did we know about love? We enjoyed each other's company. We exchanged presents on our birthdays. We went to dances and films together. His friends knew that I was his girlfriend and mine knew he was my boyfriend and they dared not trespass. Everybody thought that our relationship would continue even after we would leave high school because of the length of time we had been together. The other boys and girls were either in or out of love with one boy or the other. The way Andrew and I stuck together made the students call us husband and wife behind our backs. To us sex was out of the question for the fear of pregnancy. This was the issue that almost separated us because of taunts and pressure from our peers. When Andrew finally got me round to it, it was a sacred experience. I was so scared and told him not to take it for granted. It only showed how much we cared for each other. I cannot also say I really understood what it meant except that it satisfied some urge in us and we preferred each other to anybody else. It scarcely took place but when it did it rested in my memory for long. When I think of it now, I am surprised at the level of maturity we displayed. When it was study time we worked together.

He would scold me for being too slow to understand certain topics. He made it his duty to see that I passed my tests. He had once introduced me to his parents when they came to visit him in school. We both passed the A Levels but he did so well that he was given a scholarship to study in England. The week before he left, I was the most miserable person on earth. He assured me that everything was going to be all right. For the first two years he kept writing and telling me that he was doing fine and looking forward to our being together again. During the third year his letters became less engaging. Soon they became infrequent and formal. I replied to his letters according to his tone. In the fifth year, I received only postcards for Christmas. I also sent him postcards. I did not want him to know how I felt, for at one time I heard rumours that his parents were arranging for him to come home and get married. In fact, during his stay in London he came home twice and during this period I managed to see him. He invited me out each time he came home, but we could not be together as much as we would have loved because of the project he was writing.

I remember the last time he came home and invited me out to a nightclub. So much had happened during this time. At first we behaved as if we were strangers to each other. You know that type of reticence comes from uncertainty. So much water had flowed under the bridge. We no longer knew where we stood as far as our love for each other was concerned. He told me about London, about his studies and research and what he intended to do in the future. There was no talk about our future together. I had a feeling that he had invited me out of politeness. As the night progressed we became more intimate. He kissed me as we danced. I closed my eyes and tried to recapture our high school days. When I opened my eyes again, all the innocence, the honesty, the trust, the hopes were gone. Not only were they gone, but the Andrew with whom I had danced and the Andrew with whom I was dancing were two different people. He looked stressed. When I asked him about it he told me that it was the result of the type of life he was living. Life in London was too demanding for a student who had to spend more money on bills and producing papers demanded by the supervisor and meeting deadlines than on food and leisure. There was hardly any time for relaxation, as he had to take on an extra course to widen his prospects when he started looking for a job overseas. He also kept a moustache, which made him look older than he really was. But the aspect that had attracted me to him was not affected. He had a way of smiling which lifted the left end of his upper lip. He also had a way of looking at you when he is listening to you talk that gives the impression that he is listening with his eyes.

Looking at him now took me back to how we had met. It was during a chemistry practical lesson in the laboratory and we were doing titration. I was paired with him and he allowed me to carry out the experiment first. As I struggled to get the tubes steady on the tripod and in the right position, he folded his arms and watched me. I started pouring the liquid and midway he held my hand. I was so surprised and looked round to make sure that the teacher had not seen what was happening. Fortunately he was busy with another student.

"Let me continue," he whispered. I looked at him and he seemed to be smiling at my clumsiness. I was angry and stood sulking instead of watching what he was doing. Before the teacher came round to see what I was doing, the liquids were already in the expected positions in the test tube. He approved of what had been done then asked Andrew to dismantle the whole set up and begin his own. I watched as Andrew worked with deft fingers, and all this while he said nothing to me. I felt too mortified to say anything. After the lesson, he took away my file and I had to follow him to get it. That was the beginning of our relationship. That seemingly mocking smile had captured my heart.

After that evening in the nightclub his letters became a trickle and finally stopped. Now he had come back trying to put back the clock. He had come back one year too late. Coming back with a PhD in Engineering, he was going to have a good job. But that was not all that counts in a marriage. I had gone too far with Gabby. Better the devil you know than the angel you do not.

Gabby's people were also pressing on me to do everything to join him at the end of the year. Most of the traditional rites had been carried out and the final traditional blessing was scheduled for the month of February, just three months away. We had agreed that the civil and traditional blessing would take place on the same day. Whether there was to be a wedding or not depended on the two of us. We had discussed this option. For Gabby, it was just normal for us to have a church wedding. But first of all I wanted us to make an assessment of what it would entail. The wedding trousseau would come from America. Gabby was making arrangements for that. There would be six ladies and gentlemen-in-waiting, a pageboy and girl and six flower girls. We had to provide the attire for all these people. We also calculated the expenditure on the reception in town and in the village. The honeymoon was not left out. When the cost of all this was estimated, the amount was overwhelming. We calculated our own resources. Gabby had a substantial amount in his account. Mine was negligible compared to his. We were not ready to count on what the family was going to chip in. Gabby suggested taking a loan from the bank. In his usual enthusiasm, everything was going to be fine. But I did not want to start my married life adopting austerity measures in my daily expenditure because debts had to be paid back. Moreover, I had witnessed a wedding, which was considered the wedding of the year, crumble because of money that had been borrowed for the wedding. It had become a bone of contention between the newlyweds because the man always claimed that he could not provide what the woman needed because he was paying back the debts. If we could not finance a grand wedding, then a quiet ceremony with family members and friends was good enough for me. But Gabby did not want to hear of it. Luckily for him, the family had covered all the expenditure of the traditional rites with Pa Martin spearheading everything. He asked nothing from Gabby. We had just five months to make up our minds. Time was running out.

Meanwhile my work in the office was going on smoothly. I tried to keep everything else in the background as much as possible. It was strange that now that I was actually going to get married, not only engaged, there was no ring on my finger. My colleagues asked me about the ring and I told them a convincing story. Nobody ever suspected what had happened to the diamond ring, perhaps only Benny and Jane. We had for our marriage booked for gold finger bands with our initials intertwined on them. They were still at the goldsmith. I had suggested this and what came out at the end pleased me more than a grand wedding or the former diamond ring. Ironically, I felt more attached and committed now than when I had the diamond ring on my finger.

My relationship with my boss was very friendly. I did my work well giving him no reason to be angry with me. I even offered to stay back some afternoons to do some pressing work. He was very appreciative of my offers. He was the type of man who in his personal relationships acted on impulse when he was appreciative. He never hesitated to give me permission when I asked for it, except when there was a genuine reason for his refusing. I too made sure that I did not abuse this kindness by asking for permission too often. He used to help me out financially and used to call me into his office just to tell me if I needed help just to ask. He did this when he noticed that I was not feeling fine, when I had the problem with Gabby. But he did not probe. My colleagues could not understand the type of relationship that existed between my boss and me. But my boss was an honourable man and knew that he had lost as far I was concerned. He too had once asked me when the great day was going to be. I had promised him that he was going to be very much part of it.

My social life was becoming restricted. I realized that I could no longer do some of the things I used to do. At first I would leave the office and go out with friends, sometimes only coming back home to change and go out again. I had nobody to care for, so I could stay for days without cooking. Now I went straight home after work. I prepared meals which I had never had time to prepare. I tried out recipes I had seen in cookery books. I baked cakes, which I either took to the office to share with my friends or sent to Pa Martin. I once baked a particularly rich cake and gave it to my boss. My colleagues could not believe this and made comments to the effect that it was not for nothing. But they forgot that a good gesture smoothens and maintains a good relationship. My intention all along was to make him understand that though I had not allowed him to get closer, we were still good friends.

There were days during which I was so bored that I wondered for how long I was going to keep indoors before breaking. One evening I took a sleeping pill to help me sleep. The next day I felt so drowsy and weak that I vowed never to take one again. Weekends were the worst times. I developed the habit of visiting my in-laws on Sundays. Although they welcomed me, I felt that I was getting in their way. I even had to accompany them to places I had not planned to go.

I was dying to go to a nightclub. I enjoyed dancing and could dance till dawn. But there was nobody with whom I could go to a nightclub. I did not want to give any person reason to tell stories about me. I had declined many invitations and was no longer invited. When Martha invited me to join her at the New City Nightclub for her birthday party, I jumped at the invitation.

It was a common practice for single girls to celebrate their birthdays just to have an opportunity to get their friends together to enjoy themselves or sometimes with the hope of making a catch. On such occasions a selected cross section of the young people in town are invited. A group of girls could go to such parties without any problem. There was usually a large flask of punch to accelerate the mood of the party. We arrived at the party when it was well underway and people were dancing. We were ushered to our seats. There were empty seats near me since the occupants were dancing. I noticed that I was sitting at a table next to where the birthday girl was sitting. I did not know those who were sitting next to me. I was not sitting with the girls with whom I had come and was not pleased with the idea of starting a conversation with strangers. This was the idea, to mix with people as much as possible so that soon you find yourself getting to know the people with whom you were sitting. At one point during the party, the instructions were that you should dance only with members of the table at which you were sitting. Relationships have been known to extend even after such parties. In the semi darkness, I could not make out some of the people who were dancing. But I saw Martha, the birthday girl, dancing with a dashing young man. Vivacious as ever, she was dancing and chatting with her partner. They were dancing so close that I wondered whom this new release was. I watched them dance for some time. That particular record ended and people started drifting back to their seats. I saw someone moving towards where I was sitting. It was Andrew. I could not be mistaken. My heart fluttered. I did not know what I was going to discuss with him if his seat was at the table where I was sitting. It was and he came and sat down.

"Lizzy, I am glad to see you although you have been avoiding me."

"How can I be avoiding you when I have not met you? I did not even know that you were around."

"But Martha surely told you that I wanted to see you," he said with an accusatory tone. "You did not want to see me. I understand that you are engaged to be married. But that does not mean you should avoid me."

I felt guilty when he said this because it was exactly what was on my mind. I was at a critical stage where I wanted no distractions or situations to set tongues wagging again.

"I am not avoiding you, Andrew. I only did not have the opportunity to meet you." My placatory tone was to soften the hardness in his voice. What was the use being rude or nasty to him when there was nothing to gain by it? He continued.

"Martha told me you were engaged to be married and would not entertain any visits from me. I would have come to your office."

"Well, that was her interpretation. Why should I not want to see you? Have you done anything wrong to me?"

"I wonder. So am I allowed to visit you?"

"Nothing stops you."

I did not want the evening to be spoilt for me. I had come to enjoy myself and not to have an aimless argument. Moreover, a particularly good record was on and people were drifting to the dance floor. I invited him to dance with me. Like the proverbial cricket I had invited my own death. After the first record he made sure that we danced most of the records. During some of the records he held me so close that I felt really uncomfortable. He whispered in my ears, "It is so nice to hold you like this again, Lizzy, and do just as we used to do." When he said this I felt more uncomfortable but not wanting to attract attention to us, I just switched off to what he was saying and concentrated on my dancing.

"You have not changed, Lizzy, my sweet, you will always be the same to me." His talking was like a monologue. I made no response. As the night progressed, with the help of the punch, which was served at midnight, people became more relaxed and inhibitions were dropped and intimacies developed. This was one of the intentions of the party. Andrew was trying to recapture the past. How did he expect me to be the same? I was about six years older. The changes were both physical and psychological. My waistline had broadened. My mind was more mature. I knew what I wanted out of life. So much had been written on the pages of my mind. He too was definitely not the same. He had grown taller and broader. His voice was deeper. He had grown a moustache. This was something he did not have in high school. Much had been written on the pages of his mind too, which was surely different from what had been written on mine. I wondered what had happened to the wife I had heard that his parents were arranging for him.

The next day was Saturday and Andrew came to visit me in my house. He carried a bag, which he handed over to me.

"This is what I brought for you but did not know how to give it."

"Thank you," I replied. He held me to kiss me but I managed to escape the kiss.

"Lizzy, what is wrong? You do not want to kiss me?"

"Andrew, I have a husband and do not think that it is proper for us to kiss as we used to do. Please do understand." He looked at me as if there was something he could not understand. I wondered what Martha had told him.

"All right, I will," he said and sat down. He looked round and commented, "You have a nice setup here."

"I try to make it cosy and to my taste."

"You have always been a homely person, neat and organized. That is why I liked you so much."

I knew where the conversation was leading to and blamed myself for it. In the effort of pushing Andrew's words to the background the previous evening, I had let down the barrier that I was trying to build between Andrew and myself. I waited for an opportunity to find out why he was so insistent in putting back the clock. It soon came for it seemed Andrew was anxious to get married but he was not finding it easy. He lamented having lost track of the girls he had known in high school. I consoled him by saying that when the girls with whom he had been in high school were ready for marriage, the boys were not. So it was rare to find college sweethearts getting married.

"I was counting on you, Lizzy. You are not married yet."

"But soon will be. By the way what happened to the girl your parents were grooming for you?" Andrew smiled.

"Which girl? I don't know what you are talking about."

"Don't pretend, Andrew, you must have known what was happening. There is no smoke without fire."

"Is that why you stopped loving me?" It was my turn to smile.

"Don't talk about love Andrew. Do you know that love has to be nurtured and that without nurturing it dies?"

Andrew was not a happy man when he left my house that evening. But he was quite reasonable when I recalled what had happened to estrange us. I was grateful for this. He came to my house as often as he could until one evening I had to introduce him to Pa Martin. I had to tell a lie. I did not want any unpleasant situation to be created for I noticed that Pa Martin did not take kindly to his presence.

There are times when one remembers the past as if it happened just a few days ago. I can clearly remember what happened when I got the news.

"Jane gave birth to a baby boy yesterday," Benny telephoned to tell me. I could tell from his voice that he was very happy. He was so excited about the baby that I had to ask him how Jane was doing before he could tell me about her health. I was so grateful that everything had turned out well. I thought about the baby Gabby and I would have when we got married. We had agreed to plan for our children and I did everything to avoid an unplanned pregnancy. Benny and Jane had planned theirs. It is not by mistake that I kept referring to them. They were my scale of reference because it was from them that I learnt what love and commitment mean. I wanted to share these first days of the baby's existence with them. I wanted to go to Douala and be with them but I did not know what excuse I was going to give my boss. I knew that my boss was not going to refuse giving me permission for a day or two. But to stay for a whole week was impossible. I relied on the good relationship that existed between the two of us to get more days than he was ready to give.

On Thursday morning I went in with my application with the intention of explaining why I wanted to go to Douala. This reason had nothing to do with the baby. I had timed the duration in such a way that if I went on Friday or Saturday I could stay till Wednesday the next week so I actually asked for three days off. By so doing I was going to spend five days with the Bilas. This was enough for me.

When I walked into his office, he was busy reading a letter. When he finally took up his head he was surprised to see me. He started giving me instructions as if he had called for me. As he spoke he pushed four files towards me. He looked preoccupied. I wondered what must have ruffled his usually calm feathers. He was in quite a state. He was unsteady. The instructions were not understood because not only was he jumping from one point to the other and back again, but part of my mind was not on what he was saying. It was focused on the state of his table. It seemed as if he had been looking for something in a hurry. The usually neatly arranged files were all scattered on the table. It also seemed as if he had left the house in a hurry. His coat was creased and his tie was askew. His shirt had a layer of grime on the collar.

"Is there any way I can be of help sir?" The words were out of my mind before I realized what I was saying. I had a feeling that there was something wrong and I had to offer my help although I did not know how I could be of help.

"Just type the letters and work on the files as I have instructed."

"Sir, you are not yourself this morning. You look disturbed."

This stopped him in mid action. He looked at me for a while. I tried to maintain a concerned but calm look.

"Sit down, Elizabeth." He yawned and scratched his head. Then he realized that his tie was not straight. He straightened it and picked up his pen. He put it down without writing anything.

"Thank you, Elizabeth. Thank you for your concern. I am really in a state this morning. Thank God that you are the first person to come in. Your concern will surely ease off my worries."

"As I said sir, if I can be of help I will be just too glad." Here I was saying about the same things he had said to me.

"If you can work on these files before mid-day then you will be helping me a great deal." Here was my chance.

"We all have problems, sir, in fact I came in just now to explain the situation in which I find myself. I know that you are very understanding and I wanted to explain to you before giving my application for permission."

"Just do the work I have asked you to do. I will be away the whole of next week so just give the application and I will sign it. There will not be much work for you next week so if you can do all the work I have given you today then you are free."

"Thank you, sir. I hope that everything is going to be alright."

"I hope so."

I carried out the first set of files but realized that I could not work on them because I had forgotten certain of the instructions. As I re-entered the office he looked up. He was more relaxed and steady.

"I am sorry to disturb you again, sir. I did not quite understand how to treat these files." After showing me what to do he added two more files. He wanted to clear his table before going away.

"Please work on these two as fast as you can. You can do the others after. I am leaving the office at one p.m. and need to take them along. When you finish the ones I have just given you bring them to me."

I could sense the urgency in his voice and manner. As I arranged the files in order of priority I prayed that there should be no visitors to the office that morning. I worked on the two last files he had given me and typed out a letter and two circular letters. When I presented them to him he received them but did not dismiss me.

"I like you, Lizzy." He always called me Elizabeth. Lizzy was too intimate and Gabby was fond of calling me that way. Hearing it from the lips of another man it did not sound the same. He continued, "One can rely on you." His table was clear now. His 'in' tray was empty. He took the files out of the 'out' tray and gave them to me. I stood waiting. He pulled out his drawers and went through them. When he was satisfied that nothing had been overlooked, he took his briefcase.

"I think everything is ready. Have a nice weekend."

"Same to you sir."

He detached his office keys from a bunch of keys and gave them to me. Then he ushered me out. I wondered what he meant when he said everything was ready. He looked like a man ready for battle and I wondered what type of administrative battles he was going to fight. Talk about his having problems with his minister was whispered in the office but I had to keep my mouth shut. I read letters and typed responses, which indicated that things were not going on well. As his private secretary, I had to be careful about what I said.

The sun was unusually hot for the month of September. As is the case with Douala, it is always hot whether in the rainy season or the dry season. The heat and the smells from the gutters gave a general feeling of putrefaction. The smell was suffocating as I stood at the *Rond Point* Roundabout waiting for a taxi. The roadside vendors had their goods displayed right at the edge of the gutters and the slimy greenish waters that filled the gutters were a great contrast to the glittering trinkets displayed nearby. Even the hawkers of the famous *'pain chargé'* displayed their goods unprotected on plywood boards as near as possible to the road. Some of the boards even straddled these gutters, giving much-needed shade for the larvae and worms that found a haven in these gutters. One of the hawkers thought I was interested in his wares and encouraged me to come and buy. I looked at the gutter, then at the bread and finally at him and shook my head. The message must have gone home. But this did not mean anything to him. He looked away as if neither the gutter nor I existed.

I arrived at Jane's house in the latter part of the afternoon when Benny was still at work. I had to stop there because I was so anxious to see the baby. The choice of a gift for the baby had been made easy by my long friendship with Jane. Back in Bamenda as students in high school we had once seen a woman going to the clinic with her baby and had greatly admired how the baby was dressed. The combination of colours in the baby's attire, the carrier bag and the umbrellas was stunning. Jane had admired this so much. With the sex of the baby in my mind I had gone round looking for a similar combination in the market. Not finding it I went to May's Maternity shop located along Commercial Avenue and described to the proprietress exactly what I wanted. She produced it: a pair of shorts with its accompanying short sleeve shirt. The cap and socks were made of the same material but made thicker and stronger with stiff. I went to the market again to look for a carrier and umbrella to match. All these had a predominantly blue colour. As I looked at the gifts as I was about to pack them in my bag, I imagined the look on Jane's face when she would see them. I felt the sweet sad thug of a pointless melancholia and the light-exhilarating caress of a warm happiness.

The baby was sleeping quietly in its cot in the parlour. We stood and watched its silent breathing and impish face. It was a beautiful sight with the entire lacy frill on the cot tent and little pillows cuddling the baby's sides. Jane was so happy and excited with the gift that her eyes became misty. When I saw this I turned and embraced her. She held me tight and we started laughing. I wanted to know how everything had happened. It was a narrative filled with joy, excitement and pain. Pain was what she had really felt. But the force of the others overshadowed the pain. Even as I am telling you now my dear readers the pain really comes last because it is just a necessary prelude. When it is all over the others remain.

We were engaged in a conversation and did not hear the gate opening. We only heard the car driving in. I was anxious to see Benny's reaction to the baby and waited with a sense of suspended animation. When he came in, his elation was evident. My pen is a poor substitute to paint a good picture of the expression on his face It was like that of a man who had successfully carried out an assignment and was ready to congratulate himself if others were not going to. He embraced his wife tenderly. I watched, really amused because of the thoughts that were going through my mind. Benny had not wanted to miss all these. He wanted to be part of it all. I could not resist teasing him.

"Congratulations, Benny. But the person I should be congratulating is Jane. She went through all the pain alone."

"Just hear that," he replied as his lips curled into a smile. "You cannot imagine the agony I was in as I paced the corridors of that hospital. This lazy boy took such a long time in coming. I almost went mental."

Maybe he takes after you," Jane joined me in teasing her husband.

"The important thing is that he arrived safely, thank God." We all fell silent as the baby started to cry. Jane moved over and carried him out of the cot. She sat down to breastfeed him. He sucked hungrily making smacking noises.

"Hey! Go easy on it boy. Don't suck my woman dry. She is mine you know."

We all burst out laughing. I laughed longest because I could already imagine Benny vying for pride of place with the baby. As the baby sucked we looked on enthralled. I stole surreptitious glances at Benny. He caught me at it and gave me a secret wink.

"We should have something to eat. Jane, you need to replenish what has been taken out." He continued, "Elizabeth, are you staying the night here or are you going over?"

I knew that he was asking for the sake of asking for he knew as well as I did that Gabby would not accept such an arrangement. Secondly I wouldn't want to interfere in their intimacies. All the same I wanted to hear what he thought.

"What do you suggest I do?" He hawed and hummed and I cut him short. "I would have liked to stay but first I have to see Gabby. I telephoned to tell him that I would be here today. Maybe he is waiting for me."

A girl still getting used to the slippers she wore on her feet served lunch. I could see that she had not yet adjusted to her new environment. While the mother brought the food to the table, Jane directed the girl on how to place the plates, glasses and cutlery on the table. I could see that it was not going to be easy with Jane when her mother went back to the village. But with Benny's love and support, I was sure Jane would pull through.

The day had been a busy one for Gabby. He was so busy that he forgot I was coming to Douala. By six o'clock that evening he was an exhausted man lying on the sofa in the parlour. The door was not locked. After a knock I opened the door and walked in with Benny at my heels. The sight of his exhausted body now relaxed in sleep stopped my entrance. He lay on his back with his head propped on a chair pillow, his arm flung across his chest and his left leg slightly bent at the knee. His mouth was slightly ajar and he was breathing slowly and deeply. A weak snoring sound issued from his nose as his stomach rose and fell rhythmically. As I looked at him I wondered at the way man can be defenceless in sleep. I had watched him sleep many times but this one was arresting. He was so unaware of our presence. Sleep, the replica of death! Benny pushed passed me. His footsteps made Gabby sit up abruptly. He wiped his eyes and yawned. He stretched out his arms and yawned again.

"Welcome, Lizzy. Benny, it has been a lousy day," he said in a tired voice and yawned again.

"When did you get here, Lizzy? I am sorry I could not come to pick you up."

"It's okay. I am here and that is what is important."

"Have you seen the baby?" He was now awake and waited for me to answer, but Benny cut in.

"I must be going back. I just came to make sure that Elizabeth was not going to be lonely. If you had not come back I would have taken her back with me. Are we meeting this evening?" I expected Gabby to say yes, but he shook his head wearily.

"I do not think so. I have some work to do." I expected him to say I could go and be with Jane if I wanted to, but he said nothing. I was puzzled at his whole attitude and waited in anticipation for the surprise, which I thought was in store for me. My enthusiastic observations about the baby met only with grunts. My high spirits dropped and I was at a loss. I wanted us to talk about the baby or anything else but he just sat there pretending to read a newspaper. His behaviour was grating on my nerves and I could stand it no longer.

"It seems my presence here is not needed. You could have told me to go back with Benny if you knew you were going to be so busy. This jolted him. My tone and the sarcasm in my voice made him know that I was affected by his behaviour.

"I am sorry, Lizzy." He dropped the paper as if he were waiting for the opportunity to do so.

"I am tired. That is all."

"Are you so tired that you cannot even talk?" I had a feeling that there was something more to this. I had enough experience now not to be deceived and went for the attack.

"You are worried. You are more worried than tired. If you do not want to tell me I will not ask. But I thought that was one of our duties to each other, to share our problems."

He sat for sometime looking at me as if he was finding it difficult to make a decision, an unpleasant one of course.

"Lizzy, I do not know how to tell you this. I know that you are going to be unhappy, so will I. But there is nothing I can do about it. I have to leave for Yaounde on Sunday and will come back only on Wednesday or Thursday." Although my heart sank at this, I tried to alleviate his misery. I tried to cheer him up.

"If duty calls there is no way you can avoid it. Your job is important. You cannot jeopardize it because of me."

"There is a meeting taking place on Monday in Yaounde and my boss has asked me to represent him at this meeting. I am so tired because I have been busy preparing the documents I have to take along for the meeting. Tomorrow, I have to get some briefing on the meeting. I have to meet his counterpart in Yaounde for us to put our work together before Monday. That is why you see me so preoccupied."

Although he tried to be cheerful I could detect an underlying uneasiness. When I suggested he go back to the office to complete the work he had left, he jumped at the suggestion. I was taken aback. I wondered why he had not refused since he was so tired. I wondered what was happening. He had not allowed me to go to the Bilas just to leave me alone in the house. But I thought that if this was going to put him at ease then it was fine. I told myself to be patient and after super, which was eaten in semi silence, I took a novel to keep myself occupied. But I could not concentrate on the story. I kept reading and rereading the same pages and soon lost the trend of the story. I tried to think about a baby and how it felt to be a mother. I thought of becoming pregnant before the marriage. But this was against the custom of our people. The traditional rites of marriage cannot be performed when the bride is pregnant. A church wedding with the bride in such a state would be a mockery of the meaning and solemnity of the occasion. I had to wait. Five months was not such a long time. Then I realized that I was in my late twenties. When I met Gabby I was about twenty-six years old. By the time I would be getting married I would be past twenty-seven. All the stories about difficult pregnancies and deliveries came flooding my mind and my imagination fed on this. I imagined myself not being able to have a baby and the agony I would have to live with. I imagined how disappointed and frustrated I would be if my pregnancies terminated prematurely or if I brought forth a stillborn. I was just imagining because to conjure up an emotion you must have experienced it. These thoughts weighed on me and by the time Gabby came back I was down at zero emotionally.

Gabby came back, looking more like himself. I was still in the parlour when he came in. He thought I was going to immediately fall into step with his raised spirits. Unfortunately the tables were turned and I was at low ebb. I had metamorphosed. I felt a chill run through me when I thought of Gabby lying next to me. It was a product of mixed emotions. First there was this wish for a baby, strengthened by the fact that these were my fertile days. Then there was the fear of spoiling all the arrangements with a pregnancy. Above all, I felt far away emotionally from Gabby. I do not know why I felt that way. It was the first time in our relationship that I wished Gabby would not touch me. But knowing Gabby I knew it was a senseless wish. Surprisingly, when I resisted his touch he turned over and fell asleep. I was more than disappointed. I did not know why I had acted that way. Maybe it was the desire of the excitement of a chase and capture that makes a woman feel wanted. I examined this possibility but it was not satisfying.

Saturday passed like a whirlwind. In the heat of activities in Jane's house

I forgot the events of the previous evening. This was the first weekend since Jane gave birth and given that I was around she used the opportunity to get me to do some shopping for her. Gabby had to leave that evening for Yaounde. He hadn't much time before leaving. I tried to make up for the previous evening by trying to be cheerful and acting as if nothing had happened. But what had actually happened? A feeling, a sensation, an action, a thought were all leaving a dangerous residue in my mind. I still had this lingering sense of lethargy, which threatened to overcome me when I thought that my stay in Douala was not going the way I had expected. My premonition was coming on strong and I became afraid. At nine that morning after Gabby had left to meet Benny, I also left for Jane's house to help prepare lunch. They had invited us to eat together before Gabby's departure. I did not know whether they were to meet at home or they were to meet somewhere else before coming home. On my way I tried to keep my mind off the inexplicable melancholy that had started to entrench itself into my being. As I prepared the soup in Jane's kitchen, I kept reflecting on what might have caused the strange reactions of the previous evening. My conversation with Jane was tilted and I was afraid Jane might notice that I was not myself. At one moment, out of curiosity I asked Jane when Benny had left the house. Without suspecting anything she told me that he left the house just a few minutes before I came in. There was more than an hour's difference between when Gabby had left the house and when I had arrived. If Benny had to meet Gabby somewhere, then Benny could not have been an hour late. This further increased my fears that something was going on. Who was going to help me get to the source of it? The person who stood a better chance of doing so was going away – Gabby himself. I oscillated between the desire to tell Jane and to handle the situation myself. I was dying to share my problem with Jane but remembered what she had told me. It might have been a defence tactic to take responsibility off her shoulders but I had learnt something from it.

Jane had a way of taking you unawares with questions or statements giving you no time to formulate a lie. You either told the truth or blundered through a lie. So she did when we found ourselves alone in the kitchen.

"Lizzy, it seems you will not go back to Gabby's place this evening. Gabby's going away is affecting you so much. It is unfortunate that this trip had to come up. In five months time all this waiting will be over."

Later as we sat on the sofa waiting for the men to come back, Jane could not resist picking up the trend of her observation. The baby was asleep in its cot. The parlour was quiet. Only the noise made by the house girl cleaning the kitchen could be heard. Even the music coming from the musical set on the cupboard was tuned low. The muffled sound of vehicles passing on the street outside sounded far away. Jane's observation had called for a light-hearted response but I was not able to think of any. Even if I did, it could not have come out of my mouth light heartedly because my heart was heavy. It was burdened by things I could not explain even to myself. Apart from the fact that I could not compose my grief into a coherent narrative, I was taking a sheet out of Jane's book. I did not want to pour out my fears to her. If Jane could keep her troubles to herself, so could I. But my silence called for further probing from her.

"I am fine. There is nothing particularly wrong. I am just a bit confused. I do not know what to do."

"What is happening, Lizzy? Tell me. I can be of help."

"Thank you, Jane. I want to sort this out myself."

Jane looked at me for some time and shrugged. I felt a tiny surge of pleasure for keeping her in the dark. Then she changed the topic of conversation.

"I am sure that you will stay with us now that Gabby is going away. You will be lonely all by yourself in that house."

"I will be fine. After all it is just for one day. I think I will go back to Bamenda on Monday."

The decision just came to my mind at that moment. I did not know whether I really intended to go or it was just a way of letting her know that I was no longer interested in staying. I had wanted to stay and wait for Gabby while I spent some time with Jane and the baby. But this sudden decision put me in a quandary with myself. Was I leaving because Gabby was not there or I just wanted time to examine what was bothering me? I did not know which, but there was always this nagging feeling that all was not well with Gabby and me.

The men came back earlier than expected. As they walked in I looked from Gabby to Benny trying to read some explanation on their faces. But their faces did not betray anything. I was about to ask them what they had been doing the whole morning but could not trust my voice. I felt that I was going to sound accusatory and so kept quiet. As we ate I tried to catch Gabby's eyes. But he kept avoiding me. He kept up a lively conversation. I tried to maintain an interested front but Gabby's attitude especially towards me was disturbing. We used to gaze at each other uninhibited. Anybody watching us would immediately understand. In the company of Benny and Jane it was not an embarrassing thing to do because they were similarly engaged. What was happening to disturb the flow of current between Gabby and myself? I was determined to find out. The result was going to determine whether I would wait for Gabby or not.

As we drove back home he took a route with which I was unfamiliar.

I had mastered the road from Gabby's residence in the Akwa neighbourhood to Benny's house in Bonanjo. I asked him where we were going. He did not reply and we drove on for some time in silence.

Then he said, "I am going to pick up Jean Claude to drive me to the bus stop."

My heart fluttered. I remembered how Gabby had reacted when he heard that a man had kissed me on the street. I wondered whether Jane had told him that Jean Claude was the one. I became afraid that he was scheming at something. His next words reduced my anxiety.

"You don't yet know how to drive, otherwise you would have driven the car back after dropping me at the bus stop."

This was one of our arrangements. I would learn how to drive as soon as we got married. This was a convenient and safe topic to get us talking until we got home. His going to get Jean Claude was not in line with what I had planned. We wouldn't have enough time to ourselves before Gabby left. I would be left hanging on the precipice of anxiety. J.C. was sitting alone in his parlour when we arrived. He had taken off his shirt and was resting. He must have just come in but there was nothing to confirm this. J.C. was so happy to see me and kept asking me about Bamenda and telling me how he had a wonderful time there. I wondered why I had not seen him since I arrived. The three of them were always together. Just to say something I voiced my thoughts.

"You have been missing."

He told me that he had been out of town for the whole week. I lapsed into silence and they continued talking. They talked about things that had to be done in the office. They talked about the possible outcome of the meeting that was going to be held in Yaounde. They talked about people I did not know. I kept quiet all the way home. It was getting to three p.m. when we arrived at home. Gabby had to hurry so as to arrive in Yaounde before nightfall. He had packed in the morning when I was doing some laundry. He called me into the room while J.C. sat in the parlour.

"Gabby, what is happening to us?" I could not say 'you' because I could imagine what he was going to say. I would be asking a question which he could easily throw back at me. And he did.

"What is happening?" He repeated my question.

"Since I came you have not been yourself. This has affected me. I cannot tell exactly how I feel."

"You must be imagining things, Lizzy. Maybe it is the baby that is affecting you." He tried to make light of the situation. But I made as if I had not heard him and continued.

"Now you are going away. I don't know what to think. If you are so far away from me as you have been since I came here, then there is no need for me to wait for you. I will leave for Bamenda tomorrow." This seemed to have broken the barrier that was between us. He took me in his arms and kissed me. It was so exhilarating to feel Gabby's arms around me again. It seemed as if I had been starved. The past two days had been aching because we were together but lacked the emotion to ignite our affection. Something was always coming in the way.

"Lizzy, you have to wait for me. You promised to be here until the weekend. After all, your boss is not going to give you a query."

I regretted having told him all what had happened before I left Bamenda. He continued, "You really want to stay with Jane and be with the baby. I know you like that. Please stay."

He sounded so serious. I believed him and banished all other thoughts to the background. I was once again happy. On the way to the bus stop we talked about the baby. For the first time Gabby really talked about the baby and made some observations I did not expect from him. He pointed out certain features of the baby like his nose and ears, which he said were purely Benny's. I took note of this to verify later. J.C. was also very interested in the baby and said he would be going in the evening to see the Bilas. Gabby was fortunate to get the last ticket for the bus which was loading when we arrived. It was not long before the bus took off.

As we drove back home J.C. kept up a stream of conversation telling me about the type of people he met and the temptations he is exposed to everyday in the course of carrying out his duties. He worked with Gabby at the National Produce Marketing Board. While Gabby was involved in the administrative part of the work, J.C. was in charge of registering cocoa brought in by licensed buyers for exportation. He talked of the tricks licensed buyers play to maximize their profits. He told me the story of a licensed buyer who was in the habit of mixing bad cocoa grains with good ones. He had mastered the way cocoa bags were arranged for examination and made sure that his were arranged accordingly with the bags with bad grains kept far away from the inspection area. Checking was done randomly and if he had made arrangements with the inspector of the day his bags would pass unchecked. This unfortunate day the manager had come down to the warehouse himself so the work had to be meticulous. Usually samples were taken from the top middle and bottom of the bag. The number of good grains was counted against the number of bad ones. If the ratio of good grains was seven out of every eight grains then the cocoa was passable. But if it was five to every eight, the bag was rejected. This licensed buyer could not have his consignment signed in because sixty percent of his bags were rejected. This was later reported to J.C.

Two days later, at home, he heard a knock at his door at about ten p.m. He could not remember what had kept him in that evening.

A man walked in, looked hesitantly round and asked, "Is this Mr. Kamdem's house?"

"Yes, you are talking to him."

He was a round man and his head perched on his body like a pumpkin on a barrel. His hair had started receding but what was most arresting about him were his eyes. They seemed to absorb everything as they moved like radar round the room. Although he seemed to be looking round as he spoke, his attention was focused on him, weighing and assessing him.

"Sit down please, can I help you?"

"Thank you. Thank you. I am lucky to meet you in. I wanted to see you in the office but you were not around…"

He sat down heavily and seemed to have difficulties in breathing. He was dressed in a flowing 'danshiki' gown with matching trousers and cap. He looked quite at ease in his attire as his stomach had ample space to spread. He exuded the air of a man who knew how to carry out his business dealings and nothing could stand in his way. J.C. waited for him to continue.

"I have a problem. I brought a consignment of cocoa three days ago…" J.C. immediately remembered the report he had read and suspected why the man had come to see him. The man continued.

"My papers have not been signed for the consignment to be moved from the warehouse to the waiting room."

"Why? This should be done as soon as the cocoa is checked in."

"Yes, the cocoa was not checked in because there was a bit of a problem. This had never happened before. I don't really know what happened. But I know that you are a man and you are going to treat this like a man. Here is a small envelope for you."

We arrived at Gabby's gate at this point of the narration and he had to get out to open the gate. Once inside I did not wait for him to open the door for me. I got out of the car and he parked it by the side of the entrance. I did not invite him to come in but he did all the same. Although I did not want to give him an excuse for staying, I wanted to know whether he took the money or not. When I came back from the room where I had gone to keep my bag he was comfortably seated.

'*Tu es ravissant,*' he commented. I was caught in mid stride. Although I couldn't speak French very well, I understood what he said. I was too shocked to say anything. He continued in English, "You know you are. And you know that I love you."

"Jean Claude. please do not say that."

"Why? Because you are going to marry Gabby? Does not stop anyone else from loving you? You want to tell me that you do not know that I love you, Elisa?" J.C. was springing surprises on me that day. His variation of my name was one I hardly heard. I was forced to smile at it in spite of my indignation. He continued, "I know that you want me to go. I will not stay. But I am coming back to take you to see the baby at seven o'clock." He was out of the house before I could say anything. I looked at his retreating back wondering what he was up to. I did not dwell long on this. I was alone in the house. Gabby would be gone for three days. What was I going to do with myself? I wondered. I went back into the room and sat on the bed trying to assess my recent situation and to make a decision about the coming days. What else was there for me to do apart from going to Jane's place and spending the days with her? I had neither accepted nor refused to stay with them while Gabby was away. But now I felt the need to stay on my own at least for that evening. Gabby's presence had seemed to fill the whole house even when he was in just one of the rooms. It was not a big apartment, just a parlour, bedroom, kitchenette and bathroom. It was so convenient except in the event of his having a visitor who had to spend the night. But now it felt so large and empty. In such an apartment there is usually very little cleaning to do. At that moment I felt like doing something to keep my mind and body busy. When I want to keep my mind off thoughts that worry me, I work. I got up and looked round the room. Unlike the parlour, the room offered me something to do. I went to the wardrobe and started checking the clothes that hung there. I had washed the clothes that had been used the previous week, but there was clothing like coats, which I could not wash. These I took to the cleaners. I wanted Gabby to have clean coats to wear when he came back. As I searched the pockets for handkerchiefs or any paper he might have left inside the coats, I found an envelope. The writing was very unfamiliar and there was just a slim sheet of paper inside. Out of curiosity I pulled out the sheet of paper. It was a very short letter. It read thus.

Dear Gabby,

I just want you to know that I enjoyed every minute of the time we spent together the other night. I am looking forward to seeing you in Yaounde. We will have more fun.

I miss you.

Love, Ange

It was dated the previous day. So Gabby had been with a woman the day I arrived from Bamenda. I let the coat drop to the floor and I went slowly back to the bed, my eyes glued to the letter. I did not look at where I was sitting and sat on my handbag. I adjusted my position without taking my eyes off the letter. I read the letter again. I wondered for how long this had been going on. My thoughts started falling in line with the significance of the letter. Thoughts have a way of arranging themselves into a convincing and credible picture. Everything became clear. Gabby had another woman in his life. He had gone to Yaounde to meet her. In fact, they had arranged to meet there. Maybe the talk of going to Yaounde for work was just a cover for his real reason for going there. Maybe she is an old love, which Gabby keeps in the background. Why had I been so foolish to think that Gabby loved only me? What of the women he had known before knowing me? Has he dropped them? Have they given him up? What about myself? Andrew was still lurking at the periphery of my emotions. J.C. was making an outright attack. I did not know what to think. All that was evident was that I had given up Andrew because of Gabby. A girl may have many boyfriends and eventually marry any of them. But there is always one whom she really likes. This is the one who hurts most. I had gone through that with Andrew and did not want the experience to be repeated. After the hurt there are always memories to fall back on. I liked Andrew but I loved Gabby. I cannot really explain the difference but it seemed to me as if I had jumped from a plane of fantasy to one of reality. I was facing the reality.

Then I thought of Gabby holding that other woman in his arms the way he holds me. We were soon to be married and he treats me this way? My cold reasoning of the previous minutes melted into warm springs of anger like ice cubes in hot water. Gabby could not be doing this to me. Not when I was right there in Douala. The anger was boiling in me. I felt like smashing something. I stood up, looked around, found nothing and flung myself on the bed and burst into tears. I wept. The torment of the thoughts surged from the bottom of my stomach, raked my being and came out in deep mourns and hot tears. My body became hot as I thumped the pillows and tossed about. Exhausted, I fell asleep.

I got up when it was dark. I looked at my watch. It was seven p.m. I had slept for three hours. I lay back on the bed and allowed my thoughts to stray. I did not want to think about anything in particular. But there was one thing fixed in my mind. I was not rushing off to share my grief with Jane. I really needed to sort things out. It was not yet too late to call off the marriage if it became necessary. My thoughts wandered. They settled on Gabby. I pushed them away. I wanted to be objective. But objectivity was not so available to me at that moment. I needed to be calm. I wanted to detach myself from the torments of uncertainty. I wondered whether Gabby was serious about getting married. I remembered that he had wanted to get married to another girl but it had ended in a fiasco. I regretted that I hadn't anything to throw back at Gabby if this situation went too far. As

I thought of other reasons why the letter could have been written I heard a knock at the door. I had not locked the door when I came into the room. I could hear J.C.'s voice in the parlour as he asked whether there was anybody at home and why the door was open and no light in the parlour. I got up quickly and locked the bedroom door while I put on the bedroom light. I told him that I was going to join him soon. I had to act fast else he would have come into the room. He looked like the type of man who could take such liberties. I washed my face in the sink in the bathroom and tidied my appearance. There was not much I could do about my swollen eyes.

"Elisa, you have been crying. What is wrong?" I hated him for mentioning what I wanted to hide from him. I was prepared to tell him that it was the effect of sleep. But the manner in which he had made the statement showed that nothing could change his mind.

"Nothing," I lied.

9

J.C. had brought me to this cabaret as he said to dispel my worries. I had told him that I was worried but in spite of all his persuasions I had not told him what was worrying me. I did not want to go with him to Jane's house. But I did not have any excuse to give so I told him that I was not feeling well. I equally did not want to go out anywhere with him. But the prospect of staying at home after having slept for three hours was very unappealing. He was so insistent on taking me out, promising to be a good boy. He assured me that I was going to enjoy the place to which he wanted to take me and my fever would pass. When left the house no mention was made of where we were going. When he called out our destination to the taxi driver, I did not bother because I was not yet familiar with the city of Douala. But when we arrived at our destination, I became suspicious. A faint sense of fright started building up in me but I pushed it aside. I glanced at J.C.'s profile. He was concentrating on the road ahead while the look of expectancy kept the muscles on his face taut.

I was grateful for his foresight. I did not want to face Jane. In spite of his impulsive attitude, I prepared to enjoy myself. The clinking of glasses, the hum of voices, the instruments standing out with promise of what was to come, and the conversation with J.C. helped to dispel the thoughts clogging my mind. He was telling me about the 'Asiko' dance. It was a spectacle, which I had never witnessed, and he gave me a brief description of what was about to take place. I wondered why Gabby had never brought me here. I was soon to know why.

I did not drink beer that evening for I wanted to stay awake for as long as possible to watch the spectacle. Beer also has the tendency of keeping you ill at ease until you pass it out and I was not sure of the hygienic conditions of the toilets in such places. So I took a small bottle of Coca cola. J.C. tried to talk it out of me but I stood my grounds. When he suggested a shot of whisky, I did not object. He kept me interested by telling me stories about events in Douala. He told me about the nightlife in Douala.

At ten p.m., a man came out from backstage, which was cut off by a thick oxblood red curtain. He went over to the microphone and tested it. Then he went over, lifted his guitar and hit off a few notes. There was a stir in the cabaret as people turned to see if the show was about to begin. He was just whetting the appetite of the audience. The place was now full of men and women. It was clear from the type of women who sat on the various tables that any decent man would not want to bring his wife here. They wore close fitting trousers, which not only accentuated their buttocks, but also their Venus mounds. The plaits on their heads reached their buttocks and some of them had put on outrageously red lipsticks. I gazed with wonder at the scene before me. In the day, anyone passing by would not believe the transformation. Night has a way of concealing the drabness of a place. The dim lights and the suffused colours gave the place a richness it did not deserve. Unless one took time to look closely, one would not notice the faded cloth on the chairs, the paint peeling from the walls and the floor where the red cement was worn away in patches. But who would be occupied with such minute observations when there was so much to occupy one's senses? There was the smell of beer, perfume, and the smell of roasting delicacies, the cacophony of noises, the feeling of expectancy and the warmth of breaths enclosed by the walls.

What attracted me the most were the girls.

I took a sip of my drink. I found out that my Coca cola had more whisky in it than I had put in. J.C. was surely taking advantage of my rapt attention to strengthen my drink. After buying the first shot of whisky, he said it was better to buy a medium size for it would be cheaper. So he bought a medium size whisky, Johnny Walker red label. It had a cloying taste and seeped into my veins. It relaxed them and gave me a sense of well-being. I watched one of the girls closely for some time. She was different from the ones who looked slim. She was dressed in a pair of red jean trousers with a white blouse with straps across her back. Her shape was what interested me before I started watching her movements. The trousers were close fitting, outlining her buttocks and stomach, which seemed to strain against the material. She was heavy busted and the absence of a supporting bra made her breasts look like two balloons. She got up to go out and stopped behind the man with whom she was sitting to whisper something in his ears. His shoulders received the weight of her breasts. As she walked out she was conscious of the stares that followed her and she made good use of this attention by putting more sway in the movements of her buttocks. A strip tease dancer could not have done better. She manoeuvred her way around the chairs with such agility that indicated that she was used to doing it. As she passed by our table her eyes alighted on Jean Claude.

"*Jean Claude! Tu es rare. On ne te vois plus.*" She came over to us talking all the time. She kissed J.C. on both cheeks and then looked at me for sometime before coming to kiss both my cheeks. Her breath, heavy with beer assailed my nostrils and I held my breath until the kissing was over. She pulled out a chair and sat conversing with him in French. I kept myself busy by watching the people in the cabaret but my ears were strained to catch a gist of what they were talking about. Their acquaintance seemed to stretch far back. When she finally left I felt a sense of relief. This woman fascinated me. She looked like a '*débrouillarde*', the type of woman who had learnt to fight for survival because of the adverse conditions she had lived through. I wanted to know more about her. Both of us watched as she swung her buttocks round the tables and walked out. As if on cue we turned to look at each other. From the way she carried herself around and the way she spoke with Jean Claude, I knew she was a prostitute. But there was so much confidence and toughness in her mannerisms that I was intrigued.

"Who is she?" I asked.

Celina was a clever and hardworking girl from the village of Busa in the outskirts of Douala. When she completed primary school she wanted to go to college but her father wanted her to get married. In revolt she had told the father she was not going to get married after leaving primary school. When her father was adamant and negotiations had started for her to marry a man who lived in Douala, she escaped. Her escape was further prompted by the fact that she had not seen the man before negotiations began. When she finally saw the man he was not to her liking. Moreover she never understood the type of job in which this man was engaged in Douala. It was believed in the village that any man who lived in Douala was rich. The man used to come to the village and give expensive things to his relatives so Celina's father thought that if Celina got married to him he would have access to the man's wealth. Although there were gossips about the source of the man's wealth, to the family all that mattered was that he was rich. With the complicity of the aunt who lived in Douala and who promised to send her to college, she escaped to Douala.

Celina had arrived in Douala with the zeal of going to school but her aunt told her that she would only go to school if she helped her raise enough money to cover the expense of her education. So Celina started selling in her on-licensed bar. One year stretched into two then three. During this period her father did everything for her to go and meet her husband. But she resisted. Meanwhile she had also learnt about the dubious dealings in which the man was involved. The aunt was blamed for instigating and supporting her. At the end of the fifth year, Celina had given up all hopes of going to school.

She was introduced at an early age to the delights of a woman's body and charms. It was a thrilling experience and she enjoyed it. The prospect of staying in town became more appealing. But she never forgot that she had to make something of herself. When she became experienced she became a threat to the aunt's business. She had to strike out on her own. She started roasting fish and selling outside a bar. Then alongside selling her fish, she added all the things that were needed by those who frequented nightspots like cigarettes, chewing gum, sweets, etc. She also kept illicit gin hidden away for those who needed it. It was from the sale of the illicit gin that she made her fortune. She now had a provision store, which she controlled in the day, and at night a boy she had hired kept it open while she went back to the trade she knew best. She was building her house in the village and was telling J.C. about the cement she had bought and wanted to transport to the village. She needed his help.

I was on my second bottle of Coca cola. I glanced at my watch and this relayed a message to J.C. He got up and went out. A tray of roasted fish and fried plantains followed his return. He had not asked me whether I wanted to eat or what I would like to eat. But I did not mind the fish. He had the situation under control. He encouraged me to eat and warned me not to look at my watch again because we had a long night ahead of us. The whisky was warming me up and I felt something loosen in me.

The show began at ten thirty. The first musician came on stage amidst loud applause. They struck up a popular tune and played it to the end. They struck up another one. More people were coming into the cabaret and looking for seats. Everybody's attention was now focused on the stage. I ate the last pieces of fish and took some pepper on the last slice of fried plantains. The hot pepper and the whisky was a good blend to keep me awake. J.C. watched as I ate and only took a piece of fish now and then.

Soon the musicians stroke up an 'Asiko' tune. The large curtain parted but nobody appeared. From the edge of the curtain a girl appeared, then two, then three, then four. Four men followed them. They had heavy bands of loincloths round their waists, which increased the girth of their waists making them more fulsome to respond to the twists and turns they were about to perform. The girls had a tight piece of cloth over their breasts but the men were bare-chested. The dancers were well chosen to show the sexuality of the African woman and the virility of the African man. They danced forward and backwards with one hand stretched forward and their heads shaking like that of a cobra about to strike. They wriggled and twisted, coming forward past the musicians down to the empty space between the audience and the dais. They stood in a line facing the audience and bowed. The hitherto silent hall broke into deafening applause. This was soon followed by a fast-paced rhythm, another 'Asiko' dance. The dancers moved on, their waists and stomachs wriggling as if they had no bones in their spines. They danced their way back to the stage where they retreated to the side of the stage while one of the men moved to centre stage. A stool was brought and placed in front of him. He stretched out his left hand, lifted the stool and placed it on his head all the time dancing as if he were not performing any other action apart from dancing. When the stool was balanced on his head he danced up and down the stage shaking his head as if there was nothing there. When he went off stage the crowd applauded.

Next a woman moved forward. A bottle of beer was placed at the middle of the stage. She danced towards it, slowly went down on her knees, picked up the bottle with her mouth, and while gripping the bottle with her knees, she used her mouth to open it. Still dancing she picked up the bottle with her mouth and slowly stood up. She lifted her head and, pointing the bottom of the bottle at the ceiling, she gulped down the beer as she danced. The crowd did not wait for the end to applaud. As she danced and drank they applauded in rhythm with the music. When the bottle was empty she went down on her knees again and put the bottle on the floor. After the woman left centre stage, a man and a woman took over. The rhythm of the music picked up. They faced each other and simulated the peak of sexual orgasm and the crowd applauded hysterically. The dancing continued nonstop. Now a man came in. He was not dressed like the rest of the dancers. He was dressed in typical Douala traditional attire with a white shirt, a loincloth and a bowler hat. He came majestically to the centre of the stage, bowed and started dancing. The crowd went hysterical again. It seemed as if he was the guru of the 'Asiko' dance as the crowd started chanting, "Turbo! Turbo!" He demonstrated a few dance steps then he stopped and waved at the crowd. He came to the edge of the dais and dropped his hat to the floor. He turned round and started dancing away from the hat beckoning it. To my greatest surprise the hat started sliding on the floor following him. The crowd shouted and whistled as he disappeared behind the curtain with his hat after him. It was the end of the show and the hall was filled with a babel of voices.

All I wanted to do was sleep. I was unsteady on my legs and J.C. helped me into the room. I was vaguely aware that I was not in my room. What first came through the fuzziness of my perception was a distinct male smell in the room. But this made no lasting impression. J.C.'s proximity registered more as the natural responses to the sexually stimulating 'Asiko' dance still coursed through my body. I was lying on the bed with feet on the floor trying to ward off the heaviness in my head. J.C. was pulling off my shoes and carrying my legs up to the bed. I felt more comfortable and adjusted myself. I felt his arms go round me. He started kissing my lips, moved to my jaw and ears, then to my neck and chest. I do not know whether I responded to his caresses but I enjoyed the sensation. He unbuttoned my blouse and pulled it off. Next my bra came off. My skirt also came off and he was tugging at my pant. In the recesses of my mind, I thought it was Gabby and let myself go. He was about to plunge between my legs when I came to my senses. I opened my eyes. J.C was poised over me, his eyes closed with desire. I gathered all my strength and pushed him off, jumped off the bed and ran to the bathroom. I closed the door and locked it. I sat on the cover of the toilet seat trembling. Whether I was trembling from anger or unsatisfied desire I could tell but I soon felt a hot choking sensation swelling in me. I became angry with J.C. for taking advantage of me. I was angry at the fact that all his attention and concern for me that evening were just a means to an end.

I had been made to believe in the rewards of friendship. In the company of the three men I had come to know so well, I saw the type of communion that comes out of respect for one another. But now this belief was being destroyed. One's attitude to love and sex can be a binding as well as a dividing force. My attitude to love and sex had taken a dramatic turn when I met Gabby. At first it was just fascination and attraction. But as time passed it grew into something more binding. It was no longer the expectation of an exciting moment to be thought of no more when it was over. What I felt for Gabby was so special that I believed that the bell of time was ringing relentlessly. I had never felt like that towards a man even Andrew. Now J.C. was trying to destroy it all. His destruction was multi-faceted. He was destroying the fact that man can be true to himself. He was making me believe the dictum that birds of a feather flock together. Was he trying to balance up what Gabby was doing? Did he know more about what was happening with Gabby than I did? These questions flashed through my mind. Although he had done and insinuated that he was interested in me, I took no notice believing that he could not do such a thing to his friend. Even if his love was genuine, it was already tainted because he knew what existed between Gabby and me and how far we had gone. He was just being egocentric. Worst of all he was not only making me miserable, but he wanted to leave a load on my conscience.

I had never taken him seriously when he complimented me on my appearance. I thought it was just a way of flattering me. Although he was not yet married he looked like a married man. His whole person belied what he was. We usually joked about his single status and he took this good-naturedly. Whenever he was in our company there was always a vacuum, which he was in no hurry to fill. Benny was the first to get married. Gabby was following suit. But J.C. was taking his time. He always said he had not yet met the right woman.

J.C. was a peculiar person. Many times I looked closely at him but never understood what made him tick. He seemed not to be passionate about anything. He hardly expressed his views in a clear manner. They were always shrouded in maybes and perhaps. One thing that also struck me was that he always wanted to be in the forefront of every activity. He always wanted to help out. He spent money freely but on the contrary he was not the type of man who had girlfriends round every corner. Sometimes he invited some girls when we went out with him. But these occasions were rare and widely spaced. What intrigued me was that none of them stayed with him for long. He just enjoyed our company. Underneath all this display of *joie de vivre* I saw fear of responsibility, of being tied down to anything or anybody. He had the qualities that would easily attract a partner. J.C. was a handsome man. He earned a good salary and was a likely prey to women. How he managed to avoid them, I could not tell. He dressed well and always looked smart. Although he had a wide range of girls to choose from, I noticed that he preferred the company of married women. I am sure it gave him great pleasure to see other people's wives make a fuss over him. He was cutting the picture of a real Don Juan. Marriage would limit his exploits or even expose them. He was contented with what he was getting. Satisfaction without responsibility appealed to some men and I think J.C. fell in this category. He was also smart at turning a situation to his own advantage.

I sat there thinking about the note I had found in Gabby's coat pocket. What if there was nothing to it? Would I ever have forgiven myself if J.C. had had his way? Would I take revenge in this manner if I ever caught Gabby with another woman? Was it worth the love I had for Gabby? I then realized how love could be agony. It agonized over things that had not yet happened. The agony over possibilities that could be avoided was tormenting me. I dreaded things that were in the distant future but which the mind could take and make concrete through contemplation and precipitated action.

A loud banging at the door brought me back to the present. J.C. was calling and pleading with me to open the door. My concern at what could have happened gave way to shame. What explanation was I going to give J.C. if he started to mock me in his usual infuriating manner? What was I going to say? How was I going to face him naked when I opened the door? I burst into tears. I sobbed into my palms as I covered my face with them. The tears bore all the pain of disappointment that had clogged my life. It was the pain of longing that had been part of my life until I made the trip to Douala. It was the pain of expectation that had died out. It was the pain of hope that was being stifled. Worst of all, it was the pain of confusion, fear, uncertainty and disillusionment. I allowed the tears to flow. As they flowed they cleared the muck in my head.

I could hear J.C. pacing the room, intermittently knocking at the door and calling me to open the door. I wiped my eyes and looked round. The situation was incredible. Here I was, sitting in a locked toilet weeping for what I could not tell. Only ten hours after parting from Gabby I was already in a fix. I wondered at the surprises and complexities life offers us, which we sometimes consider little but which can have grave consequences. These surprises carry us downhill while we are occupied with our little worlds. When we touch bottom then our eyes open and we start groping uphill. But by then we are so exhausted that there is no more strength to recapture what has been lost. Then we say it is destiny.

What would Gabby do if he found me in such circumstances? What would he do to J.C.? When I thought of how Benny and Jane would react, I felt a sinking sensation in my stomach. From these reflections I knew that I could stand my ground with Gabby but would not want to destroy my relationship with Benny and Jane. What would they think of me? I shuddered at the thought. Goose bumps covered my arms. My body was now aware of the temperature of the room. The bathroom window was open and the cold air of the morning was drifting in. Goose bumps were now acting as a buffer for the cold as I drifted from the thought that had made me shudder to the welfare of my body. As I hugged myself and crouched over, there was some more warmth where my chin and my arms came in contact with my stomach and knees. The exhaling of breath from my nose kept up a stream of warm breath between my breasts. My toes were twitching in reaction to the cold tiles on the floor. My hair was in disarray.

J.C. was quiet now. I wondered what he was doing or thinking about. I called to him to bring my dresses to the door. I was prepared to slam the door in his face if he tried to push his way in. I hoped that by then he would be as sober as I was. He handed the dresses over to me in silence. I dressed quickly but could not bring myself to open the door. I sat back on the toilet seat wondering how to get home. I looked at my watch. It was three thirty in the morning. J.C. knocked at the door again. I got up and opened the door and walked passed him without looking at him. But I noticed that he too was dressed, not in his pyjamas but in the shirt and trousers he had worn. I slumped on the sofa and pretended to settle till morning. He came and sat by me. He could not understand why I had behaved that way and was trying to get an explanation from me. Could he not understand that I had a mind of my own and was able to determine what was good for me in spite of the whisky I had drunk? But how could he? When all he wanted was sexual gratification without a thought about its repercussions? It was just one of his exploits, which would soon be forgotten. But for me it wasn't. It would have been a load on my conscience. It would have been a weight on my future.

In a court of law the basis of the prosecutor and defendant's arguments would have been interesting. It could have been based on assumptions which had to be proven not by the facts of the situation but on the intentions and how the participants felt. It also could have been based on a series of 'ifs'. If she had not allowed herself to be seduced, he would not have gone that far. If she did not trust him she would not have accepted his invitation. And the argument would go on and on. Whatever verdict is pronounced in the end would not reflect the truth because the truth lay deep down in the heart of the accused and the defendant. These are the truths that are not easily said, sometimes never. Some of these situations are caused by the influence of the ego of the individual, what they think of themselves and what they think they are capable of doing.

You know there are some men who think that because a woman is nice to them she has fallen in love with them. Some think that they are so handsome that no woman can resist them. Some think that money can get any woman for them. Yet others think that a woman acting on the impulse of a rebound would give herself to any man who happens to come along as revenge. I think that J.C. hadn't any of these in mind. He was just taking advantage of a situation. He might have loved me genuinely but decency in friendship requires that you respect what belongs to your friend. For what is friendship but the acceptance of another person who has no blood relationship with you as an integral part of yourself, someone with whom you can afford to be yourself and from whom you expect honesty. Is it not often said that a good friend is better than a bad brother?

I felt that J.C. had betrayed his friend. I saw the trio breaking up if this ever got out. I imagined the unpleasantness that would exist between them. How would Benny and Gabby react to J.C. having by necessity of service to see each other on a daily basis? I looked at J.C. to see whether he was thinking along the same lines. He was not. His face showed resignation but there was a weight of disappointment on the curvature of his mouth. He was speaking again. I was not attentive to what he was saying and tried to fix my mind on other thoughts to drown his words but I heard them all the same.

He was not even trying to excuse himself or ask for forgiveness. He kept hammering on the fact that he had acted out of the love he had for me. But I was grateful for one thing. He did not mock me by telling me that I had behaved like a teenager, or the more annoying statement, which implies that women think that their husbands are as faithful as they are. He kept up the monologue until he said that if I wanted to go home he was ready to escort me home. I jumped at this opportunity and declared that I was ready to go home. I dared not mention it before, fearing that he would say that if I wanted to go home I could do so, knowing full well that I couldn't go alone. I did not want to expose myself to such ridicule.

The fear of being attacked by thieves was overcome by the fear of Benny coming early in the morning to check on me and not finding me in.

Was that what J.C. had in mind? Did he think he could keep me till daybreak thus raising suspicions about my whereabouts? Did he know about Gabby's plans concerning his trip to Yaounde? Was this a well planned move by J.C. to get me and if possible for good? Was J.C. serious or just a home breaker? Whatever he was, morning was not going to meet me in his house. I hadn't the nerve to fabricate a convincing story. I was sure that whatever I said would leave a question mark on my whereabouts that night. I wanted it to die a natural death between J.C. and me

I wanted to forget the events of the night. But how could I forget the excitement at the cabaret, the thrill of skilful dancing, and the warmth of the whisky as it slid down my neck and the total ambience in the cabaret? I did not want Jane to know. I could not trust myself not to mention it inadvertently in the course of conversation with her. I also had to avoid J.C. at all costs. I could not pretend in his presence. My actions would immediately raise questions. How could I laugh and joke with him as I used to do when the memories of what he had tried to do to me were still on my mind? I was also uncertain of how he would react in my presence, for guilt cannot be concealed for long. I wanted it to be one of those locked away secrets that people look at now and again in privacy. I had to go away.

I got up after a short sleep feeling tired and with a headache. There was a dry taste in my mouth and a feeling of nausea. I felt thirsty but did not feel like drinking water. I lay back on my bed wondering why I had not given J.C. a piece of my mind by telling him exactly who I thought he was. I could only do this when I was safe in my own house. But I hadn't the strength to do so. All I could do was to thank him. I had made my thanks to sound sarcastic. He had looked at me for some time and walked out without a word.

By eight o'clock I had already bathed and packed my things. I was arranging the sheets on the bed when I heard the sound of Benny's car at the door. Just as I had imagined, he had come to check on me. I thought of what to tell him as I went out to meet him. But his first remarks gave me an opening.

"Lizzy, I see you are going back to Bamenda." I looked at my bag and was grateful that I had kept it in the parlour.

"Yes. I think I should go back."

"Did you take this decision after Gabby had left or he knows about your going back today?"

"We did not discuss anything about it, but I know that Gabby will not mind."

The way Benny looked at me indicated that he was not convinced.

"But I would like you to stay. Jane is expecting you. She has been worried about you all night, wondering what you are doing all alone in the house."

"Benny, you and Jane have been so good to me. You have helped me a lot. I have to start facing my situations alone."

"What situations do you have to face?" I was not convincing Benny, but with the events of the previous night, I had to stand my grounds. "I do not have to come running to you people each time Gabby is not around."

"You are right. After a pause, I am going to work. I just came to see whether you are all right. But are you not going to tell Jane that you are going away? She is waiting for you."

"I am sorry, Benny. I want to arrive in Bamenda in the day. Give my love to the baby and the mother." I sounded so distant that Benny had no choice but to let me do as I wished.

"All right, let me take you to the bus stop."

I could not believe what I had done. I could not believe that I was really in a bus going back to Bamenda without Gabby's knowledge. I had lied to Benny. Maybe I should have told him the truth about what had happened. How was I going to tell him? There was no real reason why I had decided to stay on my own that evening. At least to Benny there wasn't a reason. On the other hand, he might have been in the know of what was going on. Then he would have told me a story to cover his friend. Telling Benny would have meant hiding some of the facts. I might even be made to look silly with my unfounded suspicions. My heart surged as I remembered the letter, which I had found in Gabby's pocket. More burning thoughts raced through my mind. I was ready to give rein to the anger that laid deep in me and which I had tried to keep down with various reasoning. I thought these reasons would make me feel better and give me a genuine reason for going away. I smiled when I thought of the expression that would be on Gabby's face when he came back and discovered that I had gone without leaving even a note. I included Benny in this picture because I believed that he was not completely innocent. They were up to something. Their unexplained absence that afternoon still hung over me like suffocating smoke.

When I thought of Jane's reaction to my sudden departure, I felt uncomfortable. Motherhood had mellowed her. I imagined her looking at me with what can be described as a certain serenity of eye and comfortableness of face, not allowing what she was hearing to register on her face the way I had expected it to. I became angrier when I realized that Jane was drifting away from me. I could have rushed to her with my fears. But I couldn't. I felt cut off and betrayed. My anger now had a line to hang on. Gabby, Benny and Jane had betrayed me. What was there for me to look forward to? It was not too late to call off the marriage. It seemed as if the trend was repeating itself. But this time I was not going to allow myself to be taken for granted. I wanted to find out if Gabby wanted me as much as I wanted him. I was once more doubtful on how successful my marriage with Gabby was going to be. Was it going to always be on such shaky grounds? Was I ever going to be certain of Gabby's love? Why did such situations arise to darken the light shining in my heart? This was the second time I had had reason to be angry with Gabby. But this time I had no patience or reason to stay and find out. It looked like a pattern that was repeating itself. This time there was no ring to put the blame on. There was nothing to fling back at him in anger. My anger fed on my suspicions and I was happy I was going away. But what I was actually doing was only going away from Gabby. I was not moving out of his life.

Is it departures like this one that give us time to cool down and give reason a chance? What was there to reason out if all the evidence bore some credibility, which I thought it did? Was this the type of game we were going to play all our lives? I was not ready for this. I was not strong enough for it. I could not bear to be used, betrayed and taken for granted. But I wanted Gabby. I wanted him to be part of my life. I wanted to share my life with him. I wanted to be committed to my decision in marrying him. But the mental and emotional agony that trailed our relationship was breeding doubts in my mind. First there were Gabby's accusations about my boss dating me and then the story from Martha, which almost ruptured our relationship. Our outpouring and reconciliation had ushered in a period of confidence and assurance. Now the letter I had found in Gabby's pocket and Gabby's strange behaviour had thrown my mind into confusion again. J.C.'s attempt to seduce me had created an offshoot of a major problem, which still had to be solved.

As I ruminated on these thoughts my anger increased. I was angry with Gabby. I was angry with myself for being such a fool. For the first time I really envied Jane and in the light of my present predicament saw their disagreement over where she should give birth as a minor issue. I felt I was most unlucky. Then the thought of calling off the marriage came strong into my mind. It was better to be single and happy than to be married and unhappy. This thought was like a sudden illumination. In my total confusion, frustration and anger I did not think that this was a way out. Now it looked so appealing. What arrested my thoughts in mid stride was not what the consequences of my decision would provoke but what would be left for me to look forward to. To me life has to be fulfilling. It must have an aspect on which you can fall back if all else fails.

Gabby was failing me. Who or what else was I to turn to? For the first time I earnestly called on God to help me make the right decision. I often went to church but never took the sermons seriously. It was more an occasion to meet friends. But as I lay back in the bus and closed my eyes, allowing the wind to blow into my face as the bus sped towards Bamenda, I felt a sudden need for support. But I was not sure where it would come from. A sudden calmness overcame me as the coolness of the breeze seeped into my head, soothing the ache on my temples that had accompanied the ache in my heart. Although the ache in my head continued, the throbbing in my heart ceased. I dozed off for some time. The bus sped on as its wheels ate up the kilometres, the road curling away behind us like the tail of a disappearing snake.

I arrived at my house feeling tired and dejected. When I opened the door the smell of stale air assaulted me and increased my sense of dejection. It was not a welcoming smell. The two rooms were quiet and even the sounds from outside were locked out. I wondered whether it was not my mind that was locked in. I stood at the threshold trying to adjust to this new sensation. I had to adjust because after successfully pushing to the back of my mind the thoughts that had been bothering me, I expected to find solace in my house. But standing in my parlour now and looking about as if I was not sure I was in the right room made me aware of how stupid I had been. How did I imagine that I could escape from what dominated my conscious as well as my unconscious mind? The silence in the room radiated this. It seemed to say there is no comfort for you here. I felt so strange standing there undecided as to what to do next. It was not only the desire for physical motion to make me move ahead but also an emotional one to get me out of the muddle in which I found myself. There was no peace in my decision. I had made things worse. I could have stayed back and sorted things out with Gabby before coming back to Bamenda. That would have been better than escaping from a situation that I knew clung to me wherever I went. What was I going to tell Pa Martin if he came to visit? He was bound to notice that there was something wrong as soon as he saw me. He had the habit of looking intensely into my eyes each time he visited me. When I thought of this I prayed that he would not visit me until I had arrived at a decision or worked out a plan on how I was going to handle the situation. I needed this to act as an armour to deal with whatever unpleasantness would arise, especially as far as Pa Martin was concerned. I was not good at pretence but once I had made up my mind it became a conviction.

As I unpacked my things, I kept examining and re-examining the events of the previous days and thinking of the most appropriate manner of handling the present situation. I rehearsed in my mind the scene that would take place if Pa Martin came to visit. That was my immediate concern. I had the words well chosen, but these were all responses only to some vague form of questions.

After unpacking I lay down on my bed to rest. Immediately Gabby's face flashed across my mind and memories of the night he had spent on that bed came flooding back threatening to drown me in the sweet sensations they evoked. I struggled with them trying to push them away. I did not want them to mellow the idea that was already forming in my mind. I soon dozed off into a restless sleep. My nerves were too taut to allow me to relax and sleep peacefully. The coolness of the room, the cold sheets on the bed and the quietness of the room did not have any effect on my tensed psychology and in this mood it conjured up all sorts of bizarre situations. In my sleep I kept fighting with one phantom or the other. At one moment it was a cow chasing me and Gabby blocked the only outlet through which I could escape. He was standing with his arms folded across his chest watching me run round and round with the cow after me. The smile on his face made it appear as if he was not aware of the fact that he was blocking the only exit open to me and was just waiting for me to tire out. I screamed when I realized I could not escape. As the sound of my voice echoed and re-echoed in the walls of my mind, it seemed as if the walls, which enclosed me, were crashing down. The crashing sound soon dwindled to a constant knocking. I woke with a start and realized that the sound was coming from the door. I waited for some time for the person to give up and go away. I was not in any state to receive any person especially Pa Martin who could come to my house anytime he wanted. But the sound of the knocking continued.

I had taken off my clothes, which were damp with sweat and tied a loincloth round my chest. I had also taken off my bra and had nothing underneath except my inner wear. When I got up I did not put on any dress. I went to open the door with the intention that my attire and appearance would discourage any visitor who intended staying for long. When I opened the door there was Andrew smiling at me with relief on his face. He was the last person I wanted to see.

The sun made its presence felt as its last rays illuminated the skies, giving the earth the glow of dusk. I had not yet put on the light in my sitting room and it was in darkness. Andrew was still outside and I had not said a word even to invite him in. Then I regained my composure and stepped aside for him to come into the room. He walked passed me into the room, the smile vanishing from his face. He looked round uncertainly before sitting down. For a moment he looked as if he had just realized that he had made a mistake and did not know how to correct himself. Then he sort of gathered himself together and smiled again.

"I was passing to town in a taxi and saw you alighting from another. I have been to your office two times and each time I was told that you were out of town. So when I saw you I was sure that you were just arriving and did not want to miss the opportunity to see you."

All this while, I said nothing. I turned to go into my room to get dressed. I was not angry at his presence but I was not pleased at the timing of his visit. Yet I did not want him to feel unwelcome. So I had to do or say something to make him feel at ease.

"Please excuse me for one minute. I will be right back."

"Elizabeth, I hope that you are not angry with me." I was taken aback by his response and I stopped to look back at him.

"Why do you say that?"

"A moment ago you looked as if you were going to throw me out of your house." I laughed. He too laughed and made as if he wanted to say something then thought against it.

"I am just tired, Andy. If I do not talk it does not mean that I am throwing you out of my house."

"I know that I am intruding, but I could not go back home without seeing you." I waited for him to continue and made up my mind that if he had come to talk me back into his affections or about any other man in my life, I would really throw him out with my silence.

"But if you are too tired to talk, then I will go away. But I will be back before the week ends."

I realized there was something on his mind and I decided to get it out. "No, I am not too tired to listen. While I am listening, I will be resting as well."

He launched into his thoughts. "Elizabeth, you know how much I care about you." These opening lines brought me back to the defensive. I prepared myself to listen to him but not allow myself to be affected by what he would say. He continued, "Since I came back I have not been able to get over the fact that we cannot begin afresh. I have not come to bother you with this, but I have been thinking about you from the point of view of what I thought you were going to be. There is something wrong, Elizabeth. What is it?"

I wondered where he was heading. His question was so ambiguous that I did not know what answer he expected from me. He knew that I had a fiancé but I convinced myself that he would not expect me to talk about him. I had to be sure of what he was talking about.

"What do you mean? I do not understand your question."

"I am talking about those aspirations we used to talk about so much back at school. What is happening to you?" How could I answer such a question? I was tempted to treat his question lightly and throw it back at him. I even wanted to tell him that the opportunities opened to him where not open to me. But I maintained my silence. I remembered how he used to be hurt when I drew attention to the fact that he came from a rich family. I was also becoming curious to know what was on his mind.

"I am just living my life, Andy. What did you expect me to be?"

"Have you no ambition, Elizabeth? Are you satisfied with who you are?"

"I cannot change from being the type of person I am."

"I mean what you are," he corrected.

"This is the best I could get."

"Are you satisfied with it?"

"Please, Andy, I am not in a court of law to answer questions on what I have done with my life. It is no business of yours to probe into it."

I could not believe the vehemence in my voice. It took both of us by surprise. We sat quiet for some time. I was about to apologize for my outburst when he started speaking again. His voice sounded as if things had not turned out the way he wanted. And indeed they had not as far as I was concerned.

"I am sorry, Elizabeth. I am sorry at the way I am probing into your life. It is no business of mine, but I am concerned about you."

"I appreciate your concern but I do not want us to talk about me."

"I want us to talk about us."

"I am sorry, Andy. We cannot talk about us. Us is in the past. We have since gone our separate ways. Putting back the clock would be a difficult thing to do."

"I do not mean us in the future but us in the past. The present is still as vague as air. I want us to talk about our dreams, those clean ideas we used to believe in."

"What makes you call them clean?" I looked at Andrew and the words he had once said to me while we were in high school came back to me. (We all have our dreams and until you identify yours and make it a reality then your life is just a waste.)

"They were so pure, so innocent and believed in with such fervour. At that time they looked so possible."

"What about now? I asked just to hear what he was going to say."

"That is what I want to find out."

"From me? What about you?"

He did not seem to have heard my question and continued.

"I know you want to get married. I thought we would together make our dreams a reality." Andrew had specialized in Medical Engineering, but with the existing trend in the economy in Cameroon I did not see him getting a lucrative job.

"What about you, Andy? Without me you can still make your dream a reality."

"Of course."

"How?"

"I do not want to go into an explanation. For now all I can do is go back to England and get a job with a construction company. Then I can either work in Britain or one of the commonwealth countries. Then I will be sure of where I stand."

"How could I have fit in this grand design of yours?"

"Elizabeth, you are laughing at me now. But if you had not forgotten about me you could have seen how you fit in."

"What about marriage? Are you not going to settle down and raise a family?"

"I have thought about that as well. But for now I want to consider other things first. If I have to raise a family it would not be here. But that is not what I came here to discuss. I might not have another chance. I got the message from the old man I met here the last time I came visiting. Are you sure that marriage is what you want?"

The turn of the conversation took me unawares and I was about to act off with an angry protest, but Andy cut me off.

"I know that marriage should be an essential part of our lives. To me it is not all. It is important but not all consuming. You should have something of your own, something to fill that longing in you, something on which to exercise your creative energy. I can remember how you used to talk about that in school. Don't let it die, Elizabeth. Don't let it be crushed out of existence. Think about it, Elizabeth. I know that you are capable of doing it for yourself. Go on and think about it."

I was almost making sense of what Andy was saying but in the circumstances it looked so odd. I was surprised at him. I could not believe that this was the same Andy who had come back with the hope of renewing our relationship, who even hinted at marriage and who looked so disappointed when I told him that there was another man in my life. What was he after? I wondered. He could not have so quickly swallowed his disappointment.

He sat and looked at me as if he wanted to see the effect of his words on me. I could not look at him in the face for fear he could see my confusion. I did not want to hurt him. Before Gabby came into my life, Andy had held a special place, though he was so far away. I could not completely get rid of this fact. I did not want to for his words that day were going to affect my life in a special way. But for the moment, I saw no reason for this lecture except for the fact that he had not really gotten over his disappointment. There was something he was trying to get across to me. Each time I tried to dwell on it, another thought immediately replaced it until I decided just to listen to him and not try to puzzle out what he was after. I wanted the conversation to die out. I did not want it to seem as if I was sending him away. If he had nothing more to say he would take his leave. But he changed the topic suddenly.

"How was your stay in Douala?"

"It was nice."

"That is a vague answer. Tell me about it."

"Do you want me to fill you in on the details? Do you really want to know?"

"If you want to tell me, I would not object to listening." At that moment I had an eerie desire to tell him a bit of what had happened. This was not because I expected any response from him but to see how he would react. I wanted to probe the depth of his feeling for me. Then I realized that it was a stupid thing to do. If nothing had happened I could have easily fabricated a story to see how he was going to respond and whatever question he was going to ask. But something had actually happened and I could not tell the truth and support it with lies.

"I do not think it is important for you to know. It would not help either of us."

Then I used his tactic of changing the topic of conversation.

"Let me bring you something to drink. I have just come back and there is no food in the house."

"I am okay. I just wanted to talk with you. I hope you have understood what I have been trying to tell you."

He was on his feet but I kept to my seat wondering whether I should really get up. I wanted to get to the bottom of what was on his mind. Suddenly I wanted him to stay. I had a strong urge to question him further. I wanted to ask him the question that had been forming in my mind as he spoke. I did not ask these questions as he spoke because I did not want to give him the impression that what he was saying meant anything to me. But as he stood and waited for me to accompany him to the roadside, it dawned on me that he really was saying something.

Gripped by this new realization I blurted out, "Andrew, I hope you will visit me again. I want us to talk again."

"Really, Elizabeth? You want me to come to your house again? I thought it was out of bounds. I was just taking a risk today. I would not want to meet your chevalier again. But if you say so, I will come."

We moved to the roadside. It was quite dark now and the street was filled with shopkeepers from the main market along Commercial Avenue. Those who could afford a ride in a taxi shouted greetings to their friends who were going home on foot. The lights from the taxis intermittently illuminated our faces and during one of these brief flashes of light I looked at Andrew's face. He was intent on watching out for a not yet full taxi to take him home, but his attention was constantly diverted by what was going on, on the street.

Sonac Street at this time of the evening usually presented a panoramic view, as its almost half a kilometre of straight road was a chimera of constantly changing shades, light and sound. A group of dancers coming back from a funeral celebration filled the street and their songs, laughter and unruly behaviour impeded the smooth flow of traffic. This in turn made movement on foot perilous as pedestrians avoided the group by cutting in front of taxis. The normal heartbeat of the street increased as impatient taxi men blared their horns and hurled abuses and curses at the dancers who in turn hurled abuses back at them. At one moment the taxis came to a standstill as the dancers had to cut across the road to go into the Ntamulung neighbourhood. The din was deafening, but there was nothing anyone could do about it. When the group of dancers passed by us there was a crush of human bodies and I was thrown against Andrew. Instantly his arms went round me. He pressed me to his side while he watched the constantly shifting mass of people.

"This is what I have missed all these years." I was startled at his statement. For a moment I was afraid that he was getting emotional because he was holding me so intimately. I looked at his face and heaved a sigh of relief. His gaze held a glint of excitement and wonder as he looked at the mass of humanity, which could best have been described by a tourist as picturesque.

I was not thinking of what was happening around me. I was trying to decide whether he was harmless enough for me to allow him to visit me again.

"I would like you to visit me again," I said as we parted. It was the second time that evening that I was inviting him to my house.

"Really, you want me to come?"

"Yes."

"Why?"

He might have thought that I had a special reason for inviting him. My reason might not have been what was on his mind. In spite of all I liked his company.

"Are you not still my friend? Is our friendship over?"

He hesitated before responding. "If you want me to come, I will come."

Three days later, I received a call from Jane. She tried to find out what had happened to make me leave Douala without informing her. I had to make up a plausible lie. I told her that I had promised to visit Pa Martin on Saturday and I had left Bamenda without telling him. So I had to come back. More to that, if I stayed I had just one day to be with Gabby before coming back, so there was no use staying. She was silent at my excuse and I hoped she believed me. To break the silence I asked how Gabby was doing. She narrated what had happened when he came back.

Gabby came back from Yaoundé on Thursday evening. A cold empty house welcomed him. He could not understand what was happening because he thought I was waiting for him. When he saw the letter I had taken from his coat on the bed he could not immediately connect it to my disappearance. He rushed over to Benny's house. Benny was not in. Jane told him that I had returned to Bamenda.

He had walked into the sitting room with all confidence expecting to see me. When he was told that I had gone back to Bamenda, he sagged into a nearby chair as if all energy had been sapped out of him. He tried to find out from Jane why I had left without telling even Jane. But she had no answer to give him because there was none.

Gabby sat on the chair and waited for Benny's return. He was tired and worried. Jane watched him closely and decided not to ask any questions. She did not ask because apart from his tired looking appearance there was all evidence that something had happened and she would soon know. But when Benny came back and found Gabby waiting for him, looking tired and still in his travel creased shirt, he suggested they go to his house so he could change his clothes, for he looked like a night watchman who had just come back from work. Then they would talk. They all laughed at this comparison and the two men went out. Jane never knew what had happened and when she tried to find out Benny told her categorically that nothing was wrong.

On Saturday I went to the market and bought food for the week. I was in the kitchen preparing lunch. Andrew had come soon after I returned from the market and we talked as I worked. He was telling me the story of what happened when he went to the village soon after his return from London. We were roaring with laughter when there was a knock on the door. I immediately imagined it was Gabby and my blood began to race. I did not want whatever confrontation was going to take place to have Andrew as a witness. I prepared myself to water down whatever animosity would arise especially as Gabby had never met Andrew. I put a bright smile on my face and walked to the door, but before I got there Gabby opened it and walked in. I was half way through the sitting room and we met in the centre. I took his travelling bag and wished him welcome. He did not answer. His eyes were focused on Andrew.

At that moment a strange thought came into my mind. I wanted to see how Gabby would react to Andrew's presence so I walked into the bedroom with his bag without making any introductions. In the bedroom I sat down on the bed and thought of what to do. No coherent trend of action came to my mind although I had planned what to say when he came. A frown creased my face and my heart was fluttering at Gabby's presence, but I am sure it fluttered more because of my confusion. All I could do was allow the events to develop in whatever direction, but I was prepared for and alert to whatever unpleasantness might arise. There was no sound from the sitting room and I could not imagine what was going on. Before I came out I parted the door blind to see what was going on. Andrew was staring through the window. Although his attention was focused on some clouds in the sky drifting westwards, his whole being was alert to the presence of the man sitting opposite him. Gabby was looking intensely at Andrew whose face was turned away and only his profile received the intensity of Gabby's eyes. The scowl on his face made his tension more evident. There was an underlying touch of inquisitiveness on Gabby's face and when this overcame the scowl, he looked more intrigued than angry. The muscles on his face became more relaxed. I am sure he was just waiting to hear what explanation I was going to give regarding Andrew's presence in my house. Andrew on the other hand became tenser as the minutes ticked by. When I appeared both men turned towards me as if an unseen mechanism had triggered their movement. Andrew quickly turned his eyes back to the window. Gabby was looking directly at me. The smile was back on my face and I came and sat next to Gabby. I immediately felt it was two against one from our position. Andrew did not seem to be part of it. He was as innocent as he looked.

"Welcome, Gabby. This is Andrew. Andrew, this is Gabby, my fiancé. I am sure you two have never met." I turned to Gabby. "Andrew was my classmate in high school. He came back from London three weeks ago. He's an engineer."

This just came out of my mouth. I did not know how Andrew would take this. I waited for him to correct me but he did not. I had wanted something simple enough for us to talk about. My good intention backfired. Andrew looked at me with a momentary fleet of confusion, then he smiled and looked away. He might have thought I was playing a game. Gabby looked at him as if he were seeing him in a different light. It was a sort of curiosity, which I could not decipher. It was neither condescension nor admiration.

As if to interrupt my introduction, the water that I had kept on the fire to prepare the corn-fufu boiled over, making a hissing sound as it put out the flames of the cooker. Before I rushed into the kitchen, I pleaded with

161

Andrew using my eyes not to make the situation more difficult for me than it already was. At my look he smiled at Gabby and extended his hand in greeting. Gabby hesitated before taking it. I saw this as I entered the kitchen and was relieved. Not to allow this gesture of Andrew's to die out I called out to them.

"Lunch will soon be ready. Just make yourself comfortable."

I lit the other gas spout and poured in the corn flour. As I stirred my ears were tuned to the talking going on in the sitting room. Gabby was asking Andrew questions as if it were an interview. I could sense the tension in his voice. His curiosity had gotten the better of him but he was not relaxed enough to be conversational.

When the paste was smooth enough I added more water and left it to simmer. Then I moved to the angle of the kitchen where I could see Andrew and made gestures for him to be patient. This was not necessary for I soon realized that he understood the situation and was handling it well. Gabby's was the righteous anger of a man who meets another man in his fiancée's house. While the corn-fufu simmered, I avoided going into the living room. My presence might disturb the almost relaxed atmosphere building up in the silence between them. If I went into the sitting room who was I going to pay attention to? Gabby or Andrew? There was no common topic the three of us could talk about. If I spoke with Andrew it would seem as if I were ignoring Gabby. If I spoke with Gabby it would seem as if I were trying to cover up. For it was certain that the three of us being together in the same room was abnormal. If the atmosphere continued to be strained, the situation was going to be unpredictable because in a tense atmosphere the mind is trapped by unanswered questions.

As I served the food on the table, I flashed a smile at Gabby, then at Andrew. Andrew smiled back but Gabby looked uninterested in my smile. Andrew was now really enjoying the situation and although I was grateful at his amicable disposition, I did not like it. It looked as if we were having fun at Gabby's expense and in such a situation Gabby might suspect anything. I took the smile off my face. It was not difficult to do so because keeping up this façade of a smile was already telling on my facial nerves. I felt relieved when my face relaxed and assumed its normal contours.

I had prepared Gabby's favourite meal of corn-fufu and huckleberry. I knew that he was going to enjoy it and this cheered me up a bit. As we ate I made light conversation to ease our appetites, for in spite of the fact that the food was delicious, the circumstances were such to make one lose one's appetite. They were not in a talking mood as their fingers lifted the food to their mouths, so I stopped talking and tried to concentrate on the food in front of me. I could not. The tension between the two men affected me, as I was the cause of their antagonistic feelings and the focus of their attention. Between the act of putting small lumps of corn-fufu and vegetable into my mouth, I looked at the men. I tried to decipher what each of them saw in me, for they were definitely attracted by different aspects of me. Since Andrew's return he had never invited me out. I think it was the knowledge of my engagement that prevented him from doing so. He was very calm. His attitude towards me was more of caution than cordiality. Gabby on the other hand was so vibrant. He got as much out of life as he could. Andrew had plans and dreams, which he believed he had to carry out. On these grounds I had to agree with him. But there was something irresistible about Gabby. As I looked at the two men, something fell into place. I saw what each of them was offering me. Andrew's advice during his last visit made sense at that moment. I then understood the nagging thoughts that had thrown me into such doubts. Andrew had suggested something, which I had to work out for myself to complete the other half of myself. I needed something to act as a buffer to the emotional and psychological turmoil that was sure to characterize my life, something to act as a refuge. With this realization I made up my mind to pursue the seed, which Andrew had sown in my mind.

Both men ate heartily and I prayed that Andrew should leave as soon as possible. All through the meal Gabby did not utter a word. He concentrated on his food. Each time he lifted up his head I looked at his countenance trying to find out what was going on in his mind. But his face was a blank. It was like the face of someone sitting in a waiting room, just tolerating the presence of those around him while waiting to go in and find out the solution to an incomprehensible problem.

At the end of the meal I offered to send for drinks, but Andrew declined. It was just a manner of being polite but deep in my heart I wanted Andrew to go. So when he declined, I shrugged and made as if the decision was all his. Gabby also declined the drink. Andrew stood up to go and turned to Gabby.

"Please have your drink. I hope I have not been in the way. I am taking my leave." Gabby did not respond. I was angry. I then understood why all along Andrew had such a contented look on his face. He was just waiting for the right moment to throw in his poisoned dart. We were both silent as Andrew made his way to the door. I could not move from where I was standing. I watched Andrew leave the room. Gabby was beating a tattoo with his fingers on the table. I moved over to one of the chairs and without looking at Gabby I sat down. I felt a bit guilty. But when I remembered that before leaving Douala I had spread out a letter on the bed for him to see as soon as he came in, this little nagging guilt disappeared and I sat waiting for Gabby to speak. If there was going to be any explanation, then he would be the one to begin. Gabby was still sitting at the dining table while I sat on one of the sitting room chairs. We could only bridge the physical and psychological distances between us by one of us speaking first. I was definitely not going to be the one.

Without turning round and without stopping his tattooing he asked, "So this is how you want to retaliate?"

I almost burst out laughing. It had not occurred to me that he would look at Andrew's presence in my house as a way of retaliation. It sounded so ridiculous that for a moment I did not know what to say. No answer could have sounded convincing either to Gabby or myself. If I said 'yes' I would be lying. If I said 'no' it would sound as if I was being on the defensive.

So I said, "Andrew is just a friend."

"What was he doing here on the day I arrived?"

"He was just visiting. He did not plan his visit to coincide with your arrival nor did I."

"So you are telling me that you did not imagine that I would be here this weekend."

The conversation was turning into an inquiry and I did not want to be led into any explanation. I was supposed to be the aggrieved party but he was trying to turn the tables. I did not respond to his question. I waited for him to continue, making up my mind not to utter a word if he continued with that trend of questioning. He might have noticed the determined set my lips had taken and changed the topic of conversation.

"I had to come. I cannot understand why you left the way you did." His complacent tone was making me angry. How could he be so self-righteous when he could have guessed why I left? As a last-minute thought I had spread out the letter on the bed. This must have given him a clue. But here he was behaving as if he had no idea of what might have made me leave without informing him.

"You cannot? Then I am in no position to give you an explanation."

"Just say you do not want to. Don't say you are not in the position to do so."

"Do you really expect me to give you an explanation?"

"Of course."

I could not believe what he was saying and my resolve not to be the first to mention the letter dissolved.

"What have you got to say about the letter?"

"Which letter?"

"You dare to ask me which letter?" My anger was rising.

"Ah, Elizabeth, do not be so stupid. Is that what made you leave? That letter was of no consequence."

"What do you mean it was of no consequence? It was something to me. Gabby please, don't take me for a ride. I will not stand for it. If you have nothing to say about the letter just let me know."

"What do you want me to say? It was just a friendly letter."

"A friendly letter? You call that a friendly letter? I can understand how friendly it was. I also understand what happened the evening I arrived in Douala. So that is what was on your mind. Gabby I have had enough. Maybe it was all a mistake."

At that moment there was a knock on the door and Pa Martin walked in. He looked at me briefly and turned to Gabby.

"Aha, Gabriel. Why did you not let us know that you were coming? You should have told Elizabeth to tell us." There was no response from us. We both sat with our heads bowed. He immediately sensed that something was amiss and continued, "Are you not happy to see me? Maybe I am intruding. He made to walk back to the door. I broke the silence."

"You are not interrupting anything, Pa Martin. I am sorry. It was all a mistake. It is over."

"What!" both of them exclaimed as I got up and walked into my room. Both of them stood for a moment, the impact of my words dawning on them. Before I could close the door and fall on the bed to let out the tension in tears, I felt Gabby's hands gripping me from behind.

"You don't mean it, Lizzy! You don't mean it!" I wrenched my hand from his, fell on the bed, took my pillow and covered my head with it. I wanted to weep but no tears came to my eyes. I was surprisingly strong. I had to be strong. Weeping was a sign of weakness. I did not want to be pitied, petted and coaxed. Gabby came and sat by me trying to get the pillow off my head. We wrestled for a moment and I gave up. He flung the pillow away and tried to get me to look at him.

"Be reasonable, Lizzy. Don't behave like a baby."

"So you think I am naïve. I am a baby. I do not have to be reasonable. Babies are never reasonable."

"Please calm down. Let us talk."

"We have nothing to talk about. When we could have talked we did not."

Pa Martin was standing at the door of my bedroom watching and listening to what was going on. In my frenzy I had forgotten that he was there. His voice cut into my ears.

"Gabriel! What is happening? Come out here for a moment."

I waited for him to call for me too but he did not. Gabby sat as if he was unwilling to go. Then he slowly got up and walked out. I heard the two of them go out the front door. I adjusted on the bed and took my pillow and covered my head again. My mind was a vacuum and I felt as if I had come to the end of a long line of decisions. I lay on the bed waiting for the move from them. I had taken the plunge and allowed myself to sink to the bottom. If I was going to drown so be it. I made no effort to rescue myself. I lay still. I soon heard the door opening again. Both of them came into the parlour and I could hear the chairs creak as they sat down. I waited for Gabby to come to me but he didn't. I felt disappointed but reminded myself to be calm and even to pretend to be unconcerned. Then I heard Pa Martin calling.

"Elizabeth! Come out. Come out here. I am the one asking you to come out."

How could I ignore his request? My quarrel was with Gabby and not with him. I got up and went out. I was grateful that I had not wept. My red eyes and sniffling might have created a different impression on Pa Martin. We sat for a while in silence as Pa Martin looked steadily at me. I looked at him for a while and then looked away. My eyes were clear, bright and a shade of hardness might have crept over them. For the brief moment that I looked at him, I tried to figure out what was on his mind. He did not look baffled. He looked calm as if what was happening was not out of the ordinary. But when he started talking his tone hinted on a command.

"I did not expect to come here and meet such a situation. However, as I have met it I am going to have my say. Gabriel has told me what happened. I do not want to ask for your own version. You are not children. You should know what you are doing. When I leave, sit quietly for some time and examine yourselves. Then try to talk it out. I cannot interfere. I am going back home now. But I am expecting you two at my house at seven o'clock this evening."

He walked out of the house without looking back. We both sat quietly listening to our breathing. Nobody spoke for a while. I did not want to look at Gabby but could not resist stealing a glance at him. He was staring at me as if he was not sure who I was. I asked myself whether there was anything to talk about and discovered that there wasn't. I did not want to say anything more about the letter. Gabby sat like a statue, as if he was afraid to break a spell he was trying to sustain. Our silence was becoming ridiculous. It looked so funny. Here were two people bursting with anger and indignation but unable to express how they felt. Laughter started swelling up in me. I felt relieved that I was not going to be subjected to another session of trying to sort out things with Pa Martin present. This relief fanned the flames of the humour, which was building up in me. The

166

longer I considered the predicament Pa Martin had put us in and Gabby's continued staring, the more the hilarity bubbled in me. I could bear it no longer and got up to go to my room before the laughter got control of me. In the room I started laughing but put my hand across my mouth and it no longer came out as laughter. It sounded more like a sob. Gabby was again after me. My body trembled with laughter. It felt so soothing to laugh. I allowed it to overcome me. I buried my face in the pillow and laughed. I did not want him to understand what was happening. When he finally discovered that I was laughing instead of weeping he looked really baffled. He sat and watched me laugh. When the laughter ebbed I asked him what he was going to do now. He looked at me and shook his head in disbelief.

"What is so funny, Elizabeth?"

"We are supposed to be examining ourselves. Have you finished? Because I am through with mine." I started laughing again. Gabby could not help laughing himself although his laughter had a tinge of uncertainty.

"I think laughter is the best way to examine ourselves and solve this problem," Gabby said as he held me and tried to kiss me. I tried to avoid his kiss by getting up from the bed. But he could not let me.

"We have both examined ourselves and I am sure we have both come to the same conclusion, so why don't we settle it with a kiss?"

"No, Gabby, it is not yet over. Look, time is running out. You have not completed your assignment." I continued laughing. Gabby was actually enjoying the laughter. He came closer and pulled me into his arms.

"Lizzy, what type of a woman are you? What am I going to do with you?"

"I am just what I am. About what to do with me, the answer is nothing." He was holding me close and kissing me. I resisted and pushed him away.

"Lizzy, don't you want me? Remember that we have to be at Pa Martin's at seven o'clock." He had picked a leaf out of the book I was consulting but I was not going to let him off that easily.

"I cannot allow you to touch my lips with that woman's kisses still lingering there." He looked at me again in disbelief. Then he lifted the back of his palm and wiped his lips.

"Am I clean enough now?"

"So you actually kissed her!" I exclaimed with laughter in my voice, then in a more serious tone.

"Tell me Gabby. Why did you do it?"

"Lizzy, I did not kiss her. I have nothing to do with her. She is my colleague and I had to go to Yaounde to work with her. She has shown interest in me and would like to even go further. But you know as well as

I do the type of relationship we are getting into. I cannot afford to play such games now."

Throughout this speech I watched Gabby closely. I believed him and to show this I moved over to him and kissed him on the lips.

My arms were still round his neck when he looked into my eyes and said, "I will not ask you about Andrew. I believe what you told me." He kissed me this time without restraint and I gave in without reserve. It was six thirty when we were ready to go to Pa Martin's.

As I locked the door Gabby observed, "That was a tricky assignment to handle, but you found the formula for it." We laughed again and walked hand in hand to the roadside.

When we got to Pa Martin's house he was not at home. I was puzzled. I had expected him to be waiting for us. His two wives were in their kitchens preparing the evening meal. They both had already come back from the market. They sold foodstuff in the Bamenda Main Market but made sure that they came back home early enough to prepare food for their large family. Pa Martin usually told them when Gabby would be coming and they would prepare food for him. But this was not a normal visit. It was a crisis visit. And more over this was the first time both Gabby and myself were present in the compound. Gabby usually brought gifts for them but this time he had just a small travelling bag and nothing else.

When we appeared the young children were the first people to see us. They ran to us, all of them heading for Gabby. I stood aside and let them be hugged. After they had finished with Gabby they turned to me. The enthusiasm with which they welcomed me was left over from that of Gabby's. It was not effusive. I was not a stranger to the compound but now I could not have their undivided attention as I used to when I brought them biscuits.

The women heard the shouting and came out. The first wife, Mami Glacy, an adulterated form of Grace, came out to see what was happening. When she saw us her face broke into a broad smile. She stood in front of her kitchen and waited for us to get to her. She embraced Gabby before shaking his hand. She was pleased and surprised to see us. We now turned to move towards the second wife's house. She met us at the door and also embraced Gabby before embracing me. Gabby was like their first son because Pa Martin loved him like his own son and did not hide it. They were his mothers although the second wife was his age or even younger. After greeting them he walked towards Pa Martin's sitting room expecting me to follow him. But I did not.

I was more acquainted with the people in Pa Martin's compound because he made me visit him more often than I visited Gabby's mother. As Gabby walked to Pa Martin's own parlour, I accompanied the eldest of the wives to her kitchen. She protested.

"Do not sit here. There is too much smoke. It will get into your eyes and your clothes will have a smoky smell."

"Mama, I am used to smoke. I grew up in a smoky kitchen like this. It cannot kill me." She did not listen to my explanation and brought a kitchen stool outside for me to sit on.

"Sit out here. There is not much smoke." I sat out of politeness. She went back to the kitchen and brought another chair and sat with me. She was the elder wife and had taken a liking to me and I felt a bit free with her. In a polygamous home any visitor had to be careful because there are unwritten rules that have to be respected. If any of these rules are violated knowingly or unknowingly, there is always some unpleasantness. For example if I came and went to the second wife's house first it would mean I had disrespected the first wife. If I went to the first wife's house without going to the second wife's, then I had ignored her. So after visiting with the first wife, I had to move over to the kitchen of the second wife.

She too was busy cooking. Pa Martin had made it a law that both of them should cook. In most urban polygamous homes the women took turns cooking. But Pa Martin could not allow this in his compound because his compound was the place where people from the village looking for their relatives in town usually stopped for information. None of these people would come and go without eating something. The second wife's kitchen was bigger and more organized. She invited me to come and sit inside with her. Her main preoccupation was not our unexpected arrival but what we were going to eat.

"Whei! You people have come when we have not prepared any good food."

"You did not know that we were coming. If you did you would have prepared some good 'achu' for us as you usually do."

"You do not know your father. If he comes back and we have not yet prepared food for you people there will be trouble." Pa Martin was father to everyone who came to the compound and I was no exception.

"I am sure that you have just come back from the market. You are not a magician to have known that we are on the way. We will eat whatever you have prepared."

"You are saying what you think. But that is not the case." Then she called her third son, "Cornelius! Corny! Come and take this money and run to the store and buy two tins of tomatoes."

I noticed that she was almost through with her cooking and wondered what the tomatoes were for. As the younger wife she was Pa Martin's favourite, and she had to do everything to keep that position and this included providing the best food. I was sure she wanted to prepare some stew to accompany whatever she had prepared.

I did not want to be alone with Gabby when Pa Martin arrived. I wondered what he was doing all alone in the sitting room. I wanted to keep him in a state of suspense. I wanted to hear what he was going to tell Pa Martin. I did not want to give him the opportunity to make light of the situation for he was capable of doing it, especially as I had given him the leeway by laughing. My laughter had not been from being amused but a means of releasing tension. Pa Martin had not been there when I started laughing. So he did not know what happened when he left. To me this was not a situation to gloss over. I did not want to discuss anything with Gabby. I was not one to be taken for granted. I was afraid that was just the situation I had created by laughing and I wanted to rectify it.

I was in the second wife's sitting room when I saw Pa Martin walking into the compound. The safety light in front of his house illuminated his face. The tension from his thoughts had turned the lines of laughter on his face into lines of worry. As soon as he mounted the steps to his sitting room, I got up and followed him. As soon as he saw Gabby he asked, "Where is Elizabeth?"

"Papa I am here," I answered behind him. He turned round and I could see the worry lines on his face dissolving into smiles.

"Come in, my daughter."

I followed him into the house. I made sure that I sat away from Gabby. When he sat down he looked at Gabby before looking at me. Gabby smiled but I did not smile. He looked puzzled. He was waiting for one of us to speak. It was Gabby who had to speak first. I was not expected to do so. But Gabby said nothing. He kept his gaze steady on me. Pa Martin held his peace and watched what was going on. I bent my head and hid my face. I did not want them to see my smile. I did not want it to be misinterpreted especially by Pa Martin. He might think that we had made a fool of him. He was the last person I would want to antagonize.

In the continuing silence, Pa Martin burst out, "What have you two come to do here? I told you to sort out your differences before coming here. If you have not just walk out." I held my breath and waited. I dared not lift up my head. I dared not look at the two men afraid of what I may see. From Pa Martin's voice I knew he was angry. But there was nothing I could do to ease the situation. Gabby had to do the explanation. He was the man. He began in a low voice.

"Pa, I am sorry…"

"Speak louder, I cannot hear you," Pa Martin almost shouted at him. Gabby's voice was not that low not to be heard but Pa Martin wanted him to speak with assurance. I could understand his predicament. He had gone too far in the marriage negotiations to be confronted with any setbacks. Gabby started over.

"Pa, I was saying that I, we are sorry for the scene you met today. It is unfortunate that you had to be a witness to it. I have had problems with Elizabeth but we have always sorted it out. And we have sorted this one out. We have also examined ourselves. That is why we are here."

Pa Martin turned to me and asked, "Is it true, Elizabeth?"

I lifted my head and looked at Gabby. He pleaded with his eyes for me not to say the contrary. I hesitated then said, "Yes, Papa."

"Why do you say, 'Yes, Papa,' as if you are not sure of what you are saying? Look, you two should be very careful. Gabriel, you know I am a no-nonsense man. You know what I can do even as I am sitting here. So tell me. Are you going on with this marriage or not? I am not sure that what the two of you are saying is true." Pa Martin was really angry now and I had to say something.

"It is true, Papa. We have sorted out everything. There is no problem."

He turned to look at Gabby. Gabby had to assure him too.

"Papa, everything is fine. As Elizabeth says, there is no problem."

After saying this Gabby looked at me with accusing eyes. His eyes were saying, 'You see what you have done? I had never seen Pa Martin so angry.' He had the right to be angry, but Gabby's accusing look was not justified.

Pa Martin continued. "If everything is fine then, Elizabeth, move over and sit by your husband." I was trapped. There was nothing I could do but obey him.

As I moved over, Gabby smiled and said, "Pa, I told you everything is fine. Only that this Elizabeth you see is a complex woman."

"What do you mean?" Pa asked with dread on his face.

"Can you imagine that when she went into her room, she took a pillow and covered her face and I thought that she was crying when in fact she was laughing?" I was embarrassed. I could not believe that Gabby was going to bring this up and I waited with a beating heart for Pa Martin to react to this situation.

"But that is a good thing. Don't you know that laughter is good medicine for anger and tension? If she were crying what would you have done?" Pa Martin asked Gabby.

"I would have begged her."

"That is very good. Now beg her." Pa Martin looked at Gabby to see whether he was going to resist. Gabby could not believe this was happening. He had apologized to me several times when we were just the two of us. But doing it with Pa Martin present was incredible. He hesitated. Pa Martin urged him. "Beg her." He had to obey.

171

"Lizzy, I am sorry. Please let's not let this happen between us again."

"Aha, that is what I like to hear. You have called her Lizzy. That is what I want to hear," Pa Martin said. You could hear the joy and relief in his voice.

He continued, "Gabriel, don't you know that women like to be petted. If you don't then you have to start learning," Pa Martin winked at me when he said this.

"I know, Pa. I have been petting her. Have I not been petting you, Lizzy?" Pa looked at me waiting for me to confirm what Gabby had just said.

I was careful not to hesitate. I replied immediately.

"He has been doing that," I said and the look I gave Gabby told him to stop doing what he was doing.

But he continued, "Pa, don't you see the way she is smiling. I even pet her too much."

Before I could respond to this there was a knock at the door. A little boy came in with a cane basket. It was covered with a cloth and I knew it was food. Without saying a word, Pa indicated that the boy should keep the food on the table. After the boy walked out, Pa responded to Gabby's statement. He was just waiting for the child to go.

"You should never say you pet a woman too much. How much is much? You have to make your woman happy. Petting is not the only thing you can do. There are others." There was another knock on the door. This time a little girl came in with another basket. Pa again indicated the table where the other basket had been kept. She was followed by Pa's second wife who came in to set the table. When she got the plates out of a cupboard I went to assist her. As Pa continued to talk with Gabby he was watching what we were doing.

"Set the table for five people, Paulina, and when you have finished go and call for your mother."

Pa Martin was such a disciplinarian that there could be no disorder in his compound. One way to maintain this discipline was in the respect for elders. Paulina called her mate 'mother'. This was to give her respect for her seniority in age and in marriage. With this respect well established there was no room for open confrontation between the two women although they grumbled when things were not going on between the two of them. Only something very serious was brought to Pa Martin's attention.

Paulina went out to call for her mate. When they came back I watched to see how they were going to sit. The first wife sat on his right and Paulina on the left. Gabby was asked to sit at the other end of the table facing Pa Martin, and I found myself sitting on Gabby's right next to Paulina. The table took six people and the only empty seat was next to the first wife.

After a short prayer given by Pa Martin, we started eating. The food prepared by the two women was all served. I made sure that I ate what both women had prepared. I also noticed that Pa Martin and Gabby ate from both dishes. The women did the same. This was again an unwritten agreement.

After we had eaten, each woman carried her dishes in the baskets in which they had been brought. Paulina also took along the plates that had been used to wash and returned them to the cupboard in their husband's sitting room.

Pa Martin asked us to leave the dining section and go back to the sitting section. I made sure I sat next to Gabby. Pa went into his room and came out with a bottle of wine and a bottle of whisky. He placed them on the table. Without waiting to be told I got up and went to the cupboard from which Paulina had taken the plates. I had seen glasses being taken out of this cupboard whenever I came to visit. I brought out three glasses. Pa asked me to bring out two more. When I brought them out he asked me to go and call for his wives. I went and informed them that Pa was calling for them and went back to the sitting room. Pa asked me what I wanted to drink. I did not respond and looked at Gabby. He had not poured anything for himself.

Pa saw my look and understood. He said, "Elizabeth, we are living in the white man's time. So it is ladies before gentlemen. What will you drink, wine or whiskey?"

I asked for wine. Whenever I was in Pa Martin's company I was very careful with what I did or said. Though he had lived the better part of his life in town, respect for tradition and morals was still deeply embedded in his view of life. In the traditional setting I could have been the one to serve them. But here was Pa serving me. Gabby sat back and watched as Pa Martin poured wine into my glass. When it was half full I told him that it was enough but he continued pouring.

"One glass of wine will not kill you. You are drinking in my house. If you get drunk there are many beds on which you can sleep. So do not worry."

Gabby also took wine. Pa Martin poured a finger of whiskey for himself, then he sat back on the chair.

"This is good whiskey. It is not the coloured diluted 'afofo' that Nigerians put in bottles and say it is whiskey. When I take a bit of it in the evening, I feel it warm my stomach and my bones. It makes me sleep well."

"That's Pa's sedative," Gabby explained. "Pa, I had to leave Douala in a hurry, so I could not get you the other one which you like very much."

"Which one is that?" I asked. I had to begin to know Pa's likes and dislikes to know how to humour him in future.

"Pa likes Johnny Walker, Black Label."

"Aha! That one is fire." Before he could continue extolling the virtues of the whiskey, Paulina came in. Pa indicated a chair for her to sit on. He poured some wine and gave it to her.

"Maybe you would have preferred the whiskey?"

Paulina said, "Thank you, Pa. This one is alright." She sipped the wine looking at us. I could see that she was puzzled at Gabby's sudden arrival and more so at my presence with him. She knew something serious had provoked our presence. Anything that concerned Gabby, Pa Martin took extra care to handle. She could sense that something was out of place, but she dared not ask. I could read this from her face as she often looked at Gabby then at me. But each time I tried to catch her eyes, she would turn them away and make as if she there was a speck at the bottom of her glass which she was trying to locate. Gabby was telling Pa Martin about the effects Whiskey had on the human liver. Pa was not convinced.

"If that is what it does to the liver, then I should be dead by now. But my liver is still good. I eat anything I want to and drink any beer, wine or whiskey. But I do not drink them too much."

"That is the secret," Gabby told him. "But it does not stop the liver from being affected in the long run."

"My liver is too hardened to be affected," Pa Martin assured him. We all started laughing. Pa's first wife, Mami Glacy came in when we were laughing. She looked round uncertain of what was happening and did not sit down. Pa asked her to sit. He asked her what she was going to take. She pointed at the whiskey bottle and we started laughing again. She was confused. She thought we were laughing at her. She hesitated taking the glass Pa offered her.

To ease her uncertainty Pa said, "You see, her liver is as hard as mine." This brought on another wave of laughter.

Mami Glacy looked round with an uncertain smile on her face. She realized that something funny was going on and wanted to share in the fun. She asked, "What did we eat that made our livers so hard?"

This brought up another wave of laughter.

Paulina cut in and answered, "Whiskey."

Mami Glacy looked at her and said, "So we have been eating whiskey?" Everybody was dying with laughter. She realized the error she had made and corrected herself. "I mean drinking whiskey." But it was too late. She joined in the laughter. Tears ran down Pa Martin's eyes as he laughed.

"Oh! It is a long time since I last laughed like this," Pa Martin explained. He looked at Gabby and said. "You see what laughter does. We are all happy now. There is nothing that unites people like laughter."

Mami Glacy had caught up with the spirit of the evening and added her part. "Two old people like us need whiskey to warm up our old bones."

Pa Martin burst out in another wave of laughter. Paulina looked ill at ease. She was not up to five years older than Pa Martin's first son. Whenever age was mentioned it seemed to disturb her. I could read this on her face as she listened to her husband and his first wife.

Pa responded, "Are you saying that I am old?"

Ma Glacy had to withdraw her statement. "No, that is not what I meant. What I mean is that Whiskey is good to be taken in the evening."

The conversation was taking an uncomfortable turn. I intervened.

"Pa, it is getting late and I have to go home."

"That is true, my daughter. I would have liked you to stay longer. I am sure that it is your presence that has brought so much laughter this evening."

Gabby accompanied me to the roadside. While we waited for a taxi, he remarked, "You really know how to get to Pa's right side."

"He is my first husband. Don't you know that?"

"Oh! Sorry. I did not know that you were already sweethearts."

"And what is wrong with that," I asked with laughter in my voice.

"There is nothing wrong with it, only that he is too old for you."

"Please do not go back to that," I said, pretending to be angry. "My Pa is not old. Did you not hear him say he is not old?"

"So you prefer him to me?" Gabby asked teasing me.

"Are you already jealous? I spend more time with Pa than I do with you. So you have to be careful," I warned Gabby. We were used to such bantering in the course of which many things were said and not said.

"Then I have to hurry not to be overtaken by him."

"You better." A taxi stopped and took me back home. I knew that this was an opportunity for Gabby to have a really serious discussion with Pa Martin.

10

I knew that things were really on the move when Gabby and I went to the goldsmith to collect our rings. When I held them in my palm I thought of the diamond ring lying in the sand on the seabed. I looked at Gabby. It seemed as if he too was thinking along the same lines. He smiled and covered my palm with his two hands enclosing the rings and my palm in them. He held and squeezed them together. The sense of regret that stole over me when I remembered the diamond ring was wiped away, but I could not help thinking of how beautiful it was. It could have really suited our situation now more than it did then. Now when I thought of all what Gabby and I had gone through I had the feeling I had punished an innocent person.

We had already sent out an order for the wedding gown and the paraphernalia that made up a bride's outfit. Gabby made sure I did not have to bother about the preparations for entertaining guests. He directed our conversations towards what concerned just the two of us. He was making a conscious effort for us to be concerned only with one another. The last day that I went to Douala was the day we went to collect the rings. The rest of the weeks we talked over the phone or he came to Bamenda over the weekend, and he had to do this often. Pa Martin had everything under control.

I was in Bamenda where the wedding was to take place, but his relatives made sure I did not get involved in the preparations. We had calculated all what it would entail and had made our own contribution as was agreed in a close circuit meeting of both families. But from time to time Pa Martin kept me informed of what was going on and who was taking care of what. He told me that family members had chosen a certain material for everyone interested to sew and wear on that day. He told me of the various groups that had been invited. We had to make provision for people who would come uninvited. This was one aspect of the culture of the people which town life and western culture had not wiped away. As long as you knew the people getting married or you were from the same village, you felt it was an obligation to participate in any occasion that concerned the person or the family. Although the idea of a free meal and a drink is taking over this sense of belonging, the presence of a good number of people at a ceremony is testimony of the people's feeling of concern for the family. It is also a testimony of how much the family concerned can provide as entertainment. One always hears expressions like, "The occasion was news not a tale." It was a tale when there was not enough food and drink or when something extraordinary happened. I prayed that with all the effort made to keep me off the heat of preparations, the occasion was going to be news and not a tale.

The week of the wedding Gabby had to come to Bamenda so we could see the priest together. It was an embarrassing half hour that we spent with him. We were both born into catholic families but had thought that saying yes before God and man was just a necessary part of the show. He asked us questions to which we could not give a ready answer. These were not the regular questions but those questions that we had to keep asking ourselves throughout our lives not only as individuals but also as husband and wife. Though a clergyman he knew much of what was happening in the society especially in families. He talked about the things that usually brought division in a family. He talked of money, interference from relatives, suspicion, attraction by the opposite sex and many others. He talked like a father and I ticked off the things he was saying. Some I had already experienced. The others I was already aware of and planned to guard against.

My parents were making their own arrangements as well. This was the first occasion for my mother to be doing something of this magnitude in her own compound. I knew that she would go out of her way to do things the grand way. When I visited her for the last time before the wedding, I tried to find out how she was going about the preparations. She told me that she saved enough money in one of her thrift and loan groups. She had taken a loan and arranged to pay it back when it was her turn to be given money in her 'Njangi' group. I told her that she should not get herself into too many debts. She agreed with me but it was evident in her face that she was just trying to appease me. This was her turn to marry off a daughter and she would want to hear exclamations and praises about the occasion. Although the marriage was taking place in town she insisted on providing the calabashes of corn-beer, which traditionally the bride's mother is supposed to provide. At ten o'clock on that day six well decorated calabashes of corn-beer arrived at Gabby's father's compound. Although the six girls who brought the corn-beer came by taxi they had to alight some distance away and carry the calabashes in a procession into the compound as it is done in the village. This was the bride's mother's gift to the son-in-law. When the girls arrived Gabby was called to receive them. It was an honour for any girl to carry one of these calabashes. If the marriage had to take place in the village these girls would have been leading the procession bringing the bride into the husband's compound. They were her bridesmaids and would sit with her receiving whatever gifts were given and eventually partaking in them. Now that the bride was not with them, gifts of money and kind had been prepared for each of them. Gabby had to hand over the gifts to them personally, thanking them for bringing his wife. Gabby had to drink the first calabash of corn-beer with his friends to show his appreciation of what his mother-in-law had sent. There was a subtle match-making intention in this arrangement for the girls chosen were of marriageable ages and they had to serve Gabby and his friends with the corn-beer.

The hall was full to capacity. The tables were all occupied. Even the benches that had been placed under canopies outside were filled with people. They were dressed in various outfits. But they were distinctly African or European. The blend of the two cultures lent harmony to the whole picture that seemed to say, "We are no longer at crossroads. We know what is good." The men were at ease in their three piece suits and in their flowing 'agbadas'. They moved about with conscientious satisfaction. The women were resplendent in their 'boubous' and matching scarves. The Ibo and Yoruba outfits with their skyscraper headgears seemed to be the mode for such occasions. The woman in suits and hats looked equally dashing. When I looked at them all, I wondered what was meant by modernity and tradition amalgamated. Was the European way of dressing not traditional to them as the African's way of dressing was traditional to them too? And if one group copies from the other and vice versa, is it not mutual appreciation? Then what makes one modern and the other traditional? It is how you feel in what you wear that matters. The preparations for this day had set off like a whirlwind three months ago. They were very different from what would have taken place if we were in the village especially in the days of old. Although some of the customs were maintained in the traditional weddings, the influences of western culture and materialism were quite evident in the court and church marriages. Materialism should not be viewed only in the aspect of acquiring but also in the aspect of showing off material wealth.

During the wedding reception the corn-beer turned out to be the drink in demand. It is surprising how city dwellers with their palates accustomed to beer and whisky would cherish a local drink. Of course, they consider it a delicacy. My attention was drawn to it when Gabby insisted that I should drink some before revealing its source.

I had always thought of how I would feel on this day. Each time this thought came to my mind my stomach fluttered in anticipation. What goes on in the mind is a distillation of what we anticipate, are experiencing, or have experienced. At times one gets lost in the hustle and bustle of activities.

Susan Nkwentie Nde

Some call it daydreaming. But this is not wandering in fantasy land. Most often the mind is preoccupied by a previous unexplored thought that had been provoked by a present occurrence. I had planned a number of things to think about while the ceremony was going on. But my mind kept straying. In the church I kept my ears alert to hear what the priest was saying in order to be able to respond correctly at the right time. On the way back from the altar I had to look up and maintain a smile on my face and at the same time I tried not to trip over my gown. Thank God I was seated at last. The wedding trousseau had been sent from America. Although I had sent my measurements for the wedding gown and shoes to match, it seemed as if I had put on a little more weight. I had to put on a girdle before the dress could be zipped up. The dress fit when zipped but I had to hold in my stomach muscles. This kept me really uncomfortable. While standing for the ceremonies in church I did not feel the flesh straining against the rubber threads of the girdle. But seated in the reception hall my stomach revolted against this strange contraption. When I measured the patent leather shoes, they had fit. But wearing them for a long time for the first time they had not stretched enough to accommodate the shape of my feet. They were squeezing the flesh on my feet and a blister was already forming on each. My toes were equally burning with pain. My body was revolting against this contrived imprisonment for the sake of conformity. I sat there in agony with a smile on my face.

It was supposed to be the happiest day in my life. I was happy but uncomfortable. I tried to concentrate on the speeches. Pa Martin was the first person to speak. I listened to what he was saying but my mind did not register anything. My father spoke next. I also did not dwell on what he was saying. But when Gabby got up to speak I listened keenly. He started by thanking everyone present. After assuring the people present that there was enough to eat and drink, he went on to talk about how he expects all those who care for the two of us to help us realize our dreams. Then he said something that intrigued me. He said that both of us had dreams which we cherished and it was our place to help each other realize these dreams. Though we had separate dreams they all blend to form one whole. He called on all our well wishers to help us realize our dreams. This statement registered in my mind and took me back to Andrew's challenge not to let my dreams die.

During an interlude of music during which final touches were being made for people to start eating, I tried to take my mind away from my straining stomach muscles and my throbbing feet. I did this by thinking of the dreams I had to fulfil in my life. I had always envied the men and women I saw in wedding pictures. They looked so happy. Here was my turn to have such pictures and look happy too. I had everything that went

180

to make a modern wedding satisfying. There were bridesmaids and groomsmen. The flower girls were charming. The wedding train was as long as it could be made. I had my knight, my beau sitting by me. My dreams had come true. But is this all? I thought. Is this all there is to life? Was the merging of teenage dreams and adult realities strong enough to sustain life to its full? With these thoughts in my mind I suddenly felt empty. I felt hollow. I wanted more out of life than what was going on. The wedding was just a day's event but life was an experience that had to be lived. I had expected the wedding day to be a turning point in my life. But I wondered whether it was going to be as I thought.

Gabby nudged my side. I looked up. He thought I was sleeping. I was not sleeping, not tired, but just weary. What nonsense! Elizabeth! Enjoy yourself! A voice rang in my mind. I took a deep breath and brought myself to the present. It was time for the bride and the groom to go and cut the wedding cake before the feasting could begin. I walked with Gabby down to the centre of the hall where the table with the cake had been placed. Gabby held my hand firmly in his. When we were asked to show how we were going to be the support of one another by putting a piece of cake in each other's mouth, I held my piece of cake and looked in Gabby's eyes. Before putting it in his mouth I made a silent reminder to him in my heart for him to keep to the words of his speech in which he had said we were to help each other realize our dreams. I do not know the expression I had on my face. I might have closed my eyes. I heard Gabby whisper to me.

"Open your eyes and look at me."

I opened my eyes as I put the piece of cake in his mouth. He too put his piece of cake in my mouth and before I could chew it he held me close and kissed me. There was a cheer from the crowd in the hall especially from the younger people. I almost choked and managed to swallow the piece of cake in my mouth. We were then led to the table to serve ourselves from the various dishes that had been prepared.

I settled to enjoy myself as Martha had suggested. It was a once-in a life time experience and I had to make the best of it while it lasted. But I felt miserable not because of the vows we had been making before God and man but because of their significance and implications. These vows most often are easier said than respected. In the anxiety of getting married, the joy of being a madam and the excitement of getting a wife, anything is promised. When I sit back to think of all the promises Gabby made during our period of courtship and all the thoughts I had in me when I imagined how my married life would look, I wonder at the extent to which the human being can go to get what he wants, even including making a promise to God and not living the promise.

It is a painful irony that the pomp and pageantry attached to a church wedding is more elaborate than a court or traditional wedding. But when the marriage gets sour, this important aspect of the binding process is neglected. While the couple would rush to the court to dissolve a marriage or to traditional council to ask for the return of the bride's price, nobody ever thinks of going back to church to disown each other. Or are they ashamed to do this before God? Is it really God who brings together a couple or vested interest? Is a wedding a societal convenience to boost the image of the families concerned or the fulfilment of the desire to be truly one before God and man? Was it a lifelong covenant or an occasion to remember?

We had started with the traditional wedding. It was not an elaborate ceremony but the implications go even further than the civil and church weddings. The union is between two families, not two individuals. The wife becomes the family wife, never to be separated at least in the minds of the people. No matter what happens, she remains forever a wife of that family. Her life becomes intricately woven with that of her husband, children and in-laws. She is supposed to find fulfilment in this. This is the ultimate goal.

Considering what had gone on between us so far, I was sure I was going to remain with Gabby all my life. This assurance wore an edge of doubt when I thought of husbands and wives fighting and wounding each other. I wondered what makes their love go so sour. Lovers today, enemies tomorrow. From darling, to my dear, to that man, that woman, to that devil, that Satan.

We finished eating and I sat looking at the people as they went round the tables putting food in their plates. It was a very long queue. There was not much I could discuss with the people sitting at the table with me. I felt bored. But each time such a feeling came over me I pushed it aside reminding myself that I had to be happy.

The occasion was progressing to the end and the dancing was about to begin. It was evident from the rowdiness of the people that when dancing began it would be difficult to get the complete attention of the people. Gabby, standing up to acknowledge all that had been said in the speeches, again broke into my reverie. He squeezed my hand before standing up, giving me that smile that always disarmed me, a smile that said it all. What can make me want to leave Gabby? What was it that would make me want to leave him? The answer lay right there in front of me. But at that moment I could not see it. It was there in me, in Gabby and in all those beautiful people who had come to wish us well. I listened to Gabby. His was the only speech during which I did not feel distracted. I prayed in my heart that we would keep to what he was saying. The idea of sharing everything, being considerate and understanding, and being there for each other is the ideal. There are many husbands, many whom I know, who keep their homes in a perpetual state of fear and anxiety. When the children hear the voice of the father, instead of running to greet him they escape. Some expect complete obedience from wife and children simply because he is the head of the family. I looked at Gabby and imagined him behaving like this. It was a useless thought. Gabby was never going to metamorphose overnight.

Marriage was the ultimate goal for many girls but times are changing. Housewives now work and have businesses of their own. This gives them a certain degree of freedom. Being gainfully occupied frees them from self-defeating thoughts and from developing negative complexes about themselves. They have the freedom to think that they too can contribute to the betterment of their families. This entitles them to make suggestions about the welfare of the family. Their husbands listen, but so does society, because she has something constructive to contribute.

My trend of thought was interrupted by one of the flower girls who came to whisper something in my ears. I held her close while I listened to her complaint. She was well dressed and healthy. At once the substance of my dream which I had tried to capture was there before me. As I looked at the flower girl I held in my arms, the picture of the little girl I had seen through the window of Gabby's house flooded the vision of my mind's eye. Immediately I felt uncomfortable with the image. I tried to push it away and concentrate on what the child was saying to me. I was too exhausted to start exploring exhausting thoughts. But the image stayed. It nagged at my conscience. The little girls around me had a future at least in the minds of their parents. But what about the girl I had seen on the side street in Douala and those like her? I was beginning to see where my dream lay. Where was her place in this whole societal setup? I wondered. Could I provide her and others like her a place in this setup? I chided myself for harbouring such a thought on such a day. It was inappropriate. This was not the day to think such thoughts. I had all I wanted. I had a job and a husband. I was supposed to be happy and satisfied. But I wasn't. I was strangely dissatisfied. The image of the child flashed on and off as a reminder to me about life and dreams.

"Lizzy, you look tired," Gabby whispered in my ears. "Darling, be brave, it will soon be over." I smiled at him. I smiled at people. This was my day. I was a queen. My smile was a façade. The real 'me' wanted something more. I wanted to soar above the designed roles. Holding that little girl's hand would give me added impetus.

Dear readers, as these memories come flooding back through my mind like the images on a TV screen when put on playback, I pause to ask myself many questions. I wonder if my life would have been different if I had married Andrew. I wonder what would have happened if I had not thrown the diamond ring into the sea. I wonder how my relationship with Gabby would have ended if we hadn't friends like the Bilas. I wonder whether I would have been satisfied with my life if I hadn't set up this centre for training young girls how to sew and helping to set them up after their training.

I had to join my husband in Douala as soon as we got married. There was no question of staying away from him now that we wholly belonged to each other. Although I was quite familiar with Douala, I was going there now in a different capacity. I was a wife going to begin a home of my own, to begin a new life with Gabby. It was indeed a new life. So I thought. I had a husband to love and cherish. I had to see to the daily business of attending to his needs, his food, his clothes, entertaining visitors for him, accompanying him on his visits, being beautiful for him and eventually making him a father. My mother had hinted at these things. If I had told her of my thoughts on that day she would have considered them scandalous, so I had kept them to myself.

The first three months of my married life were governed by the desire to be the perfect wife. There was everything at my disposal. Gabby had moved to a two-bedroom apartment before our marriage. The rooms were spacious. We had engaged a boy to come in twice a week to do the cleaning. I preferred to do the cooking myself because I had the time. Moreover, I wanted to put my stamp and personal touch on whatever Gabby ate. I felt that this was an important step to take at the beginning of any marriage. I waited on him. I stayed up for him. I entertained friends for him. I visited his friends with him. It is strange the way I felt during those early months. I had known Gabby for almost a year before we got married. There was not supposed to be anything new in our feelings for each other or our reactions to the basic situations we faced together. But I discovered that my heart fluttered whenever I heard his footsteps approaching the door. I shivered with excitement when he touched me. Maybe it was the notion of what a honeymoon should be that was triggering all these reactions. We had agreed not to go to any distant place for our honeymoon. What was essential was staying together and having fun. We went to places around Douala. We went to Edea and moved round the town having a great time. We made a trip to Kribi and walked along the beaches. I reminded Gabby of the diamond ring. He just looked at me and told me never to think of it. When I insisted on knowing why, he said it formed part of his past. I understood we had to keep looking forward not backwards.

During this period I went to the market. I went to the hairdresser. I visited a tailor to whom Jane had introduced me. Gabby and I visited many of his friends during the weekends. We also received visitors in our home. Jane went back to her job and I saw less and less of her.

Then I became bored. My transfer was not yet out and this was the fifth month. Having been used to going to work every morning, this idleness worked on my nerves. I was putting on unnecessary weight. If I were in the village, I would have been undergoing the fattening period, which precedes the 'good fever', but there was nothing yet to provide the 'good fever'. I was healthy and nothing had been planted yet. My boredom was leading to irritation. I actually flared up on Gabby one afternoon. He had taken his lunch and was going into the room to rest. I followed him into the room and asked whether he had checked at our delegation to see whether my transfer decision was out. He asked me why I was so anxious to get back to work. He loved coming home and finding me waiting for him. After all if the government did not want to affect my transfer then that was their problem. I was still receiving my salary. I told him that I did not marry to become a fulltime housewife. My irritation had made me say this in a defensive tone. Gabby looked at me with surprise. Then in a cool and unaffected tone he said if he wanted me to stay at home and not work he was ready to provide all my needs. After all he earned enough money to do so. I did not know whether he was just trying to tease me or he really meant it. Before we got to this stage in our relationship he understood how I felt about being a wife, a mother and a civil servant. There was no question of being a fulltime housewife.

This incident opened my eyes to what lay in store if I continued in this way. An unpleasant situation might arise that would take years to undo. Thoughts of the things I wanted to do and which I could not carry out irritated me more. I had always wanted to do things with my hands. The unfinished sets of embroidery were packed at the bottom of my trunk. I fished them out and spent hours completing them. The new chair covers on the chairs Gabby had bought before the wedding gave me a lot of pride. This was my first concrete contribution to our home. As I worked my mind searched for other things I wanted to do. These were the things that would give me deeper satisfaction, an almost sanctifying sense of being. When I told Gabby what I intended doing he looked at me as if he were not sure he had heard me properly. He went on talking as if I had not said anything. I knew from the way he hesitated in his speech that he had heard what I had said but did not want to pay heed to it. I did not pursue the matter.

The next day I wrote a detailed letter to my mother telling her what I wanted her to do for me. I sent her a cheque of three hundred thousand francs. She was to collect the money from my savings account in the Credit Union in Bamenda. The goods were to be given to a driver who plied the Bamenda Douala highway. I had made all these contacts and arrangements without Gabby's knowledge. The following week I picked up the bundle of loincloths and delivered them to the dealer in the Douala central market. Although I did not tell Gabby, I could not hide what I was doing from Jane. She encouraged me but we still had the assignment of how to tell Gabby. When I asked her advice on what to do if Gabby objected to what I intended doing, she told me that it all depended on how I reacted to the objection. After this answer she said nothing further and I was left to think about the implication of her response. Back home I thought about her response and remembered what Jane's landlady had told her. There was always a way to get round such situations.

Within a week, tailors who sewed 'kabbas' had bought all the loincloths I had supplied to the retailer. I made more than a hundred percent gain. I sent for a second supply, this time increasing the demand. My mother had good taste in her choice of Nigerian wax, which was very good for sewing various patterns of 'kabbas'. The goods did not appear on the day I was expecting them. The police had held them up at the entrance to Douala demanding to know who was carrying out a business without a permit. When I got information that the goods had been held up, I immediately contacted the Ibo man at the Douala central market who went there and said the goods were his. I waited for him in his shed with a beating heart praying that he would be able to get himself out of the situation. He was a veteran in such matters and told me that my presence would have only complicated things further. The receipts had my mother's name on it. I was so frightened. But the man got away with the explanation that it was the name of the woman who bought the cloths and sent them to him. She was just doing what he had asked her to do. To settle with the police and the customs was a difficult matter.

To get out of such situations the Ibo man advised me to get into a partnership with him, saying that he wanted to expand his business and I was acting as his partner. For this I had to give him a certain percentage. This was not a problem because if I got into the business I was going to make a good profit. I left everything in his hands. When the documents were ready I had to go to the police to make certain declarations. When I got there it turned out to be a mini interrogation because the police and customs suspected the game we were playing. I had to tell lies to continue what I had started. Telling the truth would have landed me in trouble so I continued with the string of lies I had fabricated. I was not happy with the situation but I could not just drop the venture on which I had embanked. When I eventually told Gabby what I had been doing he flew into a

186

rage. We had a row about it. He told me to stop immediately. He could not tolerate the fact that I was being interrogated at a police station like a criminal. What did I want? Was he not providing for me as a husband should? When my transfer went through where would I have the time to do business? All these questions were to discourage me. I did not attempt to explain immediately. I allowed him to cool down. This occurred just one year after our wedding. I was so upset. I did not know that doing business on such a small scale would be so complicated. I was more upset because Gabby accused me of doing things behind his back. There was nothing I could say to defend myself. For three days we did not talk to each other. I felt miserable. I tried to make it up with Gabby but he just ignored me. At one point I almost begged for forgiveness, promising to stop. But I could not bring myself to say what I was thinking because even to me it did not sound true. I was not being true to myself. I hated the idea of breaking my promise to myself so soon. I also did not want to make any promise to Gabby because I knew I was not going to keep it.

The weeks passed and this incident was forgotten. Life went back to normal. My clandestine trade in loincloths from Nigeria continued and I was making a profit. I had nothing to do with the police nor the customs. My partner handled that part and I compensated him. Within seven months I had made a profit of almost five hundred thousand francs. My transfer was not yet out. I had told my partner in the market that I would like to expand what I was doing but I did not know how. I wanted to go into business on my own but I did not know how to tell Gabby this. I was afraid that he would talk me out of it. When I thought of the last quarrel I had with him I almost gave up the idea. Something else was also preoccupying me. I was not yet pregnant. Gabby never made any reference to this even by insinuation, but it kept coming into my thoughts to add to those that were already breeding anxiety.

I bought more material and continued with embroidery to occupy myself. I had made more than I needed and took some to Jane to take to her office with the hope that her colleagues might be interested. The first batch of three sets consisting of seven backrests, four-side stool covers, one dining-table cover and a cupboard cover was bought each at twenty five thousand CFA francs. I was surprised at the response and set this idea aside as one of the things I would include in my plan. But when was I going to carry out this plan, Gabby sounded a warning. Where was I going to get the money to carry out a plan on the scale I intended? So far I had made six hundred and fifty thousand CFA francs. I still had some amount of money in my Credit Union account. I had sent some of my profit to my mother to increase the supply of loincloths. I did not want to hurt Gabby in any way. I did not want my marriage to be tainted by any ill feeling. I wanted a good marriage and this depended on an intimate and problem-free relationship with my husband. He too soon realized what my staying at home was doing to me. He went to Yaounde to see about my transfer.

My period of idleness was coming to an end. I had to act fast else my work would prevent me from doing what I wanted. I developed a strategy. I first had to win over Gabby to the idea that I was interested in doing business and that this would not disturb my duties as a wife nor my job as a civil servant. He had to see the profit I had made so far. I believed that if he saw how much I had made so far, he would not be so antagonistic. I had made a profit of eight hundred and twenty-five thousand CFA francs together with the proceeds from my embroidery. This I presented to Gabby. I knew he had always wanted a new musical set and was waiting for a time when his finances would allow him to purchase one without stress. I told him what I intended to do but added that if he still thought it was not good for me to do the business I was interested in, he was free to use the money to buy the musical set. I said I treasured my marriage and was not ready to allow anything to destroy it. When I said this I was holding the money in my hand extended to him. He looked at me for a while and made no response. He did not take the money. I left it on the table. He picked up a magazine and started leafing through it. I also kept quiet. We had to visit the Bilas that evening. He asked me to get ready for us to go. He did not mention the money. I left it on the table. I also made no reference to it. When we were about to go out I delayed in the room, giving him time to go out so I could take the money and keep it in the cupboard before joining him.

Two months after I had started work, the wholesaler in the Douala central market with whom I was carrying out the trade in loincloths from Nigeria informed me about something he thought would interest me. I was still working with him because I had a share in the loincloth business he was operating. I had introduced him to it and it was proving to be lucrative. He told me about a lady who wanted to open a tailoring workshop and wanted a partner. I met this lady two days later. I already had an inkling of what a large business entailed but still had a lot to learn. Together with the wholesaler who acted now as my mentor, we worked out a plan of action. I listened carefully to what we discussed and asked questions where I was not clear. I hadn't much to contribute but knew exactly where I was going to come in. I was not embarking on this project for the sake of money, though this was not evident from any other point of view. I hoped to get another type of satisfaction from it. I wanted to give some young girls the opportunity to prepare for their future by being able to provide for their basic needs. Madame Charlotte was a veteran in operating a tailoring workshop. She had been operating such a shop in Nigeria but because of health problems she had spent much of her money and thought it wise to come back home.

When everything had been mapped out, I told the lady to give me some time to work things out for myself before telling her exactly how much I was going to put in. This was partly true but the real reason was to get Gabby's consent and support. I gathered courage one evening and broached the matter. He did not say anything. I went ahead the next day to explain what we had planned, putting in all the background information. There was so much enthusiasm in my voice that I thought he was not going to let me down. But in a few words he told me he did not want to hear anything more about this crazy project. My enthusiasm plummeted, but I did not give up. He looked at me when he spoke. There was no anger in his voice. It was just a flat refusal. I looked at his face. It was calm. There were no hard lines of strain, the visible manifestation of restrained anger. I smiled to myself. He looked up at that moment and saw me smiling. In spite of himself he too smiled.

"What is so funny?" Gabby asked. I continued to smile and looked at him. I did not know what to say. He asked again. Sudden insight struck me. It was so illuminating that it needed just the right words to express it.

"I was just smiling at the way a little thing can create a big gulf between us."

"So you consider what you have been telling me a small thing?"

"It is not. But it is not enough to create a strained relationship between us. Our life together is much more important than anything else." I was so relieved that we were talking about it at last. I wanted to drive my point home. I had a feeling that if I did not make a break that evening then all was lost. So I plunged ahead.

"It is just another way of increasing our income." I was afraid of telling him my real reason. He might think I wanted to carry the world's problem on my shoulders and would laugh me out of the whole idea or make me look like a fool. I had to get round this I continued, "Moreover, I won't be actively involved. I will not leave my job. Madame Charlotte will be there to see about the day-to-day running of the place. I am just a financial partner. It will not interfere with my job, nor my duties at home."

"Do you know what all this entails? Have you thought about the hurdles you might encounter? What about the risks?"

"Life as a whole is a risk. It is the greatest risk. Anything else is a lesser risk. So why not take it?"

"Where are you going to get the money to be a partner in the way you have explained?"

"I was thinking of getting a loan. I can get a loan from my bankers in Bamenda. I have a bit of money saved. I am allowed to take three times the value of what I have saved." All along I had wanted to get Gabby financially involved. But since I was not sure of how he was going to respond to the whole idea, I dared not bring this up. Now was my opportunity. I continued.

"I will be very grateful if you will help me." There was silence. I waited with a beating heart. He said nothing. This was a new phenomenon I was discovering in him. When he does not want to pursue a subject further he just keeps silent. This kept me in a state of confusion because I did not know what was on his mind, whether he had taken a decision or not. I had learnt earlier on that nagging him for a response was not the best approach.

With the money I had saved I took a loan of four million francs. I needed five million. I brought the papers home and showed Gabby. They included documents for the permit to be granted. It was drawn out in Madame Charlotte's name because she was already involved in the business and had documents to show that she was just transferring the business from Nigeria to Cameroon. He went through them without a word. I explained to him that I needed one million francs to complete the five million I had put in. Before the centre went operational six months later, Gabby became very interested in what was going on. I kept him informed but I did not make it the major conversation at home. Madame Charlotte had brought her machines. There were ten sewing machines, machines for embroidery, a machine for zigzagging and one for making special buttonholes and buttons. There was also all the paraphernalia that goes to give a tailoring centre all the dignity it deserves. A good chunk of our investment went into renovating the premises and adapting it to our needs. The lighting, internal decoration and ceiling fans gave the place a sophisticated look. This was necessary to attract the type of clientele we wanted. Much attention was given to the display room. The two rooms created were spacious enough to act as workshop and showroom.

I began working as the private secretary to the director of the Institute for International Cooperation and Communication. The work was at first not as demanding as the one in Bamenda. It was not the peak period for business people, so I had enough time to take part in setting up of the centre. I opted to interview the girls who had applied to be trained. I questioned them to find out about their background. Madame Charlotte was not too happy with me when I suggested that the first trainees should pay a minimal sum. My idea was that they would eventually become workers at the shop and train other girls. She objected saying that after their training they would go away. So we encouraged the girls to sign a contract, but I knew that what was going to keep the girls was the way we treated them. Madame Charlotte herself was not in good health and my knowledge of sewing was just rudimentary. We needed girls with the know-how to continue when her health failed her. African designs were becoming popular and the 'boubous' with their sophisticated and complicated embroideries were in high demand. The girls had much to learn. They devoured the many catalogues, which Madame Charlotte had brought and those we bought together. Madame Charlotte trained the girls intensively. This was her domain so I left it to her. But I passed by when I had the chance to assist in the areas that were not too complicated.

The centre became the talk of the town. We were making a comfortable income especially from the African designs Madame Charlotte was such an expert at producing. There were many orders for wedding gowns, bridesmaid dresses and dresses for parties. What appealed to the public was her knowledge of the right combination of colours and what materials suited what styles, along with her neat sewing methods and finishing touches. She was putting in so much and working into the nights to meet the demands. She became sick again and much of her investment went for her treatment. She eventually had to borrow some money from me. In the original agreement she had more shares than I because she had the machines and the technical know-how. She was not in the position to pay back the loan, so I suggested it be converted and I take over some of her shares. Although we were business partners, we were more like sisters. We operated with the girls like a family. I was surprised at how much we achieved in so short a time. The girls were enthusiastic to learn and worked hard. With the shift in our shares I owned a greater number and was more or less the owner of the shop. But Madame Charlotte worked as usual. She is a good and talented woman. Her illness really wore her down. But there are already two well trained girls working with her.

The musical programme that was going on had come to an end. I did not notice because I was absorbed in my reminiscences. A cough from Gabby brought me back to the present. He was looking at the screen with rapt attention. I turned to see what was going on. A documentary was going on. It was about the traditional rites and customs of a tribe in Mali. What was most interesting was the commentary about traditional marriage customs. The bride and the groom only get to know each other on the day of the marriage. The commentator was saying that once these rites have been performed, the marriage becomes a lifelong union and for no reason whatsoever was the woman to abandon her husband or the man to send his wife away. All the man could do if he were not happy with his wife was to get another one. There were pictures of teenage brides and child mothers on the screen. It was such a pathetic story. From what the commentator was saying, many of the girls become older than their ages from childbearing and hard work. One old man was being interviewed about this custom. It was evident from what the old man was saying that right from the beginning of the marriage, a sense of obligation, responsibility and commitment is instilled. There is a strong belief in the involvement of the ancestors in the daily lives of the people. It was also evident that adherence to what the ancestors pronounced through the chief priests is more from fear than from any objective reasoning.

Both Gabby and I had been watching this and from the corner of my eye I could see he was listening keenly. I wanted to know what was on his mind.

"That's a good one," I observed.

"Hmm…" He grunted, stretching his legs and adjusting himself on the chair as he continued looking at the screen.

The End